# VOICE OF
# THE ELDERS

## GREG RIPLEY

**CALUMET
EDITIONS**
Minneapolis

**CALUMET
EDITIONS**
Minneapolis

To those who have come before, sounding the alarm of climate change, and those who fight for our children and future generations.

Without change something sleeps inside us, and seldom awakens. The sleeper must awaken.

—Frank Herbert, *Dune*


During your lifetime, the people of our culture are going to figure out how to live sustainably on this planet—or they're not. Either way, it's certainly going to be extraordinary.

—Daniel Quinn

# VOICE OF
# THE ELDERS

GREG RIPLEY

# 1

*United Nations Building, NYC*
*March 20, the Vernal Equinox*

"Your attention, please. The opening session of the Youth Assembly will begin in ten minutes."

Rohini Haakonsen could hardly contain her excitement. She'd worked hard, and now she was at the United Nations. Rohini walked through the lobby and gazed at all the different faces. Much like the people of New York City, the attendees came from an amazing variety of cultures and customs, some more familiar than others. An African woman in a brightly colored kente cloth headscarf spoke with a man from Scandinavia. He wore a green wool suit and had a blond handlebar moustache and a goatee. A man in a sarong and a Nehru jacket joined them. *He must be from Sri Lanka,* Rohini thought. Even in Europe and the United States, people were returning to traditional clothing.

The Youth Assembly was a program structured around the UN's long-range goals for sustainable development. Many of the world's brightest young leaders were attending the opening session. While the world had made major progress since the Paris Agreement, Earth continued to warm. Every month set new records, and every year seemed hotter than the last. Their efforts might be too little, too late. Low-lying island nations were already relocating their populations as sea levels rose.

In other places, unprecedented droughts caused major food shortages, inevitably followed by protests, riots, and political instability. Even the American public were waking up, after being duped by the fossil fuel industry, the corporate media's obfuscation, and many politicians' complete denial of reality. Around the globe, people were becoming desperate and demanding their leaders stop this existential threat to humanity, and leaders were finally starting to listen.

During her high school years, Rohini spent summers with her aunt and uncle, and she learned firsthand the plight of many in the developing world. Her mother's colorful family was from India. Her uncle Kailash ran an organic tea plantation in the foothills of the Himalayas, near Darjeeling, and her aunt Shanti worked for an NGO, empowering women in rural areas of India and Nepal and training them to be solar technicians. Many of the women were widows who lacked a stable livelihood, but who cared deeply about preserving the planet for future generations. India's burgeoning middle class was mainly limited to the largest cities, and recent economic strides left the rural poor mostly untouched. Rohini's time in India and Nepal left a lasting impression.

Rohini found her seat. She greeted other attendees and looked over the program agenda.

"Excuse me." A man waited to edge past her knees. "I'm in the next seat," he said. Rohini stood for him to pass.

"I'm Liam," he said, and offered his hand. "Pleased to meet you."

"Hi, I'm Rohini. Nice to meet you too." She shook his hand and wondered where his accent was from. *Canadian?*

"Is this your first time?" Liam said.

"Yes. I've got to say I'm excited to be here," Rohini said, beaming. "What about you?"

"It's my first time too. I'm glad to be here, but I'm not convinced anything useful will come out of this." Liam shrugged.

"A cynic, huh? You don't think we'll accomplish anything here?"

"Don't get me wrong—I certainly hope we do—but I was so hopeful after the Paris Agreement, and despite all the press it received at the time, I don't feel like much has changed." Liam frowned.

"I can see that. Well, maybe this year will be different," Rohini said.

Dr. Susan Yang, the Youth Assembly chair, stepped up to the microphone and began her address, greeting the assembled UN officials and delegates.

"Good morning, everyone. I'm so happy to welcome you all to the opening session of the Youth Assembly—" The crowd's startled gasps drowned out her words. Four people appeared directly behind her. Dr. Yang's brow furrowed in confusion as the crowd looked past her. She turned and realized she was no longer alone on the dais.

"Do not be alarmed. We mean you no harm. We are here to help," one of the intruders said, raising his open palms.

Rohini sat in stunned silence, as did most of the crowd. She glanced at Liam to find him slack-jawed. Others had jumped out of their seats. Some noticed the bright flash preceding the strangers' appearance, and others simply glanced up to see them suddenly on stage.

The two men and two women wore clothing like historical costumes. Rohini didn't recognize the style, but it reminded her of clothing she had seen in rural Nepal. The fabric looked rustic, yet refined, like the raw silk shawls she had seen in the Himalayas.

Two of the strangers wore robe-like garments. They were brown with some sort of green symbols or decorative motifs woven into the edges of the fabric. The other two wore fitted clothing, like padding or armor.

Rohini thought of the body armor she'd seen on riot police. She had observed them up close on more than one occasion, while attending protests and marches in college and high school—a family tradition.

But this "body armor" appeared to be made of a natural material, more like leather, and was padded in places. The armored man and woman flanked the two robed strangers like bodyguards or protectors. They looked relaxed but alert as their eyes scanned the crowd.

Rohini had studied some martial arts, but something about those two screamed "don't even think about it." Rohini wasn't easily intimidated, especially by other women, but the way the female "bodyguard" carried herself made Rohini think she wouldn't want to go there.

The woman looked right at Rohini and gave her a slight smirk as they locked eyes. Rohini felt frozen in place, like a child caught red-handed. After a moment of panic, Rohini was relieved when the woman broke their gaze and continued to scan the crowd. She knew it wasn't possible, but Rohini could've sworn the woman knew what she'd been thinking.

Security personnel rushed toward the podium, but they stopped at the foot of the steps and slowly retreated. Were they as shocked as everyone else?

Dr. Yang spoke up: "Who are you people? What do you want?"

"Please, allow me to address the assembly and all your questions will be answered."

The robed figure who had spoken before stepped up to the podium. Dr. Yang backed away warily, keeping an eye on the other strangers. Rohini was a little surprised at how easily she had acquiesced to the intruders. *Why isn't anyone stopping them? Something is really off here.*

"People of Earth, do not be alarmed," the stranger began. "We mean you no harm. In fact, we have come to help. We are from another world, a world much like your own. We have come many times throughout your history, but we have chosen not to reveal ourselves, until now."

The crowd reacted with a cacophony of anxious murmurs. "Did he just say they are aliens?" Rohini said.

"I think so. This is insane," Liam said, wide-eyed.

"We have revealed ourselves now because Earth is at a critical point. If something drastic is not done to reverse the runaway climate change, human civilization will be at risk.

"We have waited and watched, hoping your culture would develop the political will to make these changes, but the greed of those who control your economies and political systems is clearly too great an obstacle to overcome.

"Only now that you are at the point of no return have your governments come together in a serious way. You possessed the knowledge and the technology to avoid this calamity, but you have waited too long. Many of your future leaders are assembled here today, and much of the world is watching, that is why we have chosen this moment to make ourselves known.

"We have come to offer our assistance, so that you may avoid this fate, with which we are only too familiar. Many generations ago, our world was at a similar impasse. Some among us believed technology and unfettered growth held the promise of a better future. Others saw this way of life was simply unsustainable.

"This division in our society ran deep, resulting in the Great War. Untold lives were lost, and our civilization was left in shambles. Those who believed in a technological solution left our world in search of a new home, unable to imagine another way. Those who chose to stay healed our world and developed a new way of living, in sync with our biosphere. We chose to follow nature's example and were rewarded with a stable and sustainable future.

"We have not eschewed technology altogether, but we have developed regenerative technologies that do not harm our world. We offer you this knowledge, as well as the wisdom of our culture. To facilitate this, and to help you understand our culture, we invite you to choose a number of your people to come study our world. They will of course be returned unharmed and will serve as a bridge between our planets.

"We leave you to decide who to send. We simply suggest they be of sound mind and body and possess a certain level of physical fitness. Our way of life is, shall we say, less sedentary than yours has become.

"I know you have many questions. I assure you we will answer them upon our return. For now, I will leave you with this: Many of our kind have developed what you call 'telepathic abilities.' We can quickly convey great amounts of information from mind to mind. I will now reveal some thoughts directly to your world leaders to reassure them that what we say is true."

The stranger held a hand to his temple and closed his eyes for a few moments. When he opened them again, he rejoined the others.

Dr. Yang spoke out, giving voice to the questions on everyone's minds. "Wait, we still don't know who you are. What should we call you? When will you return?"

He opened his mouth to speak, and Rohini sensed a brightness building around the strangers. As the words left his mouth, there was a flash, and the four figures disappeared from the dais. They vanished as quickly as they had appeared. But his words remained, echoing in Rohini's mind.

"You may call us the Elders."

# 2

Rohini's mind reeled. Did that really just happen? Aliens appeared at the UN and offered to help save Earth? *And they're going to take people to their planet to learn about their culture? Are you kidding me? Where do I sign up?* If she hadn't seen the aliens, she never would have believed it.

"Please tell me I'm not dreaming," she said.

"I'd be happy to pinch you," Liam said, with a lopsided grin. "But unless we're both dreaming, I think that really just happened."

"Cute," Rohini said, her eyes crinkling.

She felt a chaotic mix of emotions. Rohini was excited by what this could mean for the planet, but she was terrified by the darker possibilities. It was all too much.

Rohini went over the events in her mind, and she realized with a start she had been right. That woman did sense my thoughts! Was that what happened to the security guards? Did one of the aliens stop them with their mind? Did their spokesperson actually communicate telepathically with our leaders? The implications swirled in her head. *If they really are going to help save the planet, how wonderful! But why? Out of the kindness of their hearts, or are they trying to pull the wool over our eyes? Can these "people" be trusted?*

Before being allowed to leave, the attendees were questioned by several different government agencies. Rohini lost track of them all. An endless stream of agents, from agencies with unfamiliar acronyms, each took a turn. Some didn't even bother identifying themselves. *Obviously, the government is taking this seriously.*

One agent stood out in her memory—a woman with green eyes, like her own, and straight red hair pulled back in a ponytail. She seemed familiar, but Rohini couldn't place her. *She must just remind me of someone.* The woman was particularly interested when Rohini mentioned one of the aliens had seemed able to read her mind.

"Tell me more about that. Were you able to sense the alien's thoughts as well?" The agent said, raising an eyebrow.

"No, but I got the distinct impression she was reading mine," Rohini said. "I thought I was imagining it until the other alien—the one speaking—said he was communicating telepathically. Then I realized it must have been true."

When she was finally allowed to leave, Rohini hoped she might run into Liam. She hadn't seen him since the agents began questioning everyone. The American attendees had been separated from the foreign nationals. *Oh well, I guess I'll see him again tomorrow.* She left the building and made her way home.

Rohini lived in Manhattan, so she was no stranger to walking, but on a typical day she would have taken the subway home. It was a good five miles back to her place in Harlem. But even though she was tired, she was also wired. Her limbs were heavy, yet her brain kept buzzing. Maybe a walk would help settle her thoughts and pump some life back into her sagging limbs.

She decided to head up 5th Ave and go through Central Park on her way uptown, as she often did when she was overwhelmed or needed to think. She could tell when she hadn't spent enough time in nature. She always got a little more stressed and anxious, and her fuse got a little shorter. She could usually roll with the punches in her daily life, as long as she got sufficient time in nature to keep herself on an even keel.

She wove her way through the park, skirting Turtle Lake, and made her way through the Ramble up to Belvedere Castle. The castle had been one of her favorite spots in the park since she was a little girl, reminding her of fairytales, princesses, and heroines on epic quests.

She climbed the hill to the castle and went inside, waiting in the short line at the one-way circular staircase. When she got to the upper level she made her way over to the wall, rested her arms on top, and sighed as she looked out over the lake at the city she loved.

Her family had moved to New York City when she was twelve, after a childhood spent in Minnesota. What might have come as a culture shock to many Midwesterners had been a relatively easy transition as her family had visited the city many times over the years to visit her aunt Priya.

Looking down at the rocks at the water's edge, a few of the ever-present turtles caught her attention. She had always been fond of turtles. There was something about the sense of peace and stillness they exuded, especially the giant tortoises; regardless of what was happening around them, they moved at their own pace. These little guys were simply sunning on a rock, soaking in the warmth of the afternoon sun.

Rohini realized she had been standing at the wall for quite some time. The rocks were now in the shade and the turtles had moved on. Somewhat refreshed, she headed home. As she left the castle the outside world crept back into her thoughts. Rohini wondered how the rest of the world was reacting to what had taken place at the UN.

She overheard a few people talking about the aliens at the castle, but not many. If they had been in the park all day they may have been out of the loop, she thought. *Or maybe word hasn't gotten out yet. But how could that be?* The meeting was streaming live around the world. Now her curiosity was piqued.

She wouldn't have been surprised if there had been a media blackout by the government, at least initially, but the agents who questioned her hadn't said anything about being quiet or not talking to the press. She pulled out her phone and scrolled through her news apps.

The initial stories from the *Times* and the cable news networks were vague and sensational, and full of speculation: Were they authentic aliens or was it some elaborate hoax? *If it was a hoax,* Rohini thought, *they either had some incredible technology no one knew anything about or they were able to hypnotize hundreds of people.* Neither sounded plausible to her. *They must have been aliens, or some kind of supernatural beings.* She wasn't sure why, but her intuition told her to take the Elders at their word.

There were lots of new voice mails and text messages on her phone, several were from her father, and a few from friends. She hadn't been able to check her phone while being questioned at the UN and when she was finally able to leave, she was so lost in thought, she didn't even think about talking to anyone until she'd recovered some peace of mind.

As an only child, Rohini kept her thoughts to herself, especially since her mother died. Most people turned to others, wanting to talk things out, but her first instinct was to think things through herself before she sought out others' opinions.

Rohini made several quick calls, reassuring everyone that she was fine.

"Hi, Dad," Rohini said when her father picked up.

"Rohini, I was starting to get worried," her father said, the relief evident in his voice. "Are you OK?"

"I'm fine, Dad. They just let me leave a little while ago. It took them all day to question everyone," Rohini said. "Is it true, Dad? That alien spoke with the president telepathically?" She assumed her father might have heard something. He was often privy to inside information, having served as an advisor to the president during his previous term. He no longer served in an official capacity, but he still had his security clearance. The president still used him as a sounding board from time to time.

"Yes, he actually did. I can hardly believe it myself. The president didn't tell me much, but what he did share was pretty incredible. He described it like getting a computer download straight to his brain."

"Wow. That must have been crazy. Sounds like that old Keanu movie," Rohini said. Her father had always had a fondness for old movies and they'd watched countless films together while she was growing up. It had been their bond, especially when their relationship was going through a rough patch. They could sit together and share each other's company without having to rehash their latest disagreement.

"Luckily for the president, I don't think it was anything so dramatic. He said afterwards, he suddenly had all this new knowledge he could access. It was a little disorienting apparently, but it didn't sound like he was worried about getting his circuits fried."

Her father's side of the family was mainly Norwegian; his ancestors had emigrated to the United States in the late 1700's as best as anyone could tell, making their way a little further west with each passing generation until reaching Minnesota. They had been farmers for the most part, though many, like her father, had taken other paths over the years. The men in his family had a taste for adventure in their youth, often joining the military before returning home to settle down. Her father liked to blame this restlessness on their Viking forebears.

His name certainly implied such an illustrious lineage. His namesake, Haakon Haakonsen ruled over medieval Norway's Golden Age in the 11th Century. But to Rohini her father was about the furthest thing from a Viking she could imagine. He was more bookish and professorial than brutish warrior. Of course, in Rohini's mind Vikings were either football players or the cartoon dragon riders of some of her favorite childhood movies, not actual flesh and blood, everyday people. If there was a genealogical connection to the legendary ruler, it had been lost somewhere in the North Atlantic.

When Rohini got home, she climbed the three flights of narrow creaky stairs in her brownstone walk-up, opened the door and took off her shoes, a habit she'd inherited from her parents. It was customary in most Indian families, but it was also something her parents had absorbed from their adopted second home of Maui.

They had been married there in a traditional Hawaiian ceremony—at least the tourist version of one—on the beach at sunset. It was a little cliché, Rohini had always thought, though the pictures were lovely, and they had gone back almost every year while she was growing up, so it felt like a second home to her too.

She learned to surf there and with her skin tone and the copper and blond highlights the tropical sun and salt water always brought out in her dark brown hair, she fit the part.

Rohini walked into the kitchen, pulled a half-full bottle of her favorite rosé from the fridge, and poured herself a glass. She walked into the small living room and flopped on the overstuffed couch. She took a long sip and thought about the crazy day she'd had.

Thinking about the Elders and what their appearance would mean to the planet, she was hopeful about the future. *Maybe this turn of events will also serve to unify mankind in a way it never has before, now that we finally know we aren't alone in the universe.* The past several years had been challenging in so many ways on a global scale.

The unusual weather patterns, which had become the new normal, brought extreme swings in temperature and torrential rains. There could be flash flooding followed by drought, either of which could lead to crop failures. To deal with this, more food was being grown indoors or in more protected ways. Greenhouses and drip irrigation or hydroponics had been replacing dryland farming for most crops. Since dryland farming depended on the vagaries of the weather, it had always been a crap shoot, but it was especially unpredictable now.

As resources were stretched thin in many places, conflicts arose. As society broke down, old feuds had resurfaced and were used as a pretext for violence. In many places xenophobia and bigotry had also been on the rise with cynical opportunists using immigrants and refugees as scapegoats. Fear of the "other" being a tried and true method of fascists, nationalists, and authoritarians of all stripes to elevate themselves to power. *Maybe with the arrival of the Elders, we can avoid more of that.*

Rohini realized she'd finished her glass of wine and poured herself another. *I'd better eat something.* Her empty stomach was making the wine particularly potent. A part of her felt the old familiar pull to skip dinner and just get drunk, but she'd been down that path before. She knew the self-destructive tendencies that could unleash. She'd let them run roughshod over her life after her mother died her freshman year of college.

That first year after her mother's death had been a struggle. She'd started drinking, then drinking too much. Not many people in her life had realized how bad things had gotten. She was always able to maintain her façade, always able to keep up with her classes. In hindsight she realized how fortunate she'd been to have come out the other side relatively unscathed.

There were more than a few fuzzy nights when she wasn't sure how she'd gotten home, and she'd woken up in some strange beds. The first time she wrote it off as a fluke when she woke up naked in her roommate's bed. At least she could remember that night. But when she woke up next to someone whose name she couldn't remember for the third time in as many weeks, she took it as a wakeup call.

She'd gone cold turkey for a while, with booze and sex. She'd had to. Over time she'd let them both back into her life and she'd been able to maintain a happy medium, but in the back of her mind she was always aware of that dark path she'd been on. The worst part was the not-knowing. There were empty spaces where there should have been memories. Although she didn't think anything terrible had happened to her during that time, those empty spaces taunted her.

Growing up, she and her father had always butted heads. Their personalities had been so similar it was inevitable. He was smart and stubborn, and she had proven to be more than his equal on both accounts. Rohini's mother had always been the mediator, keeping the peace in the family. After his work with the government had kept him in DC for longer and longer periods of time, Rohini and her father had grown apart. But when Rohini's mother died, they'd turned to each other for solace, and they'd discovered they had a much easier time relating to each other as adults. He didn't feel the pressure to parent as much and she didn't feel the need to rebel. But there were still things she'd never been able to share with him. Still so much about her he didn't know.

The next morning Rohini woke with her memory of the previous night intact. *Always nice to start the day off with a small victory.* When she returned to the conference everyone was buzzing. It felt a little surreal as Dr. Yang stepped up to the podium.

"Do you think they'll show up again?" she said to Liam, who was sitting next to her again.

"I don't think they'll be back for a while. I imagine they'll give us some time to choose people to go to their planet," Liam replied.

"I suppose so," Rohini said. She had to admit it was a bit of a letdown.

*Funny how quickly our expectations can change.* Rohini had been so excited to attend this year's meeting, but now she worried they were only going through the motions. *Wouldn't whatever knowledge or technology the Elders gave us be more important than what we're going to be discussing here?* But Rohini realized that whatever solutions the Elders had for them, it would still take humans working together to implement them. It would still take a paradigm shift in global consciousness for any solution to be a long-term fix and not a temporary bandage. And there was little reason to think those who had been the most resistant to change would be any more willing now than they had been in the past.

# 3

Dayan entered the council chambers and strode towards the Guide, who was seated in the Place of Honor at the opposite end of the chamber. "Grandmother, I have returned," he said, dropping to one knee and placing his hand over his heart.

"Please, Dayan, rise and come to me," the Guide said, unfolding her crossed legs and stepping down from her seat on the Place of Honor.

Dayan, the Speaker, walked to her and smiled. They each placed their right hands over their hearts, their left on the other's shoulder and touched their foreheads gently together, taking a deep breath. "It is good to be in your presence again, Grandmother," Dayan said.

"Yes, it is, Dayan. Welcome home. Please, tell me of your trip to Earth. What was your reception like?"

"I delivered our message to Earth at their United Nations. Those present were understandably skeptical," Dayan said.

"And what of their leaders?" the Guide asked.

"They were receptive to our message," Dayan said. "I sensed relief from most of them, although there were skeptics among them as well. There was only one among them whom I fear may present a problem, his mind was... very dark. Perhaps as our plans move forward, the other leaders can persuade him."

As Dayan spoke, the Guide's eyes glazed over briefly, but he knew she wasn't ignoring his words. Quite to the contrary, she was glancing into his thoughts as he spoke to gain a greater impression of what had transpired on Earth.

"It is only natural that they should be skeptical," the Guide said. "I am not too worried about one holdout. As the leaders of Earth see what our knowledge can do to advance their energy technologies they will fall in line. And what of the woman, did you get an impression of her, and the others?"

"I did not get a read on her myself, Grandmother, but I believe Jianhu did. Shall I send for her?" Dayan said.

"That is not necessary. Jianhu can accompany you when you report to the full council tonight. Thank you. We will speak further then. Until such time, Dayan," the Guide said, once again placing her hand over her heart and bowing her head slightly.

"Until such time, Grandmother." Dayan returned the gesture before leaving the chamber.

Later that evening, Dayan returned. He met Jianhu outside.

"I see they've already begun," Jianhu said, nodding towards the large wooden doors which usually remained open, except when the council was in session. Two Guardians holding halberds flanked the closed doors of the council chambers. "Do you know why they've summoned me, Dayan?"

"They want to hear your opinion of the woman," Dayan replied. "Did you get a read on any of the others?"

"I didn't. I noted their presence, but the woman intrigued me. I'm afraid after stopping the security guards I spent most of my time focused on her," Jianhu replied.

Dayan was about to ask what caught her attention when one of the Guardians spoke: "The council will see you now."

Together, Dayan and Jianhu entered the council chambers. The representatives of the twelve clans were arrayed around two semi-circular tables at the center of the circular chamber. One was made of a light, almost white wood, though its timeworn surface had darkened significantly, showing its great antiquity. The other table was made of a dark, almost black wood. The members of the Council of the Twelve Clans were, by tradition, made up of equal numbers, male and female, Scholar and Warrior. In the gap between the two tables, at the far end of the chamber, the Guide sat on the Seat of Honor, like a linchpin holding the council together.

Dayan and Jianhu approached and knelt on one knee, their hands on their hearts, in the formal gesture of respect.

"Please rise," said the Guide. "Welcome, Dayan. Welcome, Jianhu. The council is eager to hear of your reception by the Earthlings."

"Thank you, Grandmother," Dayan said. "Members of the Council, our message was greeted with both hope and skepticism among the Earthlings. Their leaders were eager for our assistance as the gravity of their situation has become apparent."

"They seemed willing to begin, then?" asked the councilor from the Dragon Clan.

"Yes, indeed, Councilor," Dayan replied. "I have every confidence they will begin in our absence."

"Good. We will see how they proceed in the coming months."

"Jianhu, we understand you had a chance to read the woman. What was your impression?" the Guide said.

"Yes, Grandmother," Jianhu replied. "I did. It was… interesting. Her mind was unlike any Earthling's I have encountered before. Were it not for the fact that all her memories were of Earth, I would have taken her for someone from our own world."

"Interesting indeed," the Guide said, her eyes had once again taken on a glassy look as she peered into Jianhu's thoughts. "I can see why you were 'distracted' by her." She gave a little chuckle. "And what of the others?"

"My apologies, Grandmother," Jianhu replied. "I must confess I was quite surprised by the woman. I was able to sense the presence of the other three, but I did not read them completely."

"Very well. I will ask Qaletaqa, the Earth Elder to observe the others," the Guide said. "Thank you. You may go now. The council will discuss this matter further. Until such time."

"Thank you, Grandmother. Until such time," Dayan and Jianhu replied together.

# 4

*New York City, USA*

In the days and weeks that followed, word began to trickle out. World leaders were working on an unprecedented global collaboration. There were also many wild rumors flying around and more than a little paranoia. The conspiracy theory websites were having a field day. In recent years, the lines between legitimate news sources and fake news had become badly blurred. Those who lacked critical thinking skills had become easy dupes for spurious sources shared through social media.

People who already believed climate change was a hoax thought this was simply a more elaborate version of a conspiracy to get everyone on board with renewable energy. Those who feared a One World Government run by the Illuminati saw this as the perfect pretext for that. Others, more reasonably, just feared the unknown. What if these aliens weren't the benign beings they claimed to be?

What put everyone on edge—even those who welcomed the Elders—was the fact that these aliens could blend right in. They appeared completely human as far as anyone could tell. New Yorkers usually walked the streets with blinders on, like the horses pulling carriages through Central Park, but as Rohini walked the streets of NYC in the last few weeks, she'd found herself wondering more than once whether she might be walking right past an Elder on the street. *How would you know?* She had always been a bit of a people watcher, but she noticed more people than usual making eye contact as she walked the streets of Manhattan. *They must be wondering the same thing.*

One month after the Elders' appearance at the United Nations, there was an announcement made describing some of what the Elders had revealed to Earth's leaders, as well as what those in power planned to do going forward.

That morning Rohini retrieved her Sunday *Times* from the lobby. It seemed anachronistic, in this day and age. Maybe's that's why she liked it. The *Times* was the last news outlet that still printed a paper copy, albeit only the Sunday Edition.

She unrolled the paper on the way up to preview the front page, stopping in her tracks between the first and second floors when she saw the headline "Alien Climate Plans Revealed." Bundling the paper back up, she rushed to her apartment, taking the stairs two at a time. Back inside, she poured herself a cup of coffee, settled in on the couch, and unfolded the paper.

It was being billed as a mobilization unlike anything seen since World War II. CEOs were cooperating with governments across the globe in a coordinated effort to retool manufacturing plants for production of new renewable energy technologies. While not delving into great detail describing exactly what these were, the article said that the aliens' telepathic communication had included breakthrough insights on advancing our existing solar technologies to achieve a giant leap in efficiency. It had taken some time for engineers to work out how to put this new information to use as well as to test prototypes, but the kinks had apparently been worked out sufficiently for them to move ahead with production.

The Joint Agreement, as it was being called, described how this had been part of the Elders' conditions for their assistance. Once given this knowledge, they intended for us to get the ball rolling in their absence and help ourselves.

Rohini couldn't help smiling as she recalled what her uncle Ragnar always said, "They say the Lord helps those who help themselves, course if you help yourself, the Lord can just kick back and relax."

Ragnar had his own unique take on theology. Unlike her father, Ragnar had continued the family tradition of farming, but had settled in
New Mexico after falling for a local girl, many years before.

Returning to the paper, the next article caught Rohini's attention.
It was a call for applicants for an Earth Ambassadors Program, the
individuals who would accompany the Elders back to their world.
There had been some disagreement about which nationalities would
be eligible. Some argued they should be limited to those from wealth-
ier nations—those countries with the most resources to contribute—
others argued for equal political and regional representation. The
compromise had settled on two ambassadors each from the United
States, the European Union, Russia, and China. One ambassador each
would be selected from Brazil, South Africa, Japan and India, for a
total of twelve.

Rohini assumed selections would only be open to military personnel or maybe astronauts—they were talking about going to another planet, after all—but the application process was open to anyone
between the ages of twenty-one and forty with a four-year degree and
proficiency in at least two languages. *That makes sense,* she thought,
assuming the ambassadors would study the Elders' language. *Although, they spoke English at the UN, didn't they? I was able to understand them, so they must have.*

Rohini was finishing the article and her second cup of coffee
when her phone vibrated on the coffee table. She usually kept it in
silent mode, figuring there was enough noise in our modern world.
Checking the display, she saw it was her father. "Hi, Dad. Did you
hear about the announcement today?"

"I did. Actually, that's why I'm calling. I'm not sure how to put
this, Rohini. You know about my connection with the administration?"

"Sure, Dad. I know you and the president go way back, and
there's stuff you can't talk about."

"Well, yes, but that's not exactly what I mean. I talked to the
president today. You remember how the Elders communicated with

President Johnson telepathically. Well, he told me today that when the aliens spoke to him about the ambassadors, they also told him who they would like him to send. That's why I'm calling."

"Wait, what? You mean he wants me to apply for the program? That's amazing!' Rohini said, sitting up straighter at the news.

"No, Rohini, not the president, the Elders. The Elders want you."

Rohini sank back into the couch, her mouth agape. She couldn't believe what her father was saying. *Surely, I didn't hear him right.*

"But… what about the announcement and the application process… is that just for show? I thought…"

"No, the application process is real," her father said. "The president mentioned that there were others as well. Each of the countries sending two ambassadors had one individual who the Elders requested by name."

"But how could they possibly know about me. I didn't even talk to them," Rohini said. "That's kind of creepy, like they've been stalking me or something."

Her father chuckled. "No, I don't think it's anything like that. President Johnson told me that the other individuals they requested were also Youth Ambassadors who were at the UN that day."

"Well, I did have a 'moment' with one of them," Rohini said.

"You mean the bodyguard?"

"Yes."

"That could be it, although I would think they must have known about you before," her father said. "After all it wasn't the bodyguard who communicated with the president."

"So, they *have* been stalking me."

"Well, I guess you've got me there," her father replied. "Maybe just think of it as vetting you, instead of stalking you."

"That does sound less creepy, almost flattering even," Rohini said. "But we are still talking about aliens here, Dad. How do we know we can trust them?" *Oh God. What if they abducted me and I didn't even know it?* Thoughts of hokey TV shows about anal probes and cattle mutilations flashed through her mind.

"I've thought about that too, Rohini. Listen, the president believes we can take them at their word, and I trust his judgement. He's never been wrong when it really counted."

"Well, that's great as long as the Elder's telepathy was more of a mind-meld and not a mind-trick. What if it's all a lie? And you're OK with this? You sound pretty relaxed considering some aliens want to beam me up to God knows where. I *am* your only daughter, remember?"

"I know, sweetie, and no, I wasn't OK with it—at least not at first—but I've had some time to think about it and I've come to terms with it. I've always wanted the world for you," he said, a slight quiver in his voice. "I've always wanted you to reach for the stars—I just didn't know you would actually be going there. When you went to Space Camp I had to reconcile myself to the fact that you might pursue that path. I thought you might go on the first manned mission to Mars someday, but nothing like this. When you got more involved in ecology and sustainability, I was relieved. I thought I only had to worry about you travelling in other countries, not to another planet. But I guess the real question is, are *you* OK with this?"

Rohini was more than OK with it. It was beyond her wildest dreams. While she was nervous, it was a nervous excitement. Her body buzzed with anticipation like a phone on vibrate. She had always loved to travel, delighting in seeing new places and learning about different cultures.

Her father was right. She used to envision herself traveling into space as an astronaut, but as she grew older and came to understand the urgency of the climate crisis, those dreams took a back seat to her love for the planet. Now she was being offered a once in a lifetime opportunity where those two paths converged. That evening, Rohini was on a plane to Washington DC to meet with President Johnson.

# 5

*The White House*
*Washington, DC*

"The president will see you now."

Rohini, waiting outside the Oval Office, stood, smoothing her clothes and taking a deep breath to steady herself before walking through the door. Her stomach had been full of butterflies all morning. She'd tried to stay calm after waking, while getting ready for her meeting with the president, but it was no use, her stomach was still aflutter. Her father had known President Johnson for years, but Rohini had never met the man.

Walking through the door, she saw several people gathered in the Oval Office. They stood as she entered. She recognized President Johnson, as well as the vice president, Elizabeth Powers. She was America's first female VP and was extremely popular. It was taken for granted that when the president's second term ended, she would be her party's nominee and would easily take the election.

"Ah, Rohini, so nice to finally meet you," President Johnson greeted her with a warm handshake and a gentle squeeze on the shoulder.

"Thank you, Mr. President, it's an honor."

"And this is Vice President Powers," President Johnson said.

"Yes, you probably wouldn't remember, Madame Vice President, but I met you several years ago with my parents."

"Of course I remember. I was quite taken by how precocious you were. You were still in high school, as I recall, but you seemed wise beyond your years. And your father brags about you all the time. He's extremely proud of you, dear," Vice President Powers said. She smiled warmly.

"And this is Jane Smith. She'll be helping get you prepared for your trip," the president said, introducing the other woman. It was the agent from the UN, the woman with green eyes.

"You were at the UN," Rohini said.

"Yes, I was part of the investigation that day," Jane said.

"Pleased to meet you, Ms. Smith," Rohini said, offering her hand.

"Please, call me Jane, we're going to be spending a lot of time together, Rohini."

Jane had an intensity about her. Rohini was immediately reminded of one of the Elders at the UN, the one she had come to think of as "the bodyguard." Jane had red hair, and though she was of average height and weight for a woman, she projected a larger presence. Rohini was again struck by the same feeling she'd had before, that she knew Jane from somewhere. *Who is this woman?*

The president motioned for Rohini to have a seat on the couch as the others sat back down. "Rohini, I asked you here because I wanted to meet with you personally," President Johnson said. "I'm sure you realize how momentous this is."

"Of course, Mr. President," Rohini replied.

"The fact that the Elders asked for you by name has everybody wondering," he said. "I know during your debriefing at the UN you indicated you haven't had any contact with them before, is that right?"

"Yes, Mr. President, at least not as far as I am aware. They did say that they've been here before, so I suppose it's possible they've been watching me."

"Yes, that's quite possible," the president said. "We know little of their technological capabilities, let alone their apparent telepathic abilities. It may have been quite easy for them to observe us without our knowledge. We've analyzed the video from the UN. As far as we've been able to tell they appeared as human as you or I. I don't suppose they'd have any trouble blending in.

"Rohini, I've asked Ms. Smith to act as a bit of a mentor to prepare you. She has a particular skill set which may come in handy on this trip. You didn't exactly sign up for this, but it may be helpful to think of this trip as a mission. I know you don't have any type of military background, and I'm not going to send you through basic training, but Ms. Smith will be putting you through a bit of a private boot camp. We want you to be prepared for any contingencies on this mission, and we'll want you to be able to gather as much intelligence about the Elders as you can."

"Of course, Mr. President. That makes perfect sense," Rohini said.

"While they appear trustworthy, especially to those of us whom they contacted telepathically, we have no way of knowing whether that is truly the case. We've considered the possibility that if they can speak to us telepathically, they could also be capable of implanting positive impressions of themselves or—to put it more bluntly—we could have been brainwashed," the president said, his brow furrowing. "The other world leaders and I aren't entirely comfortable with this realization—to put it mildly—so we think it would be prudent to not simply take them at their word."

"Yes, Mr. President..."

Elizabeth Powers cut in, putting a hand on Rohini's arm. "What the president is trying to say, dear, is that Ms. Smith is going to train you to be a spy."

# 6

After the meeting, Rohini went back to Blair House where she was staying as the president's guest. Located a short walk across Pennsylvania Avenue from the White House, Blair House had served as the president's guesthouse since being purchased by the government at the behest of President Roosevelt in 1942. Rohini was staying in one of its guestrooms. It was usually reserved for foreign dignitaries and visiting heads of state. Rohini felt a little out of place in the opulent surroundings.

There were no visiting dignitaries at the moment, so other than the part of the building which housed some State Department offices, Blair House was fairly quiet. She hadn't had much opportunity to look around the grounds, arriving after dark the night before, so she took the time now to wander around a little.

Rohini made her way out to the interior courtyard garden where she saw a circular fountain surrounded by a square planting of a low green groundcover. There were benches on all four sides. She took in the garden as she made her way to one of the benches and sat down. She needed a moment to let it all sink in. Listening to the splashing of the fountain, she began to relax. She rolled her shoulders a few times to release some of the tension she'd been unconsciously holding on to all morning.

Every time Rohini was starting to get a grip on what was happening, there was a new wrinkle. The Elders' arrival had been a shock to everyone, but learning she was chosen as one of the ambassadors to their alien world was something she alone had to process. She had been sitting for half an hour when she heard the crunch of footsteps on gravel behind her.

"There you are."

Rohini turned. It was Jane Smith.

"Oh, hi, Jane."

"Mind if I join you?"

"Please, have a seat," Rohini said, patting the bench next to her.

Jane sat down. They remained quiet for a moment watching the fountain. Rohini felt the need to break the ice. "Nice digs, huh?" She blurted, awkwardly.

"Yes, they certainly are," Jane replied. "I take it you don't usually run in these circles."

"Oh sure, I stay at diplomatic guesthouses wherever I travel," Rohini replied sarcastically. "No. I'd probably be more comfortable camping, to be honest."

"Me too. Although when I've been in the field for a while, I can certainly appreciate a hot shower," Jane said, smiling.

"So, what exactly do you do, Jane? Are you in the CIA or something? Or am I allowed to ask?"

"Let's just say I've worked for several agencies which like to stay under the radar. Currently I'm on special assignment for the president."

"You don't mind babysitting?" Rohini said.

"When the president says, 'jump,' you say, 'how high?' Besides, Rohini, you're not exactly a kid. When I was your age I'd been in the military for several years already."

"True. Although I felt like one speaking to President Johnson today," Rohini said, sheepishly.

"It's the power of the office," Jane said. "Not to take anything away from the president—he's a remarkable man—but anyone in that position has a certain gravitas that can be intimidating.

"Listen, we're going to get an early start tomorrow, so I'm going to give you some space tonight. The next few months will be intense. The president wants you as prepared as I can get you in that time. I'll be staying here at Blair House too. I'm right next door, so if you need me, just knock. Otherwise, I'll see you in the morning."

"Thanks, Jane. I appreciate that."

"No worries. I'll give you a knock at six. Are you a runner?"

"I ran cross country in high school."

"Cross country, that's good. Knowing you can push yourself like that will go a long way."

"Just try not to make me puke. You'll give me flashbacks of my old coach. He used to tell us if we didn't want to puke after a race, we weren't really trying."

Jane smiled. "We'll see about that tomorrow," she said. She rose from the bench and walked towards the door.

Rohini turned her attention back to the fountain until she heard Jane's voice again, right before she went inside.

"Remember, 6am sharp!"

# 7

*Who does that smug bastard think he is?* Bartholomew Simms was seething. The Joint Agreement had gotten under his skin. *I can't believe the president is cooperating with these aliens. And other world leaders are going along with this?* *How can they be so gullible?*

Simms sat at an oversized mahogany desk in the library of his Westchester County, New York, mansion which he used as his primary office, spending more time here than his office in the city. The library was richly appointed with matching mahogany shelves lining three walls, the fourth taken up by three large Tudor-style leaded glass windows.

The shelves and the desk, as well as the ornate woodwork throughout the rest of the mansion, had been made by the same craftsman more than one hundred years before. The shelves showed their age in the smoothly rounded edges where countless hands had passed over them through several generations of the Simms family and rose all the way up to the twelve-foot ceilings, requiring an old-fashioned library ladder to reach the upper shelves.

In front of the desk, a leather sofa and a pair of matching armchairs sat on either side of an antique Persian rug. Chewing on an unlit cigar as he fumed about the recent turn of events, his gaze fell on the rug, which, he had to admit, really tied the room together. He had always found it soothing. It may have been something in the mix of patterns and colors he found relaxing, or perhaps it was memories from childhood. He could almost picture himself as he played on the rug while his father sat at the very same desk during his tenure at the helm of the family's business empire.

His father had enjoyed him playing there. As long as he was quiet, of course, only shooing him out if he were having an important meeting where a small child underfoot would have been too much of a distraction. Once he was of school age he'd spent most of his time away at boarding school. Perhaps that was why he found those early memories so poignant.

But Bartholomew Simms hadn't gotten where he was by being sentimental. Never a trusting soul, he was certainly no bleeding-heart environmentalist. *All this drivel about climate change really chaps my ass.* Being the head of a multinational conglomerate with coal-fired power plants and fracked natural gas extraction among its chief assets, there was no way he was going along with this sudden "kumbaya moment" the international community was having.

The way he saw it, he had gotten his just desserts in life. *Those people suffering under climate change deserve what they get. As God's chosen nation, America has been blessed, and as the most righteous among them, the well-heeled are right where they deserve to be.*

Like many adherents of Prosperity Theology, it would never occur to Simms that it was a self-fulfilling prophecy. It was a perfect way for the rich to assuage any guilty they might have about hoarding away wealth generation after generation; wealth so vast it would take a lifetime to figure out ways to spend it. The rich themselves were not entirely to blame for this philosophy. In many ways they were also victims; patsies to those greatest of all con artists, the televangelists who promoted it, getting rich themselves in the process.

Instead of putting their wealth to good use helping others as his grandfather had, most of it sat, gathering dust, or whatever the electronic equivalent of dust was; money being an increasingly abstract concept these days. Oh sure, he gave some money to charity. They all did. *Who doesn't love a good tax write-off, after all?* But a saint he most certainly was not, nor did he aspire to be. You wouldn't catch him washing a homeless man's feet, not in this lifetime. *I'll leave that to the pope.* But washing money? That was another matter entirely.

Simms had heard rumblings of what was being discussed behind the scenes, but hadn't realized the full scope of the international community's plans until the Joint Agreement was announced. *They've gone whole-hog tree hugger.* It was as though the "Keep it in the Ground" movement had staged a world-wide coup overnight. The markets were in turmoil. Fossil fuels were tanking, while the green energy sector was through the roof.

While Simms loved a volatile market as much as the next vulture capitalist—there was always money to be made if you knew how to take advantage of the situation—he was not going to sit idly by and watch his family's empire crumble around him. He knew there were others who felt the same way about the Joint Agreement and what it heralded. He'd already reached out to some of his friends and even some of his competitors to discuss what might be done to combat this threat.

They would be meeting soon. What Simms needed now was information. He'd learned through his connections that unbeknownst to the public, some of the Earth Ambassadors had been hand-picked by the aliens. *They must have known about these aliens before the incident at the UN and are conspiring with them.* One way or another he would find out.

Leaning forward over his desk, he pushed the intercom button on his phone, signaling his personal assistant.

"Chelsea, get me Gruber."

# 8

Rohini went back to her room, but she couldn't shake her restlessness. She was getting anxious thinking about this sudden and quite unexpected new adventure she'd been thrust into. Knowing that she'd be somewhat cut off from her friends and family for the next several months at least, she wanted to reach out. She called up Jack, one of her friends in DC.

"Jack, it's Rohini. What are you doing tonight? Yes, I'm in DC! Can you get some of the old gang together? Who is still around? Awesome. Should we meet at the Black Rooster? Right, we can always go to Irish Whiskey if they're packed. OK. See you then. Bye."

Rohini was excited and a little nervous as she hung up. Jack had been one of her closest friends in college. At times they'd been more than friends. They tried dating more than once but each time it became more apparent they made better friends than lovers. She was glad their attempts at a romantic relationship had never ended badly. They were both part of the same small circle of friends and it could be awkward in a close-knit group when things ended badly. She'd seen it happen more than once.

An hour later, she left Blair House and made her way down Pennsylvania Avenue, veered left at H street and walked over to the Yard, as the campus quad was known. She hadn't been back to George

Washington University since graduation and wanted to take a quick stroll through campus before she headed north to meet Jack at the Black Rooster. It had been one of their favorite bars in college and she looked forward to seeing one of her old haunts.

She took the diagonal path across the Yard and stopped in the middle for a moment, taking in the atmosphere of the Foggy Bottom campus which had once felt so familiar. It still did in a way, but it also seemed like another lifetime, though it had only been a few years. She turned a slow circle, looking at the buildings which enclosed the Yard on three sides, leaving it open to the north.

She stopped as her eyes caught a sudden movement. She thought she had seen someone on the path she'd just walked down, but there didn't appear to be anyone there. Sundown was approaching. *Maybe it's the twilight playing tricks on me*. She recalled from one of her psychology classes that when visual information is missing, like in low light, the brain often fills in the gaps. *That must be it.*

As she continued across campus, Rohini couldn't shake the feeling she'd had back at the Yard. She was passing through Bausell Walk nearing 22nd street when the hairs started to stand up on the back of her neck. *Is someone following me or am I losing it?* Her emotions had certainly been a bit erratic lately. Being anxious wasn't out of character, but she had never been paranoid.

She took a few surreptitious glances over her shoulder as she pretended to admire some of the trees, but didn't see anyone. She was starting to feel like she was going crazy. She was approaching the street when a van came screeching to a sudden halt right in front of her. Its side door opened and two men in black tactical gear and balaclavas jumped out, grabbing her arms on either side. A third figure knelt in the open door, pointing a gun at her.

"Inside now!" he yelled.

Rohini heard several loud bangs as a series of holes appeared in a line across the side of the van. The man in the open door fell to his side and remained still. The two men holding her loosened their grip as they looked around in alarm. Rohini took advantage of the distraction to jerk her arm free, then elbowed the man on her right, before turning back to her left, kicking the other man in the groin. As he doubled over, the first man grabbed her arm again—her blow having little effect—and shoved a gun into her ribs.

"Get in the van, now," he said, menace in his voice.

Another shot rang out and the man she had kicked grunted and slumped to the ground. The last man standing swore and released her arm, grabbed his fallen comrade and helped him to his feet. He shoved him into the van and dove in after him.

"Go! Go! Go!"

The van's tires squealed as it sped away, disappearing down the street. Rohini felt frozen in time. Slowly she realized someone was yelling her name. It sounded muffled, like being underwater. As the fog in her mind began to lift, time sped up, and suddenly everything got loud again. She turned when she heard her name again and saw Jane running towards her, a gun in her hand.

"Are you OK? Are you hurt? Rohini! Are you hurt?"

"No... No... I'm OK. I just... I just..." Rohini mumbled.

"I know. It's OK. It's over. You're safe, at least for now."

# 9

"Gruber, have you secured the girl?"

"No, sir, Mr. Simms, my apologies. There were unforeseen complications."

"Unforeseen complications? Don't give me that crap. What happened?"

"We suffered casualties. One dead, one wounded. She was being tailed by security of some kind. We don't know who yet, but they were good, stayed out of sight, definitely professional."

"We've got to assume they were government. Please tell me you weren't followed."

"No, sir. We torched the van and covered our tracks well; there won't be any trail to lead them back to us."

"They'll keep her wrapped up tight now that we've tipped our hand. We'll have to get ahold of one of the others. Do we have any idea who the other ambassadors are yet?"

"We're working on it, sir. As far as we can tell the others are foreign nationals. Since the girl was at the UN that day, we're working on the assumption that the others were as well. Many of them have gone back to their own countries. We're narrowing it down as we speak."

"Alright, let me know when you've got something concrete. We need more intel before our little summit convenes with our friends. I want to know exactly what we're dealing with before we decide our next steps."

"Yes, sir."

"And Gruber… don't fail me again."

# 10

As they sped through the Washington night, Rohini sat in shock. Five minutes after her savior appeared, Jane and Rohini were in the back seat of a blacked-out SUV being whisked across the city. In the front seat sat two men in suits with earpieces who were all business. Rohini guessed Secret Service. They reminded her of the agents she'd seen around the White House. Four more followed behind in another identical vehicle.

"Where are they taking us, Jane?"

"Someplace safe. We can't go back to Blair House. The Secret Service will grab our stuff. The plan had been to stay in the city—the president wanted to keep you nearby so he could keep tabs on you—but after this I think we'll have to reassess our plans."

"Who do you think they were? Why did they come after me?"

"We don't know yet, but it must have to do with the Elders. There's nothing in your background that would account for this otherwise, unless there's something you've kept from us," Jane said.

"I don't have any idea why someone would come after me," Rohini replied.

"With your family's connections, it's possible it could have been a simple kidnapping, but with you being chosen to go with the Elders, I think it's too much of a coincidence. There's no way run-of-the-mill kidnappers looking for a ransom would have been able to pull this off anyway. They wouldn't have been able to follow you here on such short notice. They would have gone after you in New York. Whoever they are, they've also got some pull. They must have had inside knowledge of your coming to DC."

"You mean they're someone in the government?"

"No, I don't think we've got some rogue group in the government going after you—although that's a possibility we'll have to look into—more than likely it's some loose lips and greased palms; someone bought off to provide intel on you. Greed is like a virus these days, infecting everything. I'm sure you realize you can't go wandering off like that again after this. I was just being cautious following you; we had no idea anyone would come after you like that."

"Lucky for me you did. Thank you, Jane. You saved my life."

"Don't worry about it, Rohini," Jane said. "We don't know that, and besides I was only doing my job."

"Well, it means a lot to me... Oh my God, Jack! I forgot I was going to meet him. I'd better call him so he knows I'm not coming."

"Alright, but don't call him from your cell," Jane said. "Here, use mine, it's encrypted. We don't want to take the chance they could track you, in fact just to be safe let's turn your phone off for now—and don't tell him what happened, Rohini. You'll have to make something up."

Rohini took a couple deep breaths to steady her nerves, then dialed. "Jack, it's Rohini. Look, I'm sorry but something's come up... I won't be able to get out tonight after all," she said, tears starting to well up. "Ok. Yes, next time I'm in town, definitely. OK. Bye." After Rohini hung up, her tears began to flow. Hearing Jack's voice had been too much in her present state. In an attempt to hold back her emotions, she held her breath, not wanting to blubber in front of strangers. Eventually the knot in her gut felt tight enough to form a diamond. She could only hold that tension for so long, finally letting it out in a great sigh.

They sat in silence for much of the drive, Rohini trying to process what had happened, Jane trying to piece together who these new players might be. Rohini didn't know where they were taking her, but soon she noticed the scenery changing outside her window. She could tell they were leaving the city as sidewalks and parking lots gave way to more fields and trees.

Soon they were in the countryside. They'd crossed the Potomac early on, so Rohini knew they were headed south. As they drove, she thought back to her days at George Washington. She rarely went south past Alexandria back then. When she did it was usually to go to Mt. Vernon. She loved to walk the grounds and look out over the Potomac. She was always curious to see which heirloom varieties they had growing in the vegetable gardens. Many were unique to Mt. Vernon.

She would drive down and spend the day roaming the grounds when she needed a break, packing a lunch and having a picnic under the shade of the old trees lining the bowling green in front of the estate. Her favorite spot though, was the slave memorial.

She always found it astonishing how a monument commemorating those who had suffered so much could be so peaceful, as though despite whatever terror and suffering they might have endured while living, the dead were now whispering to those left behind, "Do not weep for us, we are at rest. It is the living who need your care and compassion; it is you who need each other." She found the thought soothing as they drove through the night.

"You don't suppose they'd let us stay at Mt. Vernon, do you?" Rohini said, only half joking.

"You must be feeling better," Jane said.

"A little bit. I'm starting to calm down."

"Sorry, I don't think Mt. Vernon is an option," Jane replied. "We're headed a bit farther south. Have you ever heard of Quantico?"

"Isn't that the FBI Academy?"

"Among other things. It's located on the Marine base there. Anyway, we thought it would be a good place to keep you safe now that someone has you in their sights. It's got the facilities as well as the expertise for any kind of training we might want to put you through and we're still only about an hour from the White House."

"They're not going to put me through the academy, are they?"

"No, we'll stick with our original plan, other than the location. I'll still do most, if not all, of your training, but having other students around may be useful. They often have agents or other outsiders come in to assist with training the new agents, so maybe we can bring you in from time to time in that capacity. Otherwise we'll do our own thing."

"How could I help train agents?"

"Can you act?"

"I did a few plays in middle school. I don't think I'll be up for any awards."

"It's not that big of a deal. They sometimes bring people in to role-play to help run the trainees through different scenarios. Just pretend you're at the renaissance festival, Tinkerbell."

Rohini's cheeks flushed in embarrassment. She wanted to melt into her seat. That was one of her guilty pleasures, one of the things she'd most looked forward to every fall, not just growing up, but even through college. She went all out, dressing up in costume every year. *I shouldn't be surprised. She probably knows all about me.*

"Humph, I'll have you know I go dressed as a yakshini, thank you very much, not some cartoon fairy," Rohini replied in mock indignation.

Jane laughed. "Oh, I beg your pardon," she said. "Alright, you've got me. What's a yakshini?"

"It's like an Indian dryad. You know, like a tree spirit."

"Oh, right. How could I possibly get that confused with a fairy? We should have you dress as one of these yakshini at the academy and tell the trainees they're going to practice raiding Burning Man."

"Ha, ha, very funny. Have your fun now, Jane. Maybe I'll ask the president to let me go to one last renaissance festival, in case I never make it back from the Elders' planet. You'll have to accompany me, and of course you'll have to look the part—we couldn't have you walking around looking like some government agent. I can see it now—a few flowers, some glitter and body paint—you'll blend right in."

Rohini and Jane heard a snicker from the front seat and the two Secret Service agents shared a quick look with each other.

"Alright, don't get started, you two. What's our ETA?" Jane asked.

"We should be to the main gate in five, ma'am."

"I don't know what's worse, you two picturing me dressed up as a fairy or calling me ma'am."

They were expected, so after a quick wave through at the base guard post, they headed to a second gate a few miles into the woods at the FBI Academy. They took a little longer here as the security was tighter, but being escorted by Secret Service under orders from the White House greased some wheels. Before long they were on campus and headed to one of the academy's dormitories.

Two Secret Service agents preceded them inside, scanning the lobby. Two more followed behind Rohini and Jane, taking up posts just inside the doors. The last two agents remained with the vehicles. Once inside, they were greeted by one of the dormitory's concierges.

While dressed simply in khakis and a polo shirt, he still had that FBI look about him; youthful, fit, and squared away. He reminded Rohini of friends she'd had who were military. *But there's another quality there; a curiosity, like he's thinking, "The truth is out there."* Rohini stifled a laugh as she heard the theme music from the TV show running through her head.

"You must be Ms. Smith and Ms. Haakonsen," the man said. "I'm Bob. I'll be your concierge during your stay with us. If you need anything pertaining to your accommodations, just let me know."

"Thanks, Bob. Is Special Agent Reynolds here yet?"

"He should be with you shortly. Why don't we go ahead and get you settled in?" he said.

The first two agents followed them as Bob showed them to a room, stationing themselves outside as Bob gave them the brief tour. As it was a dorm room with two beds, two dressers, and little else, the tour consisted of Bob pointing out where the bathroom was. Bob once again reminded them to let him know if they needed anything and left them alone.

"Boy, this brings back memories," Rohini said.

"Of time spent at the FBI?"

"No, just this dorm room; it reminds me of college. I feel like I should be hanging up posters or putting a quilt from home on the bed."

"Let's see, were you more the boyband type or the Bob Marley type?" Jane teased. "I'm guessing reggae."

"I like some reggae, but I think the Bob Marley posters are more of a guy thing in college," Rohini replied, putting her hands on her hips and cocking her head to one side.

"Let's see, you're idealistic… maybe Gandhi? No that would be too cliché, and probably a guy thing too. How about Malala? Does she have posters? Oh, I know. What about that woman who lived in the tree, what was her name?"

There was a knock at the door, so Jane abandoned her good-natured ribbing of Rohini and went to open it. One of the Secret Service agents was outside with a suitcase in each hand.

"They dropped off your things from DC. I can't vouch for their packing job, but I'm sure they grabbed everything."

"Thanks. Just put them anywhere."

The agent set the bags down in front of the closet and left. There was another knock on the open door as the agent was leaving.

"Jane, how are you? I didn't expect to see you here again."

"Oh, come on. It's not like they kicked me out," Jane replied.

Rohini's ears perked up. "Jane was in the FBI?"

"She was, although she didn't go by Jane back then. Anything beyond that is for her to tell, I'm afraid," the man said.

"Rohini, this is Special Agent Burton Reynolds, known affectionately to his friends as the Bandit."

"Wait, Burt… like the movie? So, you're like Smokey and the Bandit all rolled into one? Please tell me you don't drive a Trans Am."

SA Reynolds smiled. "Rohini, I'm impressed. Most kids these days don't know the classics."

"Yeah, my dad liked to watch all those old movies from his childhood with me," Rohini replied.

"While I don't drive a Trans Am, I do appreciate fast cars."

Jane chuckled. "That's an understatement," she said. "Burt is a legend on the driving course. He aced it his first attempt as a trainee and later spent time as an instructor—but we can discuss late-seven-ties cinema and the Bandit's infamy behind the wheel another time. Are you fully up to speed on this, Burt?"

"I just got off the phone with the Director," Burt said.

"Do we know anything yet about who has taken an interest in Rohini?"

"No, they don't have much to go on yet. They'll start chasing down leads and should have something solid to go on in the next few days. What are your plans?"

"I'm not sure yet. We'll stay here for now, but I think at some point we'll have to come out into the open again. I'm sure they'll want to do some publicity with the ambassadors eventually. Until then I think this is as good a place as any to keep a low profile and train Rohini."

"Alright, I'll let you settle in. You've got full access to the facilities. Give me a shout if you need anything."

# 11

*The FBI Academy*
*Quantico, Virginia*

The next morning Jane woke Rohini for their planned run.

"I'm actually glad… we're here in a way." Rohini huffed between breaths as they ran. "I mean… I'm not glad someone… tried to kidnap me… but it's nice… to be able to go… for a run in the woods… instead of the city."

Rohini felt at home among the trees, more herself. She'd always preferred running outside, especially in the woods for just that reason. Running along a trail through the trees always awakened some deep primal feeling in her. She felt less in her head and more in her body and at the same time more connected to her surroundings.

In the city, everyone was in their own little bubble, like marbles rolling around trying not to bump up against each other. She usually ran with earbuds when she jogged in the city, drowning out all the discordant noise of the streets with music, but when she was in the woods she wanted all her senses open and alive. She loved hearing the birds and insects and was thrilled when she stumbled upon something singular, like a grazing deer or a magnificent mushroom.

"You're not feeling nauseous, are you?" Jane joked, as they walked back towards the dorm.

"No, I'm fine." Rohini replied.

"We'll have to fix that. Race you to the dorm!" Jane said as she took off at a full sprint.

*Oh crap,* Rohini thought, taking off after her. They ran all-out for about a minute before they arrived in front of the dorm. Rohini started to gain on her at first, but she faded quickly. When she caught up to Jane she bent over and put her hands on her knees, taking several heaving breaths.

"You really do want to make me puke, don't you?" she said after she'd recovered enough to speak. Jane, on the other hand, hardly seemed winded.

Jane smiled. "Not necessarily, although that would have been a bonus. You never know when you might have to run flat out. If I hadn't been there yesterday that might have been your only viable option. You did good creating space with those two that grabbed you. If you had then taken off at a dead sprint you might have been able to get away."

"That makes sense. I didn't think about it, I just reacted."

"That's right. You've obviously drilled those movements enough in your life that they were available to you without thinking. If you took those drills one step further past the strikes to the escape; that would have been there automatically as well."

They headed inside to the cafeteria and grabbed some breakfast. Jane filled Rohini in on the training schedule she had put together for the next several weeks. After consulting with the White House, she had decided they would stay at Quantico for at least six weeks. Jane wanted to take Rohini out in the field eventually and she had learned from the White House that they were planning to have some public events for the ambassadors. They would hold a press conference to announce the selected candidates in two months. Then the ambassadors would be reassembled two months before the Elders' expected return to train together as a team.

As they ate, Rohini wondered who the others would be; not only her American counterpart, but also the rest of the international contingent. She always found it fascinating to spend time with people from other cultures, thriving on learning new ways of looking at things.

She had found in the past that learning how people from other cultures viewed life often gave her deeper insight and more appreciation for her own. Although coming from a family with a mixed cultural background as well as just growing up in America—itself a hybrid of many cultures—she didn't always have a clear idea of what her "culture" meant.

Rohini often felt stuck in-between growing up not quite Indian, not quite American. At least not American in the same way her father's family was. They might have Norwegian roots, but the family had been in the US for generations. After her mother died, her aunt Priya had tried to fill that space for her, becoming Rohini's link to her Indian heritage, but it wasn't the same. She loved her aunt, but never felt completely at home in the Indian community in New York.

Rohini thought of herself as a citizen of the world before being an American. The way she saw it, she was a human first, a woman second, and an American third. *Maybe I'll have to change human to Earthling. Now that we know there are other beings out there that seem to be human too.* It amazed her once again how this one bit of knowledge was such a profound paradigm shift. She imagined the further ramifications of this would be playing out for years to come.

As they left the cafeteria, Jane elaborated on their schedule. "We'll keep to a two-a-day schedule for physical training," Jane explained. "We'll alternate running and strength training in the mornings and work on CQC in the afternoon."

"CQC?"

"Sorry, close quarters combat," Jane replied. "I forget you're a civilian. First, I want to evaluate what your strengths and weaknesses are. Once we know where your gaps are we can fill them in and put it all together. Have you done any martial arts or anything?"

"I did a little Taekwondo as a kid, but that's it," Rohini said.

"Have you had any firearms training?"

"My grandfather took us shooting once out on their farm, just a couple of old deer rifles. I think a twenty-two and something like a thirty-aught-six? Is that a thing?"

"Yes, that's a thing, .30-06. What about pistols?"

"No, I've never even held one."

"Well, we'll make sure you know your way around a variety of weapons while we're here. I mainly want to make sure you understand the basic principles well enough that whatever weapon you come across you can quickly figure out how it works and how to use it effectively. That's true whether we're talking about firearms, edged weapons, or even a broomstick. Improvised weapons could be your only option in many situations."

\* \* \*

The next few days began to settle into a rhythm. In the morning they would either go for a run or head to the gym. Rohini enjoyed the contrast. As much as she liked being outside in nature, she also appreciated being in the gym. There was something empowering about lifting heavy weights, especially if they were at or near your limit.

"It's good to get back into the swing of things. I used to work out pretty regularly in New York, but after the Elders showed up at the UN, I slacked off. I haven't done much in the last month or so."

That afternoon they also continued with the CQC training they had begun earlier in the week. Jane had been impressed with Rohini's coordination, though to her it was obvious that the little bit of training she'd had was more sport oriented. There was a distinctly different character to techniques meant to maim, kill, or otherwise incapacitate an enemy versus winning a friendly bout or putting on a performance for judges.

But their training wasn't all brutality. Rohini was developing a good base in striking, but she didn't have much experience with throwing or grappling beyond a brief foray into Aikido one semester in college. It had been just long enough for her to learn how to take a fall. That came in handy when Jane started throwing her around like a ragdoll one afternoon.

"Wow, even when I know what you're going to do, I'm still surprised when that moment comes where my feet leave the ground and my body is no longer under my control and I'm flying through the air. It's like a ride at an amusement park—a really quick, kind of painful ride at the amusement park," Rohini said, sitting on the mat in the training hall where Jane had been showing her a few throws.

"Let's try a few solo drills now. You can practice these on your own as well to get the body mechanics right. We won't do too much of this but it's helpful to have something to practice when you don't have a training partner around."

Jane led her through a series of Shuai Jiao line drills across the mat that mimicked the body mechanics of performing throws.

Rohini continued with the drills until Jane stopped her a few minutes later. "OK, let's take that first movement, run through it one time for me," Jane said. She watched Rohini go through the motions. "Good. Now let me show you how to apply that pattern to a throw." Jane took Rohini through the first throw several times slowly.

"Got it? OK, now try it on me."

Rohini tried the throw several times until it was fairly smooth. "It still feels a bit awkward, but I think I'm starting to remember it," Rohini said.

"That's where those solo drills come in. This is definitely a different way of moving your body, so the solo drills give you a chance to get those movement patterns ingrained in your muscle memory until they eventually become second nature," Jane replied.

They continued for another hour or so, Jane walking Rohini through each of the drills she had taught her, showing her how they each translated into a throw. "Alright, that's it for today, kid," Jane said.

"Thank God, I'm starving," Rohini replied.

# 12

*Marseille, France*

Jean-Luc awoke in a state of confusion. He could have sworn his eyes were open, yet he couldn't see anything; it was pitch black. *Have I gone blind?* There was no sound either, or at least very little. As he strained to hear, he could make out the faint rumbling of passing traffic outside.

He tried to move and realized with a start, he couldn't, or at least not much. He could squirm around a little, but his ankles and wrists were stuck in place. He began to slowly get his bearings. *I think I'm sitting up, but why can't I move? I'm tied down. There must be a bag over my head.* He felt his own hot breath against his face. As he turned his head from side to side, a little light crept in from below. There was also a slight pain in his left arm at the crook of his elbow. It reminded him of how it felt getting his blood drawn at the doctor's office.

He heard a door squeak open, then close, followed by approaching footsteps. Then someone spoke.

"Hello, Jean-Luc, I'm your new friend. I've got a few questions for you," Gruber said, setting the stage. "How you choose to answer them will determine what happens next. I expect honest answers from you, Jean-Luc, or else we may have to pay a visit to see your mother, and little Chloe and Hugo."

Jean-Luc whimpered. His mother was a widow and had taken in his niece and nephew, Chloe and Hugo, after his older sister and her husband had died in a car accident. Those three were his whole world. "Please, I'll tell you whatever you want to know, just don't hurt them," he said.

"No harm will come to them as long as you tell us what we want to know and never mention this to anyone," Gruber replied. "Now, tell me about the aliens. Were you in contact with them before they appeared at the UN?"

"No, how could I be?"

"I'm asking the questions here, Jean-Luc," Gruber said, a menacing tone in his voice. Gruber clapped his hands loudly next to Jean-Luc's ear, causing him to flinch. "Tell me about the ambassador program. Do you know who the others are?"

"No, I was only told that there were a few others who the aliens asked for," Jean-Luc replied, hesitantly. "I don't know who they are."

"When will the ambassadors be assembled together," Gruber asked. "Have they at least told you that?"

"Yes, there is going to be an event to announce the ambassadors in the United States," Jean-Luc replied.

"Ah, good. Now we're getting somewhere. Tell me everything you know about this event," Gruber said.

And he had.

Gruber smiled to himself as he prepared to inform Mr. Simms of what he had learned. *The Frenchman was a pushover*. Although with Gruber's expertise and the latest generation of pharmaceutical interrogation aids at his disposal, he could have broken anyone. Gruber had learned over the years that torture was a waste of time if you wanted to get information. It was too unreliable. Using torture, you could get people to admit to being guilty of something they'd never done, in a place they'd never even heard of, if you wanted. *You can never trust what they're telling you.*

That was fine if you were trying to frame someone—or simply torturing them for the sake of torturing them—but if you were trying to get real information out of someone, drugs were the way to go. *Of course, a little leverage never hurts.* Gruber would never hurt a child—that's where he drew the line—but Jean-Luc didn't need to know that. Jean-Luc had told him everything he needed to know. This was solid, actionable intelligence. *Mr. Simms will be pleased.* A plan was already formulating in his mind as he dialed his employer.

* * *

Jean-Luc woke to find himself sitting cross-legged on a dirty blanket, slumped against a wall. A wide-brimmed hat tilted low over his face and a large plastic cup sat in front of his legs. As he stirred into consciousness, the cup fell over and some coins spilled out onto the sidewalk. One rolled across the sidewalk and off the curb, clanking as it bounced twice on a storm drain before disappearing into the depths below.

In his initial confusion, Jean-Luc wondered, Am I a homeless person dreaming I'm an ambassador chosen to visit an alien world, or am I an ambassador to an alien world dreaming I'm a homeless person? Then, with a start, he remembered his abduction.

As the sudden memory of what had happened sent a rush of adrenaline coursing through his veins, he realized he must have been left there to look like a sleeping homeless person. *No one would pay any attention to me at all.* He was just another one of those nameless, faceless people that society turned a blind eye to, scurrying past, eyes glued to their smartphones.

The realization made him wonder about the actual homeless. *Who knows what kind of awful things may have happened to them?* He'd never be able to callously walk past them again without at least acknowledging their presence, and trying to help them out in some small way. While not rich by any means, he realized he could certainly afford to give a few dollars whenever the opportunity arose. *What's one less pint or cappuccino in the grand scheme of things?* Certainly his humanity and compassion were worth more.

Jean-Luc checked for his cell phone, which he found in his left front pants pocket where he normally kept it. He fished it out and checked the time. It had only been three hours. He'd almost be willing to think he had dreamt the whole thing except for his splitting headache and the fact that he couldn't imagine any other explanation for waking up here, like this. He'd never been a black-out drinker and he'd never taken any illegal drugs. There was a slight twinge in his arm when he put his phone back. He rolled up his sleeve and there on his left arm was the telltale mark where the IV had been.

# 13

*The FBI Academy*
*Quantico, Virginia*

Jane had been keeping Rohini very busy. It was partly due to the importance of her mission and the relatively short time they had to prepare for it, but Jane also had another motive. She knew Rohini wasn't used to dealing with the kind of trauma that came with attempted kidnappings or seeing someone get gunned down in the street. The best way to keep Rohini together mentally, Jane thought, was to keep her busy and let her subconscious process what she'd been through while she kept Rohini's attention on the present. So far, it had been working but Jane knew, at some point, Rohini would have to face what happened.

Their first rest day at Quantico, Rohini had finally allowed herself to feel those emotions, letting the events of that fateful night in DC hit her. When she found herself with some time to think, it all came flooding back. She had a good cry in the shower, hoping Jane hadn't heard her, but when she finally came out of the bathroom, one look at Jane told her it was probably written all over her face.

"How are you doing, Rohini?" Jane asked.

"I'm sorry, it all finally hit me today, everything that's happened," Rohini answered, tears beginning to well up again as she gave voice to the swirl of emotions she'd been suppressing.

"Hey, don't worry about it. I'm surprised it took this long, to be honest. I figured it would have to happen sooner or later. You can't keep that stuff bottled up forever or it eats you up inside."

"I guess so. I'm just not used to blubbering in front of other people."

"Here, have a seat," Jane said, patting the bed next to her. "It's healthy to let it out. I'd have been worried about you if you never did. I thought you were a bit of a stoic, but I knew you weren't a sociopath. I know you probably think of me as just some spy, but honestly, Rohini, I'm a human being too. I'm here for you. You can always come to me."

"Thanks, Jane, I appreciate that," Rohini said. After a bit of hesitation, she reached over and hugged her. As soon as she did the tears began to flow once more. Jane just held her, letting Rohini cry on her shoulder.

* * *

After they had been at Quantico for a few weeks, Rohini's training entered a new phase. Instead of their usual morning run they headed for the obstacle course.

"OK, we're going to start changing things up," Jane said. "I'm feeling pretty comfortable with your fighting skills and you are definitely starting to build up your conditioning; you're not nearly as out of breath after our runs as you were when we first got here. We're going to move on to the obstacle course for our runs."

The first day they focused on the obstacles, practicing each one many times as they went through the course, taking an easy jogging pace between obstacles. Their goal was to focus on the quality of Rohini's movement before adding too much intensity to the equation.

As Rohini found out early on, even the simplest things like balancing became much more challenging once fatigue set in. To combat this, they also worked on recovery techniques between drills on the obstacles. Jane taught her a simple technique she called tactical breathing.

"So, you can see how much harder that balance beam was after you were out of breath—that's why recovery is so critical—maybe as important as the movement skills themselves," Jane said.

"Wow, you're not kidding! I practically felt drunk trying to keep my balance on that thing," Rohini replied.

"That's not a bad analogy," Jane said. "This won't help you with a breathalyzer, but it might get you through a roadside sobriety test, not that I'd recommend you try it.

"In combat or any other stressful situation, it's your ability to recover that will allow you to function at a high level. When all those fight or flight hormones flood your bloodstream, you need to be able to weather that initial adrenaline storm. Otherwise, the skills you're developing won't be available to you when you need them most."

"It sounds like dealing with an anxiety attack," Rohini said.

"It's similar. It's a matter of getting back a little conscious control of your nervous system before it goes completely haywire. It'll save your health over the long run too. It's not stress that gets you—it's not being able to compensate for it that does you in."

Jane led Rohini through a few rounds of tactical breathing. "So, the simplest version is this: count to four on your inhalation, hold the breath for a count of four, exhale for four, and finally hold for a four count before your next inhalation. This is also called square breathing since you've got four equal parts like a square."

"That makes it easy to remember," Rohini replied.

"You don't want anything too complicated to remember when you're trying to get your wits about you. If you're in an explosion or something that really throws you for a loop you need something simple that's going to come to you automatically. This works great for that."

"So, you've been in a situation like that?" Rohini asked.

"More than once."

"Could you tell me about one of them? If you don't mind."

"I guess so," Jane said, her voice taking on a more somber tone. She was silent for a moment as a faraway look came over her face. "When I was still in the Marines, we had received intel that the Taliban had been using this village in our area of operations as a cache for IEDs. The militants stayed holed-up in the surrounding hills and would come down at night to build IEDs, planting them early in the morning before returning to the hills.

"Dozens of villagers in the area had been killed over the previous months in IED attacks as well as several Marines. Between the Marines and the other coalition forces in the area we'd hit about 30 bombs over the previous six months.

"We entered the village quickly that night, and began our sweep. Typically, we'd go house to house, make a quick check for any kind of rigging on the doors then knock 'em in. We hit this one compound that way, and everything was going smoothly. We found a cache of ammonium nitrate fertilizer and big bags of sugar—common components of IEDs—as well as some old AKs and ammunition. We thought it had been a good score, until the cache blew up. It turned out they had set up an ambush, sucking us deep into the village before springing their trap.

"When they blew the cache in the courtyard, I was outside the door, so I was somewhat protected, but the blast still slammed me down. It was the first time I'd been hit that hard and I was knocked senseless for a few seconds until my training kicked in.

"After a few breaths, I'd gotten myself together enough to roll over just as a militant came around the corner. I'd be dead now if I'd been a second slower. As it was, I was ready as he came into view and I took him out first. We regrouped and soon had things under control, but it was touch and go for a while," Jane said. "They set a good trap for us."

"What happened to your guys in the compound?"

"Everyone in the yard died. We lost five Marines and a translator, just like that," Jane said, snapping her fingers.

They were silent for a moment as the ramifications of their training sank in. Jane's story made it all real for Rohini. This stuff could save her life. "Thank you, Jane, for sharing that with me."

Since they'd met, Rohini had been curious about Jane's background. She'd felt surprisingly comfortable with Jane, and it felt perfectly natural to want to get to know her better, since they were spending so much time together. She was almost beginning to feel as though Jane were the older sister she had never had.

For the first several weeks Jane had deflected most of Rohini's questions about her background, but she slowly began to open up, a little at a time. She kept things vague—understandable for a spy—but instead of satisfying Rohini's curiosity, Jane's attempts at placating her only served to pique her interest more.

As time went on she tried to piece together what little she had learned about Jane in her mind. She knew she had been a Marine. *She must have joined quite young.* And Jane had also apparently been in the FBI, but wasn't doing that any more either. She figured Jane couldn't be much over thirty. *So, maybe a few years in the Marine Corps, a few years in the FBI, and a few more at whatever spy agency she worked for now? That would probably be about right.* One night she was determined to learn more.

"Jane, did you join the Marines right after high school or did you go to college first?" Rohini asked.

"I went to college for a year and a half first. I didn't really know what I was doing. I was getting to the point where I needed to pick a major and no one thing was calling me. I had too many interests and I don't think I would have been happy settling on one at the time."

"Why the Marines? Why not another branch of the military, or even the Peace Corps or something?"

"I had a lot of family in the Corps. My dad, my uncles, my grand-father—back several generations, in fact. It was kind of expected for the men in my family, both of my brothers joined, though no one ever expected me to go that route. They probably figured I'd marry a Marine, not become one. My mother went to college, but on my dad's side of the family I was the first one to go to college."

"Are your brothers older or younger?"

"Both older. One's still in the Corps, the other died in Afghani-stan."

"Oh, I'm sorry, Jane."

"It's OK. It's been awhile now. I guess it's easier having been in, myself. I always thought it must be harder for civilians who have lost loved ones to war. It's such a different life. I think my dad and brother and I have an easier time with it than my mom. We used to be much closer, my mom and I, but once I joined the Corps, we sort of grew apart. I'm much closer now with my dad and brother than I am with my mom. We get each other in a way she'll never quite understand."

"How did you end up doing what you do now?"

"While I was in the Corps I ended up in Intelligence, and then when I got out I applied for the FBI," Jane said. "After a few years I was loaned out to work with another agency. When it was time to go back, they offered me the chance to stay, and I took it."

"I don't suppose you regret dropping out then, after all of that," Rohini said.

"From college? No. It was the right thing to do at the time. I would have been wasting my time and money if I'd stayed. Besides, I finished a degree while I was in the Corps."

"What in?"

"Psychology."

"Really? I would have expected criminal justice or something law enforcement related," Rohini said.

"That would have made sense, but psychology has actually come in quite handy," Jane said.

"Did you work as a profiler or something, like in *Silence of the Lambs*?"

"Nothing so dramatic. It's been useful in my own personal growth, as well as understanding how people tick—what motivates them and their thought processes. Anyway, that's enough picking my brain for tonight. We've got an early start in the morning, as usual, so let's hit the sack."

"Alright. Hey, can I borrow some lotion? Mine ran out."

"Sure. Here you go," Jane said as she tossed a bottle of lotion to Rohini. "Just put it back in the basket when you're done."

"Or else I get the hose again?" Rohini quipped.

"When you least expect it, Tinkerbell."

# 14

*Grand Palace Hotel*
*Gstaad, Swiss Alps*

"Good evening, gentlemen," Bartholomew Simms said, calling the meeting to order. "I've called you all here to discuss our mutual interests in light of recent events. I'm sure you are all aware of the threat the aliens pose, not only to our livelihoods, but also to our very way of life."

One of the members of the newly formed cabal, James Van-Houten spoke up. "How sure are you that they pose a threat beyond our fossil fuel holdings? I understand your reluctance to reinvest in the green sector with the history of your companies—I know you feel a sense of tradition in maintaining your family's legacy—but times are changing, Bart."

VanHouten had begun divesting from fossil fuels and moving into the green energy sector several years before. While certainly not an early adopter, he saw the way the winds were blowing.

"Yes, James," Simms replied, "I'm quite sure. I've learned through my sources that these so called 'Elders' have more than simply 'saving' us in mind. I've learned from my operatives that once they establish our trust, they plan to take over our world and enslave us."

While not strictly the truth, Bartholomew Simms knew the more reluctant members of this gathering would need more than a threat to their bottom line to get on board with his plans. *If they need an existential threat to move them to action, I'll give it to them. True or not.*

It certainly wasn't the first time he'd lied through his teeth to get his way—in business or in his personal life—and it certainly wouldn't be the last. Besides, in Simms' mind he felt justified by the certainty that—although he had no proof—what he was saying was true. He felt it in his gut, and his gut had rarely steered him wrong.

"If we are to support you going forward," another member began, "we will need certain assurances. I for one must know that any actions we agree to cannot be traced back to us."

"Not to worry," Bartholomew replied. "My security team will coordinate everything. They are several steps removed from me through an untraceable series of dummy corporations. They will have no connection whatsoever to any of you."

A third member spoke up. "Bartholomew, when we last spoke you mentioned your desire to contact certain of my associates in the Middle East. Is that still the case?"

"Yes, Mahmoud, we will need to set up contact between them and my team. From what you've told me about their channels of communications, it should be a simple matter to keep ourselves insulated from any of their actions. If we play this right, the authorities will never have any reason to suspect our involvement, let alone our true intentions. As you have done in the past we'll use these terrorists as a means to an end. While you've helped them achieve their objectives in the past, they've never suspected that your motives were purely financial in nature. Or perhaps they have, and simply didn't care as long as your assistance was beneficial to their cause? Regardless, that same trust will allow us to use them in this case. Even if they don't view the aliens as a threat the way we do, I'm sure they'll jump at the chance to attack the West."

"That is certainly the case," Mahmoud replied. "But I'm sure it won't take much to convince them of the aliens' threat. After all, they would be in direct competition for control. I somehow doubt these aliens share their views about the need for a new caliphate."

As the meeting continued, the newly formed cabal hammered

out their goals and their plan of attack. Mahmoud would use his Middle Eastern network of contacts to put Gruber and his team in touch with the terrorist group Soldiers of the Caliphate. They had been fairly quiet over the last several years after drone strikes had decimated their leadership and their attempt at establishing a new caliphate had failed.

Their first action was to be their most audacious, striking right at the heart of power, the "Great Satan" itself, Washington, DC. How could they possibly resist such an opportunity? This would send a clear message that the aliens were not welcome and that those who cooperated with them would be held accountable as traitors and infidels.

Phase two would involve attacking the soft targets of the new Green Energy sector. The new spirit of cooperation between the various world leaders left them with a serious blind spot. While the world rejoiced in a newfound sense of unity and a common cause in the face of climate change, many of the newest renewable energy projects were going up in such a hurry that security was an afterthought. Of course, this had always been the case. The power grid had always been a vulnerable target. When Simms began considering his present course of action he was surprised how seldom it had been targeted in the past. Attacks on infrastructure weren't as shocking as slaughtering innocent civilians, but if a terrorist's aim was to disrupt the engines of empire, the grid was a target-rich environment.

Gruber had been instrumental in the planning. He made a suggestion, which impressed Simms, both for its brilliance as well as its cunning. To further assuage suspicion from Simms, or any of his circle, they all agreed to sacrifice a few smaller assets of their own to attack, thereby camouflaging their involvement—or so they hoped. *Besides, their losses will be offset by the arms and munitions sales to their new friends in the Middle East. The aliens and their turncoat allies will never know what hit them.*

# 15

*The FBI Academy*
*Quantico, Virginia*

Over the next several weeks Jane continued Rohini's physical training in close quarters combat as well as running her through the obstacle course. She also began exposing her to a wide variety of firearms. While she was not training Rohini for war, it never hurt to be
prepared.

Jane had been impressed with Rohini's aptitude at the shooting
range. She wasn't terrible the first day. Jane expected everyone to be
terrible, especially someone with so little previous exposure to shooting. Rohini had been able to hit the target that first day, at least most
of the time, and as time went by she continued to improve until she
was as good as your average law enforcement or military personnel.

Rohini still had a way to go to rival Jane's level of marksman-
ship, but Jane could tell she had the potential. Whether in their hand-
to-hand combat training on the mats, their movement training on the
obstacle course, or their firearms training on the range, Rohini had
shown a high level of coordination and physical awareness. She was
a quick study in more cerebral ways as well.

In between their physical training Jane had been exposing Rohini to various types of awareness training. She felt this would be
critical to laying a foundation for anything that came after. Rohini
was bright, there was no doubt about that, but at times she could lose

focus or miss out on important details. At other times she could be too hyper-focused and miss the forest for the trees.

"Have you ever practiced any meditation, Rohini?" Jane asked one day.

"Not really," Rohini replied. "I've started it a few times but never developed a habit of it. When I was in college I'd hear about various meditation teachers coming through town and I'd check them out sometimes. I always enjoyed the events themselves and found them inspiring at the time, but I was never able to turn that into a consistent practice."

"That's the most challenging part.," Jane said. "As I'm sure you discovered, most traditions of meditation are deceptively simple. The hard part is sticking with it. And, of course, the everyday part of your mind you are most familiar with loves variety and distraction. It gets bored easily and loves moving immediately to the next thing. A practice like meditation can become boring or monotonous in no time if you aren't able to turn that part of your mind off."

"Yeah, I'd go see these teachers and be so inspired, then I'd try to replicate the experiences of contentment and happiness at home and just get bored and restless," Rohini replied.

"It's tricky," Jane said. "One of the best suggestions I can make is to observe your mind when you're in those states, when you've found your happy place. Try to feel that feeling in your whole body and remember what it feels like. If you can do that, you will find it becomes easier and easier to remember it. When you remember that feeling, you bring that feeling into your consciousness of the present moment. It begins to feel like you are flipping a switch and turning on the neural pathways for that experience."

"I hadn't thought about it like that, but now that you mention it, when those guys tried to kidnap me, there was a moment when time slowed down so much for me it practically stood still. It wasn't a blissed-out kind of feeling, like I remember from meditation, but it was somehow, still... I don't know... peaceful. Does that sound strange? It doesn't make any sense, my life was being threatened, someone was pointing a gun at me and yet, if I think back to that moment, it was almost enjoyable in some strange way."

"It's not strange at all, Rohini. I know exactly what you mean. I've had that experience many times in combat. Your senses feel heightened and your sense of time gets wacky. It can slow way down and then speed way up, or else it can feel like you are moving lightning fast while everything around you is moving slow, like it's moving through water. It's a type of flow state. You took some psychology classes, right? Was it all pathological conditions or did you get into positive psychology at all?"

"Not much. I feel like I remember something about flow, though. Wasn't it that guy with the unpronounceable name?" Rohini asked.

Jane smiled. "It's not as hard as it looks, but yeah, Csikszentmihalyi," she said. "The other big name in positive psyche is probably Maslow, but there have been others since."

"I didn't study positive psychology much," replied Rohini. "The thing I identified with the most was Ecopsychology. I love being in nature so much, I could totally relate to the idea that our relationship with the environment affects our psychological wellbeing."

"Yeah, I always could too," Jane said. "It intuitively makes sense. I mean, we evolved in nature, so it makes sense that removing ourselves from that setting would have a negative impact on us. Although, then I think about the fact that we are always continuing to evolve, so maybe some people are adapting to being in more of an artificial environment."

"Maybe," Rohini ventured, "but even though most people live in cities their whole life, their health suffers if they stay inside all the time. And there is more pollution and stress from noise and who knows what else. If it wasn't for Central Park, I don't think I could have handled living in New York for too long. The park was like a sanctuary for me."

"True. Anyway, getting back to meditation, I've noticed that you often have very good focus when we're doing something physical. You do a great job getting dialed in when we're training hand-to-hand or on the obstacle course. I want you to try to notice that feeling when you are totally focused and in the moment and try to bring it to bear in silent, still moments," Jane said. "Why don't you try that now?

"Close your eyes and imagine yourself balancing or doing something else we've been practicing. Really feel yourself there and think about how you feel in that moment. Now try to take that feeling and hold on to it, so to speak. Not too tightly, or you'll get tense and anxious. Too loose, and your awareness will wander off. Got it? OK, now try to keep that feeling in the background of your awareness as you focus on your breathing. You can do the tactical breathing pattern or breathe naturally, whatever feels more comfortable."

Rohini recalled her time balancing on the obstacle course, that was a good suggestion. It was one of the things she most enjoyed on the course, and one of the things which got her the most focused. *Jane is perceptive, I'll give her that.* After thinking this she realized her mind was wandering and she brought it back to her meditation.

After a few moments of visualization Rohini grabbed onto that feeling of focus and concentration and brought it to her current surroundings. She was sitting upright on her bed in the dorm room she and Jane shared at the Academy. Her legs were crossed, and her hands were on her knees.

Little was happening—she was simply sitting and breathing, but the moment gained that intensity, that vibrancy that she remembered feeling a few times when she had meditated with some Buddhist teachers who had passed through DC in her college days.

Rohini started to get that feeling of bliss which had been so fleeting in her own aborted attempts at establishing a regular meditation practice. She held onto it for a few minutes and then realized she had begun to think about the feeling, instead of just experiencing it, and before she knew it, it was gone."

Rohini opened her eyes and looked at Jane, who had been watching her. "That was one of the best meditations I've had in years."

"Great. I thought that technique would work well for you," Jane replied. "You don't have to sit for hours, especially if you're just daydreaming the whole time. Just try to bring that feeling into your awareness, then keep it as long as you can. If you lose it, try to get it back. Even if you can only keep it for a few minutes at a time, it will do wonders for you. It's the best way I've found to decompress after a particularly stressful assignment."

"Like this one?" Rohini quipped.

"Well, it has had its moments, especially that first night, but no, overall this one has been quite un-stressful, compared to what I'm used to. I've actually been enjoying the time we've spent here."

"I have too, Jane. This place has almost come to feel like home somehow. It kind of reminds me of my time with my aunt and uncle on their farm in New Mexico."

Rohini recalled the year she had taken off to stay with them on their organic farm, becoming lost in thought for a moment.

"Hey, you still with me, buddy?" Jane asked, snapping her fingers in front of Rohini's face. "I thought I'd lost you there for a minute."

"Sorry, I was just remembering when I spent time in New Mexico with my aunt and uncle and then my mind started wandering. I used to go meditate in a kiva there, but it was a totally different kind of experience than this kind of meditation. It was more like a trance or something. I'd lose awareness of my surroundings, and I'd even hear voices sometimes."

"Were you by any chance smoking something at the time?" Jane asked, only half-jokingly.

"No. I've tried a few mind-altering substances in my day, but not then."

"No history of schizophrenia or anything in your family?" Jane continued.

"My mom thought my dad was nuts," Rohini quipped. "But, no. Nothing real. Nothing certifiable."

"So, what did these voices say?" Jane asked.

"I don't know, to tell you the truth. I never remembered much. It was like when you wake up from a dream that you can't quite remember. I had this vague recollection that I'd heard a voice—or voices—talking to me. Even now, I feel like I can almost hear it, but I can't quite make out the words, like when you hear someone talking through a wall. But I feel like at the time, I could understand it. I always figured it was my subconscious talking to me or something."

"That makes sense. I wonder if it was something special about the place itself or if you could repeat the experience somewhere else?" Jane mused.

"I've often wondered that myself."

* * *

While Jane kept up Rohini's training six days a week, they had for the most part taken Sundays off. Jane felt certain their location had remained a secret, so one day she took Rohini off-base for the day, thinking she could use a change of scenery.

Jane hadn't told her where they were going as they drove north on I-95 briefly before turning west on Highway 234. At first Rohini thought maybe they were headed into the city, but when they turned she really had no clue. They passed through Manassas before merging onto I-66 and continuing west. Once they turned onto I-81 and started into the mountains Rohini figured out it.

"Are we going hiking?" she asked.

"Nice job, Nancy Drew," Jane quipped. "You figured it out."

They continued for a little longer, winding up into the mountains past Woodstock before parking at Wolf Gap Recreation Area. Climbing out of the car, Rohini took in a deep breath of fresh mountain air and sighed. "This was a great idea, Jane," she said. After gathering up the daypacks Jane had prepared, they headed to the north end of the campground and the trailhead for the Mill Mountain Trail.

The first three quarters of a mile or so was a bit of a scramble, but nothing they had any trouble with. Rohini had always been a bit of a mountain goat, even if she had gotten a bit out of shape in the last few years. She still had the mountain walker's stride she'd picked up in Nepal when she spent the summer with her aunt Shanti. Many of the rural villages they visited with her aunt's NGO required more than a bit of hiking to access, some so remote that foot traffic was the main form of travel. Even when villages were accessible by road, many still only had a single bus passing through each day, and once off the bus it was all on foot.

As they gained some elevation—taking the right-hand path at a fork—the trail started to follow the ridgeline, and they began to catch glimpses of picturesque vistas opening up on both sides of the trail.

"Wow, this is a great spot, Jane," Rohini remarked, as they neared their destination, the rocky outcropping of Big Schloss. "I bet you can see into West Virginia from here."

"This ridgeline actually marks the border, so we've been straddling it the whole time."

They only encountered a few small groups of hikers coming down the trail and there was no one at the top when they arrived, so they had it to themselves. Rohini took off her pack and spun slowly in a circle, taking in the panoramic view.

"I packed some food, if you're hungry," Jane said.

They ate mostly in silence as they took in the peaceful atmosphere. To the west, a lone turkey buzzard circled, effortlessly riding a thermal updraft, rising higher and higher until it was almost out of sight. To the east, some low misty clouds hung in the valley, partially obscuring the view. Rohini had always loved this kind of scenery. It reminded her of Chinese landscape paintings, especially the sparse minimalistic ones where so much of the image was implied and much of the canvas was taken up by empty space. That void somehow always felt full to her, pregnant with possibilities, like almost anything could be hiding in those mysterious clouds.

Rohini recalled one of her favorites, a scroll painting from the 11th Century called *Nine Dragons* by Chen Rong. She'd seen it once while on vacation with her family in Boston where it hung at the Museum of Fine Arts. The scroll, which was almost thirty-six feet long, depicted the nine sons of the Dragon King from Chinese mythology, writhing through swirling clouds, white-capped waves, and churning whirlpools. It had left quite an impression on her. She could almost see the dragons now, flying through the misty clouds in front of her, while she sat silently on that rocky ridge along the Virginia border.

After they'd eaten and enjoyed the view, Jane said she had something she wanted to show her and took Rohini down the trail a short distance.

"I've been thinking about the experience you had in that Kiva. Part of why I chose this hike was because of this spot over here," she said, as she led Rohini to a flat area which was partially protected by a semi-circular rocky overhang.

"This would make a great camping spot," Rohini said. As she looked around, she saw signs that it had been used as such before, probably many times: some trampled brush and some boot prints scattered around, and more obvious signs, like the ring of stones marking a fire pit. A few charred ends of blackened logs protruded from the muddy center of the fire ring, indicating that the last campers must have been there fairly recently. There hadn't been any rain in the area for over a week.

"I thought you might try another meditation here and see if we can recreate your experience in the kiva. You've gotten me intrigued with your story about the voices," Jane said.

"I'd be happy to give it a shot," Rohini replied as she slowly walked around the site. "This looks like a great place for it."

She found a spot that spoke to her, and made herself comfortable below the deepest part of the overhang. It seemed like the most appropriate place to sit. She couldn't have articulated what it was specifically about that spot, but she let her intuition guide her.

She took a few deep breaths, shrugging her shoulders a few times to release any tension, and turned her focus inward. Slowly at first, then more quickly, the outside world around her, the world of her senses, receded until she was barely aware of it. She began to lose track of where her body ended and the earth below her began, feeling a sense of losing herself, yet the loss was actually a gain, as suddenly, she felt like she was a part of a much larger whole.

Faintly at first, then more and more clearly, she began to sense, it seemed, rather than hear, a voice. It had that familiar quality to it that Rohini recalled from her meditations in New Mexico, sounding at first like a muffled voice heard through a wall, then suddenly she heard it, crystal clear. She was so startled that she was immediately thrust back into her senses. That peaceful place she had experienced, so vast and expansive, was suddenly a tiny human body of flesh and bone. Her senses felt so acute that the light was almost painful as she blinked her eyes, and she felt intensely every tiny rock beneath her in what had been a smooth, comfortable place to sit moments before. She tried to get up but found her limbs sluggish as she tried to stand.

"Whoa, take it easy there," Jane said, putting a hand on Rohini's shoulder to steady her. "Don't rush it. You were under for a long time."

"What do you mean, how long was I sitting for?" she asked. She looked around and realized the light had totally changed. There were lengthening shadows all around her and the sun was low in the western sky, the clouds beginning to take on the first rosy hues of dusk. When she had sat down to meditate the sun had still been high in the sky.

"It's been almost three hours, Rohini. What happened? You were so quiet, I thought you might have fallen asleep, but you stayed sitting bolt upright the whole time. Then you jerked and gasped so suddenly, you almost made me jump."

"I went deep. Really deep. Like I did in the kiva," Rohini responded.

"Did you hear the voices again?"

"I did," Rohini whispered, her voice barely audible.

"And? Do you remember anything this time? What did they say?"

"I… I only remember one thing," She began, hesitantly. "It said, 'Rohini, we've been waiting for you.'"

# 16

*The Simms Estate*
*Westchester County, New York*

Bartholomew Simms was in his office, pacing back and forth. He was so full of anticipation for what was about to transpire that he couldn't sit still. He went down to his exercise room that morning, something he rarely did anymore, thinking that some time on the treadmill might burn off some nervous energy. But it was no use. He spent a good forty-five minutes there puffing away to no avail.

After showering and a light breakfast of fresh baked croissants with butter and blueberry preserves he had shipped in from Maine, he sat sipping coffee and reading the *Journal* in his mansion's conservatory. He had no particular fondness for nature, but his mother had loved to spend hours here every day tending to her plants, especially her treasured orchid collection which featured specimens from every corner of the globe. The conservatory reminded him of her, so he had taken to eating his breakfast here most mornings. As he flipped through the paper he could hardly keep his mind on what he was reading. He was too preoccupied with the day's coming events.

Simms was rescued from his futile attempt at reading by his assistant. "Sir, you have a phone call. It's Mr. Gruber," she said. "Would you like to take it here or in your office?"

"I'll take it here. Thank you, Chelsea," he said, taking the phone from his assistant.

"Gruber, have all the necessary arrangements been made?"

"Yes, sir. Everything is in place."

"Excellent. Nothing left to do but sit back and watch the world burn—I'll bring the marshmallows," he said, chuckling to himself as he ended the call.

He'd laid his plans carefully. This was one show he didn't want to miss. Walking quickly to his office—handing off the phone to Chelsea on the way—he picked up the television remote and turned it to one of the 24-hr cable news networks to watch the morning's events unfold. It was one of the few modern touches in the otherwise classic room.

He usually kept it tuned to the business channel where he could keep an eye on the markets, as his family had for generations. At one time his grandfather had kept a ticker tape machine for that purpose. The machine still sat, unused, on a corner table near the window, a nod to the past. As he changed the channel, a panel of talking heads were already previewing the day's events, giving their two cents on what it all meant. *You have no idea,* he thought. *In a very short while, all hell will be breaking loose.*

# 17

It was a warm sunny day in Washington, DC. A light breeze was blowing, just enough to take the edge off the typical summer humidity. They were headed to the first of what Rohini assumed would be many press events for the Earth Ambassadors. She wasn't looking forward to all the attention, but she was eager to meet the others who had been selected for the program.

As Rohini and Jane rode towards the city, ensconced once again in the backseat of a blacked-out SUV, Rohini couldn't help but be reminded of their sudden, unexpected departure from DC two months ago. The events of that night were still fresh in her mind, as though they'd happened just yesterday.

Her memory of that night almost seemed clearer now. In the immediate aftermath of the attempted abduction, it had all been a blur. She had still been a bit shell-shocked that night, and for the first few days at Quantico. Her daily training with Jane had been a welcome distraction from the trauma of the event.

But truth be told, Rohini was fairly impressed with herself in dealing with it all. She had always thought she was reasonably easy-going, able to adapt herself to changing circumstances with some degree of aplomb, but she'd never had to deal with something quite like this. Rohini was glad she hadn't become a cowering mess when it counted most. *If I had, I might have ended up in the back of that van, despite Jane's efforts.* Her quick reaction had given Jane the time she needed to do the rest.

When they arrived in DC, Rohini and Jane were taken to the White House first, where they met briefly with the president. His national security advisor filled them in on the progress of the investigation into Rohini's attempted abduction. They had come up with dead ends for the most part. They thought they had a solid lead when they found a partial print in the van the kidnappers had used—which had somehow survived the fire—but according to their records it belonged to a deceased Army sergeant who had died in Iraq years before when his Humvee was blown up by an IED.

After that lead fell through, they'd hoped to pick up something through the vast web of electronic surveillance programs which had become ever more pervasive over the years, but there was so much chatter about the Elders and the Earth Ambassadors from everyone around the globe that it was still like trying to find a needle in a haystack. The trail had gone cold.

"We'll be heading over to the Lincoln Memorial shortly for the press conference," the president said. "I know you're anxious to meet the other Ambassadors, but don't worry, we've scheduled a casual luncheon in the State Dining Room for you all after the press conference. You'll have plenty of time to get to know them before they all head back to their respective countries. Are you nervous, Rohini?"

"Yes, Mr. President. Is it that obvious? I'm always like this before public speaking."

"Relax, Rohini. You won't have to do anything but stand there and wave to the crowd. We didn't plan on having any of you speak today. This is just a way to announce that we've found our team. The public will have plenty of chances to get to know you all over the next few months. We'll have more events and we're even going to embed a film crew with you all during your training once the team is together. This is historic. Everyone will be interested in keeping up with you all, especially as we get closer to E-Day," the president explained.

"E-Day?" Rohini asked.

"That's what we've taken to calling the day the Elders return. It has a ring to it, don't you think?" President Johnson replied.

There was a knock on the door as the president's assistant poked her head in, "Mr. President, Martin Franklin is here."

"Excellent, send him on in."

A man with glasses and a shortly trimmed beard entered the Oval Office. He looked like a mix of lab rat and gym rat to Rohini. Like a physicist who did CrossFit. The president introduced him as the other Earth Ambassador chosen to represent the United States.

"Martin, welcome, this is your counterpart, Rohini, and this is Jane Smith. I've got another quick meeting, I'm afraid. Why don't you all head on out to the motorcade, you can meet some of the other ambassadors while you're waiting. I'll be there shortly, and we'll be on our way."

Rohini, Jane and Martin chatted as they made their way through the halls of the White House. "So where are you from, Martin?" Rohini said.

"I grew up in Northern Iowa, but I live in Tennessee now," Martin replied.

"Oh really, I lived in Minneapolis until I was twelve," Rohini said.

"Nice. I went to the U for my undergrad," Martin said. "I love the Twin Cities. I try to get back and visit when I can. A lot of friends from college still live there."

"My dad and I go visit every year on our way to my grandparents' farm. It's changed a lot since I was a kid, though," Rohini said. "What are you doing in Tennessee?"

"I work at the Oak Ridge National Lab," Martin said.

"What sort of research do you do there?" Rohini said.

"I work in the Energy Efficiency and Electricity Technologies Program. We focus on making existing technology more efficient and reducing energy consumption. I was mainly focused on our program to design and build affordable, carbon-neutral homes."

"Did you work with the Elders' designs? I heard they had provided some sort of way to make solar panels more efficient," Rohini said.

"I didn't work directly with that group, but it was part of what led me to apply for the ambassador program. I thought the opportunity was too incredible to pass up, and I'm assuming my work in the lab won't be as vital now that we're receiving the Elders' assistance. What about you, Rohini? Why did you apply for the program?"

Rohini looked over her shoulder at Jane, who was trailing behind them and raised her eyebrows in a questioning look. "You can tell him, Rohini," Jane said. "I'm sure it will come out among the other ambassadors eventually, if it hasn't already."

"I would have applied for the program," Rohini said. "Like you, I thought it was an amazing opportunity. As it turns out, I didn't even have to apply, I was chosen for it."

"What do you mean?" Martin said.

"There are four of us among the ambassadors who were specifically asked for by the Elders," Rohini said.

"Really? Do you know why?" Martin asked, incredulously.

"I don't," Rohini said.

"Do you know who the others are, or why we were picked?" Rohini asked, turning back to Jane again as they continued to make their way towards the waiting motorcade.

"I know who the others are, but if the president knows why they were chosen, he hasn't said," Jane replied.

"Who are they?" Martin asked.

"Besides Rohini, the others are Jean-Luc from France, Guangming from China, and Oksana from Russia," Jane said.

"I wonder what the common thread is." Rohini said.

Rohini and the rest of the Earth Ambassadors, had been presented with a white blazer for the press conference when she arrived that morning. It bore an embroidered United Nations design on the left breast, with the words "Earth Ambassador" emblazoned below.

Once outside at the motorcade, they saw the rest of the Earth Ambassadors —easily identified in their own white blazers—already waiting. There were lots of quick handshakes and bows as they introduced themselves, along with a few kisses to each cheek from the two members of the EU contingent, Jean-Luc from France and Heinrich from Germany.

Rohini paid special attention when she met the others Jane had named, but if there was anything that distinguished them from the rest, she wasn't able to divine it from their initial meeting. After a few minutes of small talk, they were ushered into their respective vehicles. Soon after, President Johnson arrived, flanked by several members of his Secret Service detail, and the motorcade departed.

Rohini, Jane, and Martin had the special honor of riding with the president in "the Beast," as the presidential limo was known. As they drove towards the Lincoln Memorial, people waved at the motorcade. Thousands of people were expected on the National Mall that morning as the whole world turned its attention to the press conference announcing the final selections of the Earth Ambassadors.

The excitement had been building ever since the program was announced and now all eyes were on Washington, DC. No other heads of state had accompanied their respective nations' selections, but all the countries constituting the program had sent an official representative of their governments to the event. Being in DC, this was President Johnson's show. He would be introducing the ambassadors to the world, acting as master of ceremonies for this most momentous event.

When they arrived at the memorial, they were led through a back door into the building where they would wait in the wings until they heard their cue. Rohini didn't mind if the president took his time, this was one of her favorite places in Washington. She'd visited it for the first time with her family years ago, long before coming to college at GW.

Rohini had been struck then, as she was now, by the mood of the place. Being modelled after a Greek Doric temple, she thought the builders had managed to create a sacred atmosphere. While there was plenty of symbolism built into the structure itself, such as the thirty-six columns for the number of states at the time of Lincoln's death, Rohini had always been most fascinated by the monument's murals. They depicted some of the timeless values the country was founded upon, and that Abraham Lincoln had embodied in his life. As they waited for the event to begin, Rohini found herself with a good view of one of them.

"Emancipation," as the mural on the south wall was called, was located above a copy of the Gettysburg Address. Its central image portrayed the Angel of Truth freeing slaves from bondage, representing Freedom and Liberty. On either side of this were two additional images which Rohini had always found intriguing. Justice and Law were represented by the image on the left, a woman seated on a throne. She held a large sword in one hand representing Justice, and a scroll in the other representing Law.

The other end of the mural depicted a figure representing immortality. This figure was again a woman sitting on a throne, this time surrounded by three figures said to represent Faith, Hope, and Charity. While she knew these were specifically Christian theological terms, she had always felt they pointed to something more universal, almost like a threefold version of the Golden Rule.

She had never made the connection before, but now looking at the figure Immortality, depicted in the mural, she recalled how the saints of Daoism were often called immortals. Immortality in Daoism was sometimes thought of as a physical immortality, but it was also seen as a state of spiritual immortality or enlightenment. The woman on the throne took on a greater significance when she saw her anew in this light.

The three figures surrounding her, Faith, Hope, and Charity, also reminded her of a similar set of three virtues expressed in the Daode Jing. A passage came to mind, which surprised her, as she hadn't read it in years.

I have three treasures which I hold dear.
The first is compassion.
The second is frugality.
The third is humility.
With compassion one can be brave.
With frugality one can be generous.
With humility one can lead others.

As she mused on the murals, she realized Jane was by her side. "Beautiful, aren't they?" Jane said.

"Yes, I've loved these since I was a kid. I haven't thought about them in years. It's nice to see them again. I used to pretend I was Justice over there, running around playing with a wooden sword," she said, pointing.

"Interesting. It must be genetic," Jane replied enigmatically.

"Why do you say that?"

"Oh nothing. It's not important."

Rohini was going to explore this further, wondering exactly what Jane meant, when they were told to get ready for their entrance. The event was about to begin.

# 18

Rohini and Jane heard a cheer go up from the assembled crowd outside as President Johnson walked to the podium, waving as he went. The president would be giving his address from the same place Martin Luther King, Jr had given his famous "I Have a Dream" speech, one of many historic events at the memorial over the years adding to its significance, especially to the Civil Rights movement.

Although many events followed it, none was as momentous as the March on Washington for Jobs and Freedom, the occasion for MLK's speech. *None until today,* Rohini thought. She found it appropriate this location had been chosen. *This is a moment of unity for all mankind, or at least all Earthlings. Were the Elders a part of mankind?* Rohini still found herself stumbling at times, making the mental adjustment to this new reality.

"Thank you. Thank you. Thank you all for coming," the president said, beginning his speech. "Thank you for sharing this moment of Faith, Hope, and Charity with your fellow humans," Rohini's ears perked up at his mention of the exact same virtues she had just been contemplating.

He continued. "Faith in our ability to come together as one and accomplish what needs to be done. A renewed sense of Hope that a bright, livable future for our children and grandchildren is not only possible but probable. And the spirit of Charity which allows us to put our own pettiness, our own egotistical sense of self-importance aside, so that we may focus on the needs of the least among us and the welfare of us all.

"While these values are most familiar to those of us coming from the Christian tradition, these are universal spiritual values that all of the Great Faiths of the Earth share." The hairs on the back of Rohini's neck stood up at his words. She felt like he was channeling the same thoughts she had been having moments before.

"Today we have come together as one human family to celebrate the selection of a group of exceptional individuals who have been chosen by our various nations to represent us, to represent all of us, to represent the Earth herself, on this unprecedented mission.

"When our new friends, the Elders, appeared to us that day at the UN, I, like many of you, I'm sure, was shocked. I was also, of course, suspicious and skeptical of their claims. But when the Elders' spokesman communicated with me directly, I and the other world leaders knew that this was an opportunity unlike any which has come before. Not just an opportunity to save the planet, but an opportunity to save humanity from the dark days ahead we had all assumed were inevitable.

"It had begun to seem like the dystopian nightmares of many of our most popular books and films of the past few decades would be inescapable. I think I speak for all of us when I voice my relief at the renewed sense of hope we all feel, as well as our sense of gratitude to the Elders, not just for offering their assistance in saving our planet from the chaos of climate change, but also for delivering the kick in the pants we all needed to make it happen!"

There was a loud raucous cheer at his last line, the president expertly tapping into the pulse of the people. He had always had a natural gift for it, always seeming at ease, able to relate to any crowd without seeming to be pandering. It was a fine line. Many attempted this high-wire act in an obvious, ham-fisted way, but he was a master of walking that razor's edge.

"And now the moment you've all been waiting for. The reason we are here today. I'd like you all to join me in welcoming your Earth Ambassadors!" The president partially turned his back to the crowd, extending a hand up the steps towards the monument, where Rohini and the other ambassadors were being ushered down the steps behind him. Jane, waiting near one of the pillars bordering the entrance of the memorial, gave Rohini a thumbs-up as she began down the steps.

As the ambassadors descended, the president clapped along with the rest of the crowd, gathered in the hundreds of thousands, filling the area in front of the reflecting pool and flanking it on either side as far as Rohini could see. The ambassadors began to fan out across the steps, forming a line a few steps above where the president stood behind the podium. Rohini felt a flush in her cheeks as she, Martin, and the other Earth Ambassadors exchanged smiling glances, emotionally overwhelmed by the outpouring of goodwill from the assembled masses.

The next few moments were a blur. An Elder appeared next to President Johnson at the lectern. At least Rohini assumed it was an Elder as he seemed to materialize out of thin air. He wasn't dressed as the Elders at the UN had been. Instead, he appeared to be an old Native American man, his gray hair in a single braid down his back and a red bandana tied around his head. He wore a button-down shirt, like those you would find at a Western wear store—the kind with faux mother-of-pearl snaps—and blue jeans.

"You're in danger! Go back into the memorial!" the old man yelled as he attempted to hustle the president up the steps.

A deafening boom split the bright, sunny morning like a clap of thunder, sending everything into chaos. Rohini felt like she'd been struck by lightning. One moment she was watching as President Johnson and the Elder began to climb the steps, the next they were gone in a bright, blinding flash as the force of the explosion threw her to the ground.

She had been at one end of the line of ambassadors, standing next to Martin. As she rolled over, lifting herself onto an elbow, the taste of dust and the feel of grit filled her mouth. She coughed on the clouds of smoke and dust hanging over the steps as she attempted to get her bearings. Her hearing was muffled while at the same time her ears rang, like she was on a plane with a head cold after being at a concert all night.

As the horrific scene unfolded before her, she saw bodies strewn over the steps, as well as something new—a crater at the center of the landing where the podium had been. Lincoln sat looking down over them through the smoky haze, his likeness still recognizable, but his statue, as well as the columns of the Memorial, now pitted and pock-marked.

Rohini struggled to make sense of it all until everything clicked into place in her mind. *There was an explosion.* As reality began to come into focus again, she recalled the tactical breathing technique Jane had taught her, closing her eyes and counting off a few cycles as she got a grip on herself.

She opened her eyes with a start as a hand on her shoulder brought her back to the moment. Looking up she saw Guangming, the ambassador from China looking down at her, his face streaked with blood and dust. She saw his mouth moving, but she couldn't make out what he was saying. That's when she noticed his eyes—*they're green.*

The recognition of his eyes sent a new wave of adrenaline coursing through her veins, snapping her out of her fog. She hadn't noticed them that morning outside the White House, but the contrast with the blood and dust coating his face set the color off.

"Rohini, can you hear me? We've got to get out of here," she heard him say, as she realized Jane was also by her side.

"It's OK, Rohini, you can trust him," Jane said. "Come on, we've got to move now."

As Rohini struggled to her feet, Jane had moved away, crouching down over another figure sprawled on the steps. Rohini realized from where the body was that it must be Martin, the other American. Rohini inhaled sharply as Jane stood, shaking her head. "He's gone," Jane said, then turned and stepped quickly across the debris-strewn steps, before crouching down again.

Rohini and Guangming followed. Rohini could tell it was one of the other ambassadors, his white blazer recognizable even though it was anything but white now. She thought back to meeting the others at the motorcade as she tried to place him. It was Jean-Luc, the French member of the group.

As they crouched down around him, she realized he was trying to speak. It was just a croak at first, but then his words became clearer, more distinguishable. "I'm so sorry," he said. "I had no idea they would do this."

"Who, Jean-Luc?" Jane asked. "Who did this?"

"I don't know," he groaned. "I never saw their faces... I had no choice... they gave me drugs... said they'd hurt my family if..." His words were cut short as he gasped, his body seizing, his eyes growing wide. Then, just as suddenly, his body went limp, his eyes staring into the void, beyond this world. Jane closed his eyelids and they stood, looking at the carnage around them.

"The other ambassadors... the president... they're all dead," Jane said.

# 19

*Chinatown*
*Washington, DC*

"A short time ago, in an undisclosed location, the former Vice-President, Elizabeth Powers, was sworn in to become the forty-sixth President of the United States by the Chief Justice of the U.S. Supreme Court, Alicia Fernandez."

Rohini, Jane, and Guangming sat on a musty old couch in the living room of a rundown apartment above Dragon Star Asian Foods, a small corner grocery in what was left of DC's Chinatown, their eyes glued to the screen of a shiny new flat screen TV. It was about the only thing shiny or new in the apartment, which by the looks of it, was used more as storage space for the market downstairs than anything else.

They'd entered the apartment from the market, passing through a scuffed set of double doors at the back which swung both ways like saloon doors in the Old West, past rows of shelving in the storeroom and up a flight of stairs, the only access to the apartment other than a fire escape from the bedroom which led down to the alley in back. Cases of ramen noodles filled one corner of the room, while boxes of fish sauce and sriracha took up most of the countertop that separated the small kitchen from the living room where they now found themselves.

As soon as they came upstairs, they checked the cable news channels to see what was happening in the aftermath of the attack.

They'd been there themselves, of course, but seeing it on TV gave the morning's events a surreal quality, like it had all been a dream. But it hadn't. Elizabeth Powers being sworn in as the new president confirmed that beyond a shadow of a doubt. President Johnson and the rest of the Earth Ambassadors were dead.

As the news networks had all been covering that morning's event at the Lincoln Memorial, there was no shortage of footage of the blast. They continued to show the explosion over and over from multiple angles as the talking heads analyzed the action on the screen, speculating about who was responsible, while the news ticker scrolled across the bottom of the screen.

While everyone had witnessed the sudden appearance of the Elder next to the president, only the ambassadors had been close enough to hear his words. The news analysts were evenly divided as to whether the Elder had been trying to help President Johnson or whether he was somehow responsible for the explosion.

Rohini expected they would regroup with the Secret Service after the explosion, but Jane had assured her they should follow Guangming's lead. "Just trust me on this one, Rohini, we can't go with the Secret Service right now. I'm worried this was an inside job."

The three had used the chaos and confusion following the explosion to blend into the terror-stricken tumult of the crowds scattering in every direction. They made their way east past the reflecting pool and across the National Mall, blending in with the fleeing masses.

They stopped before getting too far and attempted to clean themselves up—at least as well as could be expected under the circumstances—splashing water on themselves from the reflecting pool, then hurrying on with the crowds. As they got farther from the blast site, they didn't want to stick out any more than necessary. Some of the closest members of the crowd had felt some of the impact of the explosion, many covered in cement dust as Rohini and Guangming had been, but the Elder, the president, and the ambassadors had taken the brunt of the blast.

"Ditch your blazers," Jane said as they cleaned up. "They'll be too easy to pick out of the crowd." Rohini's blouse underneath was in better shape and her dark slacks hid the blood, dirt and smoke stains fairly well. They'd been charcoal gray before the explosion and now were only more so, if a bit tattered and torn. *If you're ever dressing for an explosion,* Rohini thought dryly, *remember charcoal gray.*

Having been up in the memorial during the blast, Jane was relatively unscathed, and Guangming wasn't too worse for wear other than a gash to his scalp an inch above the hairline, the source of the blood on his face following the blast. It looked worse than it was—as head wounds often do—and had stopped bleeding by the time they'd gotten to the reflecting pool. His short black hair hid the wound fairly well unless you were looking for it.

Guangming had made a quick call on his cell phone as Jane helped Rohini clean up by the Reflecting Pool. The quick conversation was in Chinese so Jane and Rohini were in the dark, but after hanging up he told them, "I've got us a ride, let's go."

After passing between the red sandstone of the Smithsonian Castle on the south side of the Mall and the pedimented portico of the Museum of Natural History to the north, they turned left on 7th Street, just before the National Gallery. Rohini was still in a bit of a fog, mostly from the physical effects of the blast, but also the emotional shock of what had occurred. Looking up as they passed, she couldn't help thinking how nice a stroll through the gallery would be right now. *You're definitely a little loopy.*

Twenty minutes after the explosion, they crossed Constitution Avenue and piled into a silver SUV which had pulled up to the curb. The driver, an associate of Guangming, took them on a circuitous route north into Chinatown, eventually passing under the Friendship Arch, traditional entryway to the once-thriving neighborhood. Rohini couldn't help but marvel at the arch as they drove through, impressed by the length of its single span. It was covered in golden dragons, which wasn't unusual—dragons being a common motif in Chinese culture. What struck her was a row of nine dragons across the middle of the arch, reminding her again of the scroll painting she'd remembered on that mountain ridge in Virginia.

Washington, DC's Chinatown had been home to as many as three thousand residents in the past, but only a few hundred remained. Much of the district had gentrified, filling with upscale clothing stores, restaurants and boutique coffee and tea shops. But some of the old flavor of the neighborhood still lingered in the air, like smoke from an incense stick, in the few temples and Asian Markets that remained. Such as the one where they were now laying low.

Rohini hadn't asked many questions during their flight from the scene of the bombing. She'd been dazed enough that she followed Jane's lead almost mechanically. Their sole focus had been on slipping away and keeping a low profile. All Jane had told her was that she was worried about it being an inside job and that they had better go underground for a while.

While that made sense, it didn't explain everything—like how Jane knew Guangming, or why the three of them all had green eyes— it didn't explain much of anything. Rohini felt like she was on a runaway train with no idea how to stop it, or even where it was headed. But she was pretty sure they did. Now that they were safe, at least for the moment, she needed some answers.

"OK, guys," Rohini began uneasily, standing and pacing in the small apartment. "I need to know what's going on here. You two obviously know each other. Are you a spy too, Guangming? And why do we all have green eyes?"

"Actually, we've never met before today, but Guangming and I did know of each other," Jane replied. "And you're right, there is more going on here than you've been told. I didn't think I would need to tell you about all this. I was going to let the Elders handle it once they returned, but obviously things have gone way off the rails."

"What are you talking about, Jane? What's really going on? Was this the same people who tried to kidnap me? Are we caught in the middle of some war or something?" Rohini asked.

"That's not too far off," Guangming said. "I think we may be at war, we're just not exactly sure who we are fighting."

"This isn't the Elders, is it? That Elder that appeared at the memorial—it seemed like he was trying to warn the president."

"No, this is definitely not the Elders, Rohini," Jane said.

"But how can you be so sure, Jane? I led a pretty boring life until they showed up. Now someone has tried to abduct me and when that failed they tried to blow me up! What aren't you two telling me?" she said, looking back and forth between them.

"Rohini, we know it's not the Elders... because we are the Elders."

# 20

*The Elders' World*

The Guide awoke suddenly. *Something is very wrong,* she thought. She reached out with her mind to the members of the council. *We must meet.* Early the next morning, in the Council Chambers, she told them what she had sensed.

"I awoke greatly disturbed last night. I'm afraid the Earth Elder, Qaletaqa is dead," the Guide said. There was a murmur among the councilors as they reacted to the news.

"How, Grandmother?" the councilor from the Horse Clan asked.

"As you know we had asked him to watch over the bloodline. He sensed they were in danger, but he was too late to avert it. He died trying to save one of the Earth's leaders, and the bloodline," the Guide replied. "Unfortunately, the leader of the United States was killed, as were many of the Earthlings chosen as ambassadors, including two of the bloodline. Two survived, however, the woman Rohini and one other, as did the Earth Guardian, Sinéad."

The councilors exchanged nervous glances. They all knew the implications. If the sentiment of the Earthlings turned against them, their long-range plans could be threatened. While Earth needed the Elders, the Elders also needed Earth.

"Do you have any insight into who might be responsible for this attack, Grandmother?" asked the councilor from the Snake Clan.

"I do not, though there was something Speaker Dayan said to me when he first returned which might be important. He said one of the Earth leaders had a very dark mind. Dayan was worried he might not go along with our plans. This must be investigated further. This may be our only lead."

"What do you advise, Grandmother?" asked the councilor from the Snake Clan.

"We must summon Zhongkui," the Guide said.

"I didn't think he was willing to serve the council any longer," the Snake Elder replied.

"It's true he asked to be left in retreat after his beloved returned to the One, but I believe once he hears what has happened, he will be willing to serve again. After all, it was Zhongkui who trained the Earth Guardian, Sinéad. Despite his great loss, I believe his compassion and sense of duty will outweigh his grief. Zhongkui has always been a man of action." the Guide said. "Are there any opposed?" she asked, scanning the faces of the assembled representatives. Seeing no objections, she closed the assembly, "Good. We are in harmony. Until such time."

# 21

Rohini was floored. Then Jane elaborated.

"I'm from Earth, but I am also an Elder—as are you, Rohini," Jane began. "We carry the Elders' bloodline. We have their genes. That's where the green eyes come from. I was found by one of the Elders when I was a teenager and told about the Elders' world and their bloodline on Earth.

"I was taught about their ways—our ways—to a limited degree, nothing like the full training we would receive on their world, but enough to have a general understanding of their culture and traditions. I can't travel like they do—at least not yet—but one day the three of us will most likely develop that skill."

Rohini sat back down in stunned silence. She couldn't believe what she was hearing. Nothing made sense anymore. She wrapped her arms around herself as she began to cry silent tears.

"Rohini, I know this is a shock, but just try to hear me out for now," Jane said, putting a hand on Rohini's shoulder. "My mentor, the Elder who taught me, also gave me a mission, a duty to fulfill, which was to become your guardian. While the three of us all carry the Elders' genes, I was told that you carry it from both sides of your family. This has never happened before—at least not as far as the Elders are aware—so they were especially keen on finding and protecting you.

"My career in the military, law enforcement, and intelligence has ultimately had this as its goal—to position myself to best serve in this role. At the same time, it was also a happy coincidence that the president's relationship with your father led him to feel especially protective of you, which was a perfect way for me to get close to you. The Elders certainly used that to their advantage when they chose you as an ambassador."

"So, this whole Earth Ambassador thing was just an elaborate ruse? They were only trying to get to me the whole time?" Rohini replied in disbelief.

"No, no, everything the Elder said at the UN was true. They—we—are going to help protect Earth. The Elders do possess more advanced renewable energy technologies which will help regenerate Earth—as you've already seen—and they did feel that the time had come to make themselves known. It was either that or watch the planet go down the drain. They care about us too much to simply sit back and watch us commit a slow suicide."

"How do you know all this, Jane? Did your mentor tell you?" Rohini asked.

"Yes," Jane said. "I haven't seen him in ten years, but the last time we spoke, he told me they would come to Earth's aid, if things got to this point."

"Why wait until now, Jane?" Rohini said. "Couldn't they have prevented all of this if they had simply helped us years ago? Climate change has caused so much suffering in the last few years. If they care so much, why not help us sooner? Why let us walk right up to the brink?"

"The Elders tried to help us before, in a more surreptitious way, a way more in keeping with their values. One of their most strongly held values is non-interference. They don't believe in forcing things. They usually try to influence people in subtler ways, hoping to guide them to discover truths on their own. It is more like a process of trying to create the right conditions for things to emerge on their own, so people assume they thought of something all by themselves. Are you familiar with Nikola Tesla, Rohini?"

"Wasn't he an inventor of some sort, like Edison?" she replied.

"Yes, they were rivals, and there was no love lost between them by all accounts. The Elders attempted to impart some of their knowledge to Earth by assisting Tesla in cultivating his genius. They saw in the Industrial Revolution and its increasing reliance on fossil fuels the seeds of our self-destruction being sown. They knew the path we were heading down and where it would eventually lead from their own history.

"Tesla didn't realize what was happening, at least not at first. Initially the Elders' assistance took the form of subtle suggestions here and there, a few leading questions in conversations to steer him towards a certain train of thought—that sort of thing. They knew he was brilliant and might have come to some of these ideas on his own eventually, but with their prompting his progress was greatly accelerated."

"Didn't he invent a machine that supposedly heard ghosts?" Rohini asked.

"You mean the Spirit Radio? The Elders didn't even anticipate that one. He managed to create a device which gave him the ability to hear them directly. A few of the Elders who are most gifted telepathically were able to speak with him through the device," Jane replied.

"I always thought it was written off as some sort of parlor trick, like the things Victorian hucksters did at séances. I guess the Elders weren't ready to let themselves be widely known yet," Rohini said.

"Yes, that's true. The Elders were still trying to keep a low profile. It also helped that when he initially designed the device, nobody he shared it with understood what they were hearing, so they thought it must just be a fluke. A lot of people found it spooky and didn't want to get involved. My mentor told me a story about this, actually—I haven't thought of it in years—but it might have some bearing on what happened today at the memorial.

"After Tesla built the machine, word spread through the grapevine until one night an old Hopi man showed up in Colorado Springs, where Tesla had built a lab the year before in 1899. He'd heard that Tesla could also detect thunder from approaching storms when they were still hundreds of miles away through his device, and so the Hopi man thought maybe it was the Kachinas—the ancestral spirits of the Hopi who maintain balance in the world—who Tesla heard speaking through the Spirit Radio, at least that's what he told Tesla. After hearing his idea, Tesla let him listen to the radio. As they sat listening, the old man asked Tesla if he could understand what they heard, and he said no. "It is because you don't know how to listen," the old man told him. Then he taught Tesla to meditate in a particular way while listening to the radio. "If you learn to empty your heart, and sit and forget everything, you will be able to understand," the Hopi said. Then, standing and saying his goodbyes, he left as abruptly as he had arrived, disappearing into the night."

"Wait, an old Hopi man? You don't think that could have been him today at the memorial?" Rohini said. She sat up straighter at this thought as her emotions took a back seat to her curiosity.

"The same thing occurred to me when I remembered the story about Tesla," Jane said. "I asked my mentor if that old Hopi was an Elder when he told me the story, but he wouldn't say. I always assumed he must have been, or at least a human who carried the bloodline. Maybe he has been watching over the Hopi all these years.

"Anyway, Tesla practiced meditating in the way the Old Hopi man had taught him until the voices he heard became clear enough for him to understand, something he never shared with anyone else at the Elders' request," Jane said. "The Elders assumed that if they encouraged his exploration of free energy devices, they might discourage the use of fossil fuels which would lead Earth down the path of runaway climate change. What they didn't anticipate was the level of greed and the lust for power which kept his ideas locked away, out of the hands of the public."

They were silent for a moment, each lost in their own thoughts. "But what about this mentor of yours, Jane, can't he help us out of this jam?" Rohini said.

"I wish he could," Jane said. "I don't have any way to get in touch with him."

"How did you contact him before?"

"I didn't. He always showed up out of the blue. It could be after a few weeks or a few months—I never knew when to expect him next," Jane replied. "But since he's been gone so long this time, I'm a little worried he's gone for good, I'm afraid he's returned to the One."

"What does that mean?" Rohini said.

"That is how the Elders refer to dying, they consider it a return to being one with the universe. As I understand it, the Elders who have mastered the ability to travel energetically are basically immortal, unless they die violently, or they choose to die of their own accord."

"How do you fit into all of this, Guangming?" Rohini asked, turning to face him.

"My relationship with the Elders is quite different than either of yours'," he responded. "I belong to an ancient secret society from China, what's commonly known in the West as a Triad."

"Wait, like the Mafia?" Rohini asked, surprised.

"No, but that is the image we have in the media—that we are like the Sicilian Mafia or the Japanese Yakuza. While some Chinese secret societies have degenerated into little more than criminal gangs in the modern era, many of the ancient ones like ours were established for very different reasons. They were founded along religious lines or for patriotic ideals, intended to help resist foreign invaders or over-throw corrupt regimes.

"Jane mentioned our green eyes as being a sign that we carry the bloodline of the Elders. In our society we have a different explanation for green eyes. We say those with green eyes carry the bloodline of Zhongkui, the demon hunter, one of our patron saints. We call them yin-yang eyes. According to our traditions it is a sign of having great-er innate potential for wisdom and psychic abilities."

"Yin and yang, like the taiji symbol," Rohini said.

"Yes, just as yin and yang are used to describe the relative re-lationship between things like light and shadow, male and female, day and night; we use it to describe the ability to sense not only the yang realm of the living—our ordinary everyday perception of the physical world—but also the yin realm of ghosts, spirits, and psychic phenomena.

"Within this spiritual realm we talk of yang spirits or Immortals who have become pure yang, pure energy, and confused spirits who have become pure yin or ghosts. We have traditionally thought of yin ghosts as connected to the earth and yang spirits or Immortals as be-ing connected to higher celestial realms.

Since we now know the Elders have been to Earth many times, our traditions may be related to their visits in the past, our Immortals may actually be the Elders. Our society's leader, the Guanzi, thinks this might be the case."

"I'm guessing this leader of yours must have green eyes too, then," Rohini said.

"Yes, having green eyes is one of the criteria necessary to be considered for the role of Guanzi. They are also the person from each generation whose wisdom and compassion is most universally acknowledged by our society. Their potential is usually recognized from a young age and cultivated by teachers and mentors within the society. When the time comes to appoint a new Guanzi, they are chosen by consensus. The name Guanzi is a title. It means something like "The Seer" or "The Watcher".

"Traditionally we have always thought our Guanzi had the ability to communicate with the Daoist Immortals. Now that we know about the Elders, we'll have to reconcile our traditional ways of looking at things with this new knowledge. Jane, did your mentor ever teach you anything that would shed light on this?" Guangming asked.

"From what I understand, in the past when the Elders located one of their bloodline on Earth—he called them Earth Elders—they sometimes sent a mentor like they did with me, someone to train them. They often appeared in the guise of a teacher or a religious figure from whatever culture this Earth Elder grew up in. So, I don't see why they couldn't have appeared as a Daoist Immortal. Earth Elders like the three of us are supposed to have greater potential than other humans to gain the powers of the Elders, if given the proper training."

"That's why I took you to that cave in Virginia, Rohini. After you told me about the experience you had in the kiva in New Mexico, I thought you might be able to take advantage of the cave to tap into that potential," Jane said.

"So, you mean the voice I heard, it was the Elders?" Rohini replied, a little taken aback. "Like you were saying Tesla heard the Elders through his radio?"

"I think so, based on what my mentor taught me. It's one of the signs of progress he told me about. He said that eventually I would hear the voice of the Elders and after that my practice would progress much more swiftly. Tesla didn't carry the Elders' bloodline—he was just a genius—but the device he designed must have compensated for the difference, giving him an artificial means to hear it."

"It sounds similar to what your Guanzi experiences also, Guangming," Rohini said. "But I'm guessing he doesn't need a radio."

"The kiva you mentioned, is this a cave?" Guangming asked.

"It is in a way, like a man-made cave," Rohini said. "It's like a pit dwelling dug into the earth. I used to meditate in one which always led to very strange experiences."

"We have a similar tradition," Guangming said. "We think that caves can act like a sort of amplifier—or a receiver—like this radio of Tesla's you mentioned. Anyway, it is thought to enhance one's ability to resonate with the earth and in turn with the Dao, or the whole cosmos.

"There was a famous Daoist named Hao Datong—he founded the lineage of Mt. Hua in China—following in his teacher's footsteps, he decided to dig a cave in which to practice his self-cultivation. When he had finished his cave, an old hermit wandered up and said, 'Oh, what a nice cave you've made.' Hao Datong in his compassion for the old monk offered it to him to use, starting work on a second cave for himself. When this second cave was nearing completion, the same thing happened again—another practitioner came and admired the cave, which Hao Datong once again gave away, beginning yet another cave for himself. This happened again and again until Hao had dug seventy-two caves before eventually becoming an Immortal himself."

"As fascinating as all of this is, Guangming—I mean that, I'd really love to hear more—how does this all relate to whoever is attacking us?" Rohini asked.

"Since our society's founding we have fought against injustice and the forces of greed, hatred, and ignorance in our world. Our two main patron saints are Zhongkui, who I mentioned before, and Guanyin. There are many stories of Zhongkui. His name has become synonymous with 'a person who has the courage to fight against evil or injustice.' He also embodies wisdom, as he was a great scholar before becoming an Immortal.

"Guanyin is seen as a goddess, a bodhisattva, or an Immortal—she is actually quite popular among both Buddhists and Daoists in China—her full name is Guan Shi Yin, which means 'one who sees the suffering of the world.' She is an embodiment of compassion. These two represent the values that our society was founded upon.

"At times our society has been more active in the world, though usually at these times we blended with other groups, in order to keep our true identity and mission secret. Over the years we have aided many of the revolts throughout Chinese history, which overthrew dynasties that had become too riddled with corruption to be allowed to stand. Keeping to the shadows, we have always had an extensive intelligence network. We have eyes and ears throughout the Chinese government as well as in the many Chinese communities overseas," Guangming said.

The look on Rohini's face told Guangming she was losing her patience again, so he cut himself short. "Sorry, I so rarely get to talk openly about our society's history, I tend to get carried away when I do," he said, grinning sheepishly.

"Anyway," he continued. "A short time ago we began to hear rumors about a terrorist attack against the West from our sources in the Muslim communities in Xinjiang Province in the far west of China. There was talk about striking at the heart of the West, but we didn't know where or when, and we didn't realize there was any connection to the Earth Ambassadors or the American President."

"I suppose it's still possible this was simply a convenient event to target the president," Jane began. "But it seems like the ambassadors were targeted as much as, if not more than, President Johnson."

"I think you are correct, Jane," Guangming replied. "Especially after the attempt on Rohini earlier. Unless we find evidence to the contrary, I think we have to operate on the assumption that this was an anti-Elder attack."

"It sounds like whoever tried to get to me got to Jean-Luc," Rohini said. "I feel so bad for him, but at the same time, I'm so relieved it wasn't me."

"That's perfectly natural," Jane said, putting a caring hand on Rohini's arm. "Don't feel bad about that. We're all lucky to be alive after that blast. That has me thinking, though. Jean-Luc was also one of the ambassadors chosen by the Elders, and like us he had green eyes. I wonder if the two of you were targeted because of your connection to the Elders or if it was simply because the remaining ambassadors hadn't yet been selected?"

"I'm not sure we'll be able to ascertain that with any degree of certainty until we figure out who our adversaries are," Guangming interjected. "The intelligence we did receive pointed to a group we thought was no longer active. Do you remember the Soldiers of the Caliphate, Jane?"

"The SOC? Really? I haven't heard of them in years. I thought they were long gone, but I'm only too familiar with them," Jane said. "Their leadership ranks were decimated after their failed attempt at setting up a new caliphate, and the mood in the Middle East has been trending more moderate ever since. I thought we were heading for a Reformation in the Islamic world, not a return to the violence of the past. Why would they come out of the woodwork again now, after all these years?"

"That's what we wondered as well. Our sources thought it was a mistake at first. It could be someone with little or no connection to the original group. Someone may have simply taken up their mantle again, perhaps as a reaction against the momentum of the moderates. Maybe this is the last remnants of fundamentalism lashing out before it takes its final breath," replied Guangming.

"One can only hope," Jane said. "I guess we don't have much to go on there yet. I'll check with a contact I trust, and see what they've come up with. I'm sure Burt will know something soon."

"You mean the Bandit," Rohini said, smiling.

"The very one," Jane said, getting up, before yawning and stretching. "It's getting late. We should probably get some sleep and see where we stand in the morning."

"You two take the bedroom," Guangming said. "I will be fine on the couch."

"Goodnight."

# 22

That night, despite being exhausted, Rohini slept fitfully. She had strange dreams which left her feeling like she'd hardly slept. When she woke the following morning, Rohini found Jane was already awake. Hearing the shower running, she got dressed and wandered into the living room, rubbing her eyes. Guangming was also awake, standing in the kitchen pouring coffee into a chipped ceramic mug. "Want a cup?" he asked.

"Thanks. That would be great," she replied, sliding a few boxes of fish sauce off the counter, clearing a space before sitting down on one of the old barstools there. Guangming set a steaming cup of coffee on the counter in front of her, which she took in both hands, inhaling the aroma deeply before taking a small sip. "That's not half bad, considering," she said. "I was afraid we'd be drinking some of that instant coffee from downstairs."

"I can't drink that stuff. I had them bring us some fresh beans from the coffee shop down the street, they roast their own," Guangming replied. "This is Yemen Moka."

"I'm just happy it's not freeze-dried sludge," Rohini said, smiling.

"Is that coffee I smell?" Jane said, walking into the room a few minutes later.

"Have a seat, I'll pour you a cup," Guangming replied.

"Any news yet?" Rohini asked.

"Yes, though I'm afraid it's not good. I talked to Burt. They want us in for questioning—I would've expected that—but the overzealous jackass at the FBI who's been put in charge of the investigation has decided to treat us as suspects."

"What? Why would they do that?" Rohini asked.

"The group Guangming mentioned last night, the Soldiers of the Caliphate," Jane began. "The reason I'm familiar with them is that at one time I dealt with them covertly. You may recall they overthrew a dictator before attempting to launch their caliphate. Well, unfortunately, we helped them accomplish that. Our government thought they would be more amenable to our interests after they gained control of the country, but obviously we bet on the wrong horse, as we soon found out. They played us. If it is the SOC that's behind this, and the FBI find out about my past link to them, it will only reinforce the idea that we're involved."

"So, if they found us…" Rohini began, realization dawning on her.

"We'd be treated as terrorists suspected of killing the President of the United States. It would be shoot first and ask questions later. We'd be lucky to be taken in in one piece." Jane said.

"Can't Burt tell them what's going on? He's got to know we wouldn't have anything to do with this," Rohini ventured.

"That would only make things worse, I'm afraid. The agent heading the investigation is a SAC named Edward Rooney. This guy is a real tight-ass and he hates Burt with a passion. You remember I told you Burt was a driving instructor at the academy, right? Well, before the trainees get to try the driving course themselves, they ride along with one of the instructors. Ed Rooney was already rubbing people the wrong way, not only his fellow trainees but the instructors as well. He was talking a lot of crap before the driving course, so when Burt took him on his orientation run, he really pushed it. This guy didn't know whether to piss himself or throw up when Burt was done with him. He's held a grudge towards Burt ever since.

"And he's no fan of mine, either. We were in the same class. I was one of the people he didn't get along with, and it probably didn't help that Burt and I did. Burt took me under his wing, along with a few others, which made Rooney hate us with the same venom he had for Burt.

"The one upshot might be that he doesn't know me as Jane Smith. But I'm sure they'll make the connection eventually. When they do, he'll be only too happy to believe the worst about me. He's a smarmy bootlicker who's managed to climb his way up the ladder, ingratiating himself to all the right people. No, I'm afraid that's a dead-end."

"What about President Powers? She must know we're innocent," Rohini said hopefully.

"You're probably right, Rohini, but we've got no way to get to her directly. As soon as anyone spots us we'll be lucky to get to tell our side of things before we're in a deep dark hole. If the real perpetrators aren't flushed out, eventually they'll need someone's head on a platter, and they might just settle for ours," Jane replied. "Our biggest problem is that I was working directly for the president. There was no one else in the chain of command to vouch for us. As far as anyone knows we could have gotten close to President Johnson in order to carry out the attack."

"Can't we just turn ourselves in and get this all straightened out?"

"I wish we could. What's got me worried is that someone on the inside could be responsible for this, or at least helped pull this off.

"For all we know, the same people could be framing us, in which case we're screwed. It would be a piece of cake to manufacture a story that I was some sort of traitorous double agent, especially with my link to the SOC and—no offense, Rohini, but you *are* brown—even though your mother isn't Middle Eastern or Muslim, there are still plenty of ignorant fools in this country who will be more than happy to see you as yet another homegrown terrorist if it fits into their narrative."

"I'm sure I don't help in the mix either," Guangming said, joining the conversation. "There have been quite a few Chinese students caught spying over the years."

"Industrial espionage and patent infringement are one thing, assassinating the president is something else entirely," Jane said. "I guess we'll just have to hang tight for now."

They sat in silence for a few minutes, each of them deep in thought, trying to come to grips with the predicament they found themselves in. A dark mood had descended until Rohini changed the subject.

"Did you go to college here, Guangming? Is that why your English is so good?" Rohini said.

"I did. I was also an exchange student in high school, so my English was already quite good by the time I started college," Guangming replied.

"Where did you go to school? And where did you stay with your exchange program?" Rohini asked.

"I went to USC, which was a bit of a culture shock. Although most of the cities in China are quite large, Jinchang, the city I am from, only has a population of about 200,000. My exchange program was less of an adjustment. Gansu Province has sister cities in Oklahoma, so that is where I stayed. Jinchang's sister city is Shawnee, Oklahoma."

"Whoa, I would've thought that would have been a bigger change than going to Los Angeles," Rohini said. "I think Shawnee, Oklahoma, would be a culture shock for me."

"Perhaps, in some ways," Guangming said. "There was a larger Chinese-American community in Southern California. But, oddly enough, Shawnee felt familiar. The Native Americans there reminded me of some of the ethnic minorities in my region of China. So did the cowboy culture.

"The part of Gansu I am from is in a narrow passage called the Hexi Corridor which made up part of the Northern Silk Road. It's tucked between several minority autonomous regions; Tibetans, Mongolians, and the Hui people all live in the area. Although they are less nomadic than in the past, the area is still well known for its horses.

"There is a famous place, Shandan Horse Ranch in the Qilian Mountains west of Jinchang, which was originally founded by General Huo Qubing all the way back in 121 BC, to raise horses for the Chinese army after he defeated the Xiongnu people and forced them out of the area. They have been raising horses for the military and royal families throughout our history."

"Isn't that also where the Dunhuang Caves are?" Rohini asked. "I thought they were along the Silk Road somewhere in that part of China."

"You know about the Dunhuang Caves?" Guangming asked, surprised.

"Just a little, I hadn't thought much about it in years, but I was really into the Daode Jing in high school. I seem to recall them mentioning the Dunhuang Caves in the translator's introduction to the edition I read. That's where they found a lot of ancient manuscripts like the Daode Jing and the Diamond Sutra, if I remember correctly."

"Yes, in fact Wang Yuanlu, the Daoist monk who found the cave with the manuscripts, was a member of our society. He was practicing as a wandering Daoist at the time and came upon the Dunhuang Caves one day around dusk. Seeing light coming from one of the caves, he headed towards it, hoping to find a meal and a warm place to sleep for the night. As he approached the mouth of the cave, an old monk with wild hair and a big bushy beard popped his head out. He said he was the caretaker of the caves, and invited Wang to stay the night.

"That night as they were sitting around the fire after dinner drinking tea, Wang realized the old hermit had green eyes. Naturally Wang thought he might be a member of our society, so he made some overtures to see if he was—members of our society often make ourselves known to one another through hand signs or code words.

"The old man feigned ignorance, so Wang figured it must simply be a coincidence. The old man told Wang he was getting too old for the job of caretaker and perhaps it was time to leave the caves' welfare to someone else. He asked Wang if he would consider the job, saying surely it must have been the currents of the Dao and destiny that brought Wang to him. Wang, in his humility, told the old man that he was not worthy of such an honorable responsibility. After repeated requests from the old monk, he said he would consider it, and they retired for the night.

"The next morning when Wang awoke, the old monk was gone. Wang searched the nearby caves, but could not find any sign of him. Returning to the cave in which they'd slept, he noticed the thin ribbon of smoke from what was left of the previous night's fire streaming towards the back wall of the chamber, as though drawn by a draft. Investigating, he found there was air flowing into a crack in the wall. Figuring there must be another chamber behind it, he set to work knocking it down, revealing another room stacked to the ceiling with ancient manuscripts which had been hidden away from the world for over a thousand years.

"There was a story in our society of a library somewhere in that part of the country which had been sealed up for protection after the neighboring kingdom of Khotan was sacked and burned by the Karakhanids in 1006 AD. Its location had been lost to the sands of time. People had come to think it was only a legend. Looking over the manuscripts in the days that followed, reading through their titles—at least of those he could, as many were in languages other than Chinese—he realized that this must be that library. But that was not his greatest discovery, at least not for the society.

"In the back of the chamber, set into a niche in the cave wall, Wang found a lacquered wooden chest, decorated in designs similar to those sometimes used by our society. Opening the chest, he found histories of the early years of the society and its founders, as well as many of the prophecies of our early Guanzi. Until then, what we knew of the earliest years of our tradition was somewhat murky. All our histories were written after 1000 AD, at least three hundred years after the time of Zhongkui."

"I thought all of the Dunhuang Manuscripts had been collected and digitized years ago by a research consortium," Rohini said.

"That's right, at least all of the manuscripts they were aware of. Wang Yuanlu realized the importance of keeping the manuscripts relating to our society a secret. He kept them separate from the rest, hiding the chest away until he could return them to the Guanzi. He knew the remaining documents—of which there were thousands— would be of historical significance to the entire world. He contacted local officials, offering to send the manuscripts to the provincial capital. This was right in the middle of the Boxer Rebellion, however, so they weren't terribly interested in a bunch of old scrolls at the time.

"As word of the library got out, much of the collection was spirited away over the next ten years before the government finally transported the remaining manuscripts to Beijing, but I realize this isn't terribly relevant to our current predicament," Guangming said, trying to contain the obvious pleasure he took in telling his tale.

"Don't worry about it, Guangming, it's a welcome distraction while we're stuck here, biding our time," Jane said, grabbing the carafe from the coffee maker and pouring them all another cup. "We're going to need another pot. Have a seat, Guangming. I'll make this one."

"Jane, what year did you say that Hopi man met Tesla?" Rohini asked.

"1900. Why?" Jane replied, pouring more coffee beans into the grinder before putting on the lid and pushing the button. The apartment once again filled with the aroma of fresh ground coffee as Rohini exchanged a meaningful glance with Guangming. She waited to speak until the buzzing of the grinder subsided. "That's the same year that they found the Dunhuang Manuscripts."

# 23

"That can't be a coincidence," Rohini said. "I'm adding that one to the list."

"What list?" Jane said.

"I've been having a lot of weird déjà vu moments lately. I'm not sure I'd call them premonitions, but I've been having a lot of... I guess I'd call them synchronicities."

"Like what?" Jane asked, intrigued.

"Well, like yesterday at the memorial. Remember the murals we were looking at?"

"Sure. What about them?" Jane replied.

"Do you remember the president's speech about Faith, Hope, and Charity? I had been thinking about them like President Johnson mentioned in his speech—about how they were universal values. I know that doesn't sound like that big of a deal, but when I heard him speak, it felt like he was saying exactly what I'd just been thinking," Rohini said.

"He was probably inspired by the memorial when he wrote his speech, just like you were," Jane said.

"I know, that's what I thought too, but it was so striking at the time," Rohini said. "OK, here's another one. When we were hiking in Virginia, I remembered this Chinese painting I had seen in a museum in Boston years ago—Nine Dragons by Chen Rong— then when we drove into Chinatown yesterday there was a line of nine dragons on the arch. Again, maybe not that big of a deal, but I got that same feeling at the time, like it was more than just a coincidence."

Guangming, who had been sitting quietly listening, staring con-templatively into his coffee mug, straightened suddenly. "Did you say Nine Dragons, Rohini?"

"Yes. Why?"

"You may be onto something, after all," Guangming said.

"Why do you say that?" Jane said.

"I don't believe I've told you the name of our society yet, have I?"

"Don't tell me it's Nine Dragons," Rohini said, her eyes widening.

"Not exactly, but close enough. We're known as Long Sheng Jiuzi Hui; the Nine Scions of the Dragon Society, and Chen Rong was one of our members."

"OK, I'll grant you that one, Rohini. That's too much of a coin-cidence to write off," Jane said.

"Well, now you've got to tell me about Chen Rong," Rohini said. "All I ever knew about him is that he was famous for painting dragons."

"Yes. That is his main claim to fame. What is less well known about him is that he was also a scholar in the court of the Song Dy-nasty and a warrior known for his great virtue and integrity. Like Zhongkui, he achieved the highest degree by passing the exams at the Imperial Palace.

"In his younger years, he proved himself a great warrior, once leading an army against the Mongols in the Yin Mountains at the east-ern end of the Gobi desert, keeping them beyond the Jade Gate Pass, west of Dunhuang.

"It wasn't until later that he achieved fame as a painter while at court. The Song Emperor at that time was named Lizong. He had a favorite concubine who convinced him to lend his ear to her brother, a man named Jia Sidao. Jia was a cruel and conniving man who even-tually rose to the Premiership, virtually controlling the court and the Empire along with it.

"He was a corrupting influence who eventually became little more than a mob boss, enriching himself by selling government goods on the black market. He kept a collection of rare curios and antiques which his underlings would procure for him by any means necessary.

If objects were not given to him willingly, his thugs would take them by force. Jia Sidao tried in vain to enlist Chen Rong into his schemes, until Chen had finally had enough.

"One night, Jia invited him to a sumptuous feast, intent on convincing him to join Jia's nefarious plotting. Chen, who was miserable simply being in the presence of someone like Jia, became increasingly drunk over the course of the evening, draining his wine cup every time it was filled. Eventually, he couldn't abide it any longer. He called Jia out for his double-dealing and plotting behind the Emperor's back and left in a huff.

"The following day Chen Rong sought an audience with the Emperor, attempting to warn him about Jia Sidao's conniving ways. Chen's entreaties fell on deaf ears, however, the Emperor wrapped completely around Jia's finger by this point. As it became clear he would not be able to extricate the court from Jia Sidao's grasp, Chen retired from the court and left the Emperor's service. After a short time, the Song Dynasty fell to Kublai Khan, uniting the whole of China under the Yuan Dynasty. Most historians hold Jia Sidao responsible for the fall of the Song, with good reason. Chen left the court knowing it was too late to save the Dynasty."

"What happened to Chen Rong?" Rohini asked, intrigued by Guangming's tale. "What became of him after he left the court?"

"Well, it was during his time in the northwest that he was recruited into our society, but his home town was in the opposite direction, in Fujian, in southeastern China. After his retirement from the court, he returned there and continued to serve as our eyes and ears in that region."

"So, tell me more about the green eyes in your tradition," Rohini said.

"Well, I already mentioned the yin-yang eyes. We also call them jade eyes for obvious reasons. Another story about the green eyes relates to the area in which our society was founded. The area around my hometown. There has been a much higher concentration of green eyes there, as long as anyone can remember. There is a theory among historians that the reason for this is that a lost Roman Legion of a

General named Marcus Crassus had wandered east along the Silk Road after his defeat in what is now Turkey.

"The story goes that after his defeat—one of the worst in the history of Rome—the remnants of his legions either wandered east or were captured and assimilated with the local population in what is called Zhelaizhai village, a part of Jinchang City. It used to be called Liqian, which historians speculate is a name which sounds like legion, pointing to the Roman theory. They have performed DNA testing on some of the residents there and many were found to carry Caucasian traits, but this is the area of the Silk Road and the edge of the Gobi Desert. People such as this have existed there long before the time of Marcus Crassus."

"That name sounds familiar for some reason, but I've never heard that story," Rohini said, furrowing her brow.

"He is most well-known to history for putting down the slave-revolt of Spartacus," Guangming said.

"That must be it," Rohini said. "I've always been a sucker for anyone who fought against slavery; Harriet Tubman. John Brown. Spartacus. But please, continue, this is all fascinating. I think last night you said the green eyes had to do with Zhongkui also. What is it you called him, the Vampire Slayer?"

"I think that's *Buffy* you're thinking of, Rohini," Jane said and smiled.

"A modern classic, to be sure," Guangming said. "But no, Zhongkui is usually known as the Demon Hunter or the Ghost Hunter. I suppose the idea is basically the same, but I think he would be closer to the character Angel. In some stories Zhongkui is made king of the ghosts, responsible for hunting down unruly ghosts who are bothering humans, like the vampire Angel fought other vampires."

Jane and Rohini looked at each other and smiled. "You really know your *Buffy*," Rohini said.

"It was one of my earliest exposures to American television. The host family I stayed with in Shawnee had a teenage daughter who was obsessed with it. She had a DVD boxset of the entire series which we watched during my stay."

"So, with Zhongkui, is this literal ghosts and demons we're talking about?" Rohini said.

"Well, not in the way you might think. According to our Guanzi there are energetic forces which could be described that way, but we usually think of them in more psychological terms; the negative emotional states like greed, anger, and hatred, for example, as being like demons which possess a person's mind. We also think of memories which you are haunted by, which you are unable to let go of, as being like ghosts," Guangming replied.

"Was Zhongkui an Elder, do you think?" Rohini asked.

"Well, not that we knew. But I suppose it's possible, or more likely that Zhongkui became an Elder—as Jane mentioned was possible—and that our founder carried the Elders' bloodline," Guangming said. "Our leaders, starting with our founder, often had the ability to sense the future, sometimes in the form of premonitions that something was about to happen. Occasionally they left more detailed prophecies of events which were expected to occur far into the future.

"One of these prophecies—which incidentally was among those Wang retrieved from the Dunhuang cave—spoke of a time when green-eyed people from many different nations would come together to save the world from a great calamity. When the Elders appeared, we were as shocked as the rest of the world, except for our Guanzi. Having read the ancient manuscripts. When we found out I had been requested by the Elders, the Guanzi immediately put us to work finding out who the other ambassadors were and whether they, like me, had green eyes. When we did, her suspicions were confirmed."

"Well, if that's supposed to be us, I'm not sure how we'll be able to do that holed up in Chinatown," Jane said.

"I think I can help with that," said Guangming. "The society can certainly assist us in getting out of the city, the question then becomes what our next step should be. I propose we go speak with the Guanzi. Whatever the best course of action is, the Guanzi will know. If nothing else, the society could keep us hidden until the Elders return."

"And where is the Guanzi now?" Jane said.

"In China. In the Qilian Mountains."

# 24

Rohini, Jane, and Guangming stayed holed up in their Chinatown apartment for the next several days while arrangements were made. Running with nothing but the clothes on their back had left them unprepared for an extended stay underground, let alone the traveling they were preparing to do. Fortunately, his DC contacts kept them clothed and fed and were working on getting them the fake passports they would need to get out of the country.

Even this wouldn't be enough to get them through most airports with the tighter security that had now become the norm. What began as a knee-jerk reaction in the wake of 9/11 had never let up. Once a whole new level of bureaucracy was created, it had quickly become entrenched, and would remain so for the foreseeable future.

The plan was to take a private plane from a small airfield, something the society fortunately could provide with their extensive network and deep pockets. Taking a private plane granted them a lack of scrutiny usually reserved for billionaires and celebrities. One of the society's members would be flying in to pick them up, taking them first to Hong Kong before continuing on to Gansu Province.

While the necessary arrangements were made, they spent most of their time watching the news and trying to catch what little information Burt was able to relay to them about the investigation. Not being a part of it himself, what he was able to glean was coming in dribs and drabs.

The first day, no one claimed responsibility for the attack, but in the days that followed, word began to spread that the Soldiers of the

Caliphate, long thought defunct, had claimed responsibility. Guang-ming's sources were right. The terrorists released a video of a masked spokesperson reading a prepared statement in front of a black flag bearing the symbol of their organization, the Hawk of Quraish with crossed scimitars.

When they saw the video for the first time, Rohini couldn't help thinking how generic it was, like it could be anyone behind that mask. *All you need is a ski mask and a camera and you can take responsibility for anything you want. They have yet to develop facial recognition software that can beat a balaclava.*

Then again, terrorists had gotten smarter over the years. They'd learned from their mistakes. It hadn't taken them long to realize the slightest clue in a video could give away their location. A seemingly nondescript building in the background or a recognizable feature of the landscape, even an unnoticed reflection in a window—any of these might tip off investigators, which meant drones wouldn't be far behind.

There was nothing Jane, Guangming, or Rohini could see to go on in the video. The speaker's features were well-hidden. The flag appeared like the ones the group had used in the past. One might assume that the group would be active in the same area as in the past, the area which they had claimed as their new caliphate, but Jane thought there was no way they would be stupid enough to operate out of the same area. That would simply make them too easy to track down.

Rohini, on the other hand, thought that since they were stupid enough to be terrorists in the first place, she wouldn't put it past them. "I thought we'd gotten beyond this," she said. "I mean, I understand some of the civil strife that's been going on lately with the weather being so crazy. All the droughts and food shortages driving the refugee crisis are understandable reasons for unrest, but I've never been able to understand religious intolerance or racial and ethnic tensions before."

"I don't think it's necessarily accurate to consider these guys religious fanatics. While they have tried to wrap themselves in a cloak of religiosity and holiness, the world sees them for what they are—

power hungry thugs and murderers. Their actions when they ran their supposed caliphate bore that out. They never attempted to live up to their own ideals. Their hypocrisy was as remarkable as their brutality," Jane replied.

"I suppose so, but they certainly were able to use others' beliefs to fan the flames. The thousands of fighters that flocked to them proved their genius, diabolical though it may have been," said Rohini.

"It's true what you're saying," Guangming chimed in. "But it is not unique to them. It is reminiscent to me of the mob mentality which prevailed in China during the Cultural Revolution, or the Red Scare in your own country during the McCarthy Era.

"Take this man for instance," he said pointing to the TV. "He is playing on the fears and insecurities of your people for his own gain, simply to enrich himself, and yet his followers are unable to see through his charade."

On the screen was an older white man in a shiny gray suit with a red power tie standing behind a podium. Although his suit was probably expensive, he still managed to look dour and frumpy. He was obviously overweight, and had a bizarre hairstyle, somewhere between a comb-over and a pompadour. The sound was muted, so they couldn't hear him speak, but by the spittle leaving his mouth and the wild gesticulations of his arms, they could tell it was probably his usual vitriolic rhetoric.

"If the SOC is the last gasp of terrorism—like you were saying—I hope Terrence McDonald's candidacy is the last gasp of racism and misogyny," Rohini groaned.

"One can only hope," Jane agreed. "What amazes me about him though, is how they can't see right through him. He's always been a bully and a con man, to me he instantly comes off as a total bullshit artist."

Terrence McDonald was all those things. While he always painted himself as a successful businessman, using his name as his brand, attempting to make it synonymous with class and success, he was anything but classy.

"You're right. He even talks like one of those pitchmen from late-night infomercials," Rohini said. "Don't they realize he's selling something? I mean I guess any candidate is selling something, but he sounds like a carnival barker, and his ideas are like a word salad. How can people take him seriously?"

"I guess they're buying what he's selling. They are willing to overlook his hyperbolic rhetoric because they have identified with him. They believe he can save them from the boogeymen he has created," Guangming said.

"I suppose so. There is a certain authoritarian personality type that likes that whole 'strongman' thing, whether it's dictators or sugar daddies," Jane said. "There's also another group which he appeals to because of his wealth. They're the kind of people who want low tax-rates on the wealthy—even though they are poor themselves—because they think they'll win the lottery someday. It's the same people that still buy in to trickle-down economics."

"When he announced his candidacy and he said he was going to build a wall, a great wall, I thought, oh please, the Great Wall, that's our thing," Guangming said. The three laughed together for a moment, the joke a welcome relief.

"He's a real peach, as my uncle would say," Rohini said, shaking her head. "I guess he comes from a long line of peaches though. Did you know his father was arrested at a Klan rally when he was young? And his grandfather made his fortune running brothels during the Gold Rush after skipping out of Scotland to avoid conscription during World War I.

"He even went to a military academy, but then he got five deferments to avoid the draft during Vietnam. You're right, he is a real peach," Jane said. "He certainly has used recent events to his favor though, hasn't he? He was already whipping people into a frenzy about immigrants and refugees, and then when the Elders arrived, it was like immigrants on steroids. I mean you can't get much more 'other' than aliens."

"They represent everything he is opposed to. He is even still a climate change denier, is he not?" Guangming said. "Even as some of the low-lying island nations are already relocating their populations from sea-levels rising, and the coral reefs are dying due to ocean acid-

ification. How can anyone be so obstinate in the face of such undeni-
able evidence?"

"Well, I guess it's the inevitable result of half of the electorate
moving away from 'fact-based' politics," Rohini said. "If the facts get
in the way of your ideology or your bank account, you can just pretend they don't exist. Isn't a lot of his fortune tied up in fossil fuels? I
can't imagine the sudden shift in our energy policies has sat well with
him. I know he's always been accused of grossly inflating his wealth,
but even he must have taken quite a hit when fossil fuels tanked."

"You're probably right," Jane said. "And now with the renewed
threat of terrorism in the mix, it's just adding fuel to the fire."

# 25

"Terrence, I thought we agreed you were going to tone down the rhetoric?" Bartholomew Simms said. He sat in his office as usual, talking into the speakerphone at his desk. He'd been ready to tear McDonald a new one after watching the morning's campaign event, but he'd stayed civil.

"I thought it went great," Terrence said. "They love me out there. My supporters are the greatest. No one has ever had supporters like me."

After a few more fruitless attempts to talk some sense into McDonald, Simms gave up. It was no use. There was just no getting through to him. He only heard what he wanted to hear, and he'd say anything to placate you, saying the exact opposite in the very next breath. *Oh well, McDonald is serving his purpose.*

He'd thrown a total monkey wrench into the elections. Simms had hoped McDonald would be able to challenge Susan Powers in the upcoming election, and he might have, if he were capable of sticking to the script for more than twenty-four hours. He'd had serious reservations the first time McDonald went rogue. Now that he'd gone completely off the reservation, Bartholomew had resigned himself to a Powers' presidency. *There's no way this clown can win anymore.* Not after all the damage he had done with his support among women and all the crazy things he'd said over the last few months. Now that Susan Powers was the president, she'd be unbeatable as the incumbent.

It wasn't widely known that Simms was the main benefactor behind McDonald's candidacy. He'd made sure of that. Most of the money he'd allocated to backing McDonald had gone into dark money pools through bundlers and super PACs. He'd taken full advantage of the murky new world of campaign finance created by *Citizens United* many years before, but now that McDonald's campaign looked sure to crash and burn, Simms had begun scaling back his support. *No use throwing good money after bad.*

*Perhaps he might still be useful in dealing with the Elders.* When they first showed up, most of the public reacted like it was the Second Coming—the answer to the world's prayers in dealing with the specter of climate change. Where McDonald had been especially useful to Simms had been in his ability to tap into the vein of xenophobia that was McDonald's bread and butter, and extending those irrational fears to the aliens.

To Simms, as well as McDonald and his supporters, there was nothing irrational about those fears. Not having been privy to telepathic communication with the Elders, they had no way of knowing whether the Elders could be trusted or not. McDonald was their ideal spokesman, not afraid to voice the fears they all felt. The crowds at his early rallies had focused their disdain on minorities, immigrants, and President Johnson. But their scorn had become increasingly focused on the Elders in recent weeks, and since the attack, President Powers.

*What strange bedfellows*, he thought, realizing that McDonald was successfully turning a large portion of the population against the Elders in almost the same way he was using the terrorists. It had been a bonus when word leaked that two of the Earth Ambassadors were unaccounted for and were suspected of being involved in the attack. That helped draw attention away from his team, further covering their tracks.

Gruber learned the investigation had turned up a past connection between the agent who had taken out his team and the terrorists. Perhaps they could use that lead to track her down. While Simms couldn't have cared less about the man who had died in Rohini's failed abduction—Gruber's team members were disposable in his mind—it irked him that his plans had been thwarted. He never let people get in his way, in business or in life. If his men were able to find her, he'd make sure she'd never get in his way again.

# 26

When Rohini heard about their travel arrangements, she couldn't help but feel some trepidation. She loved to travel, but this sounded like the sequel to *Planes, Trains and Automobiles*.

"It won't be that bad. Especially not the first leg of the trip. We'll be flying in a private jet, after all," Guangming said, attempting to reassure her.

"That's not the part I'm worried about," she said. "It's everything after that."

"I'm sure it will be fine, it's not like we'll be riding bareback," Jane said. "Now, that I would have some issues with. I don't even want to think about the chafing.

"What we should probably be the most worried about is making it onto the plane in the first place. There's only one nearby airport outside of the Special Flight Rules Area around DC—Stafford Regional Airport, which unfortunately is just south of Quantico."

"Seriously?" Rohini said.

"As long as we keep a low profile we should be fine. Between our new identities and the transportation Guangming has arranged for us, I don't think they'll even give us a second look."

"I hope you're right."

Jane and Rohini altered their appearance for the trip. They both dyed their hair and eyebrows black, before taking photos for their new passports, but all three of them thought it best to wear colored contacts. Three people with black hair and brown eyes would certainly stand out less—especially once in China—than three people with green eyes, and Jane's red hair would definitely not have gone unnoticed.

After everything was arranged, the morning of their departure arrived. The son of the elderly Chinese couple who ran the market knocked on the door to the apartment, letting them know it was time to go.

Grabbing their gear, they made their way downstairs to the storeroom, past the rows of shelves, and out the back door of the market, which opened to the alley. A black limousine with a pair of small Chinese flags attached to the hood was there waiting, the engine still running. The driver held open the rear door as soon as he saw them, ushering them quickly inside. They left the alley and made their way toward I-95 and Fredericksburg, Virginia, where they hoped a plane would be awaiting them at Stafford.

The society had provided them with a car from the Chinese Consulate in DC, complete with diplomatic plates. It would work wonders in avoiding any undue attention from the authorities. Most law-enforcement personnel knew not to go after such vehicles unless they were willing to risk their jobs. Their occupants typically had diplomatic immunity from prosecution and messing with them risked an international incident. It had come as a boon to their escape plans.

"Fingers crossed," Rohini said as they left Chinatown, once more passing under the Friendship Arch.

The drive was as uneventful as it was nerve-racking, especially the fifteen minutes or so driving past Quantico. Every time they saw a police car, Rohini was about ready to jump out of her skin. She felt certain the agents at the academy must know they were driving by, her paranoia growing by the minute.

Even as they'd safely reached the gate to the airport, Rohini had imagined police cars, their lights flashing and sirens wailing, rushing out to stop the plane before it could head down the runway and take off. Once they had successfully passed through the gate, after signing in under their assumed identities, they drove right to the plane. They grabbed their bags and headed towards the Gulfstream's airstairs which were already deployed. A face popped out of the open hatch.

"Welcome aboard, friends!"

Rohini stopped dead in her tracks. Standing in the open door of the plane was the Hong Kong action star Jimmie Yan. "I know, just keep moving," Guangming said, as he passed her, stepping onto the airstairs. "You can get his autograph on the plane."

She wasn't usually one to be star-struck—and truthfully wasn't even now. It was just the unexpected juxtaposition of someone she'd seen in so many movies suddenly standing in front of her—there of all places, in the middle of all this craziness—that had stopped her short. She recovered her wits and followed Guangming onto the plane. Jane brought up the rear, scanning the area one last time before ducking inside the plane.

The pilot closed the door behind them and disappeared into the cockpit to prepare for takeoff.

"Please, have a seat," Jimmie said, after they stowed their gear. The cabin was configured for 11 passengers, the minimum available as it had all the bells and whistles, including a conference table, a pullout couch, and even a bar. "Make yourselves comfortable. Can I get anyone a drink before we take off? We've got a fully stocked bar in the back."

They were all more than ready to take Jimmie up on the offer, ready to finally let down their guard for a bit. The three of them took seats around the conference table while Jimmie grabbed drinks. Guangming opted for a beer. Jane joined Rohini in drinking a glass of rosé, her standby.

"Guangming, is Jimmie in the loop?" Jane asked.

"He is. You can speak freely. He's not fully up to date on all that has happened, but he's a member of the society. You can trust him implicitly."

"How did you end up being the one to come pick us up, Jimmie?" Rohini said.

"Just a happy coincidence, I guess," Jimmie said." I happened to be in New York, so when I received word that a society brother needed a lift, I flew on down."

Rohini smirked at Jane and Guangming, "Yeah, we don't really believe in coincidences anymore, at least not as far as all this is concerned," she said.

"If it's not a coincidence, does that mean we were destined to meet?" Jimmie said, fixing Rohini with a sidelong glance.

Blushing slightly, she smiled. "We'll just have to wait and see, won't we? I understand it's going to be a long flight."

"You're not kidding. What's our flight plan anyway?" Jane said.

"We're headed to Vancouver first, to get over the border and refuel before crossing the Pacific. Then it's on to Hong Kong. We'll deal with customs there and refuel again before flying on to Lanzhou," Jimmie replied.

"How did you get involved in all this secret society stuff?" Rohini asked.

"My family has been involved with the society for several generations. They were originally from Gansu, but my grandparents came south during World War II. Most people who are part of the society have normal everyday lives. We don't spend all of our time dealing with society business. It just so happens that my normal life is in film. It can be useful for the society to have connections in any industry, so they were happy to support my career. It was a connection from the society that got me my first big break, but after that things took on a life of their own."

"I bet having an actual double life might give you some insight into some of your roles," Rohini said.

"I get a kick out of it actually. It's like an inside joke that only other society members get. I've done a few spy thrillers, but I thought it was really funny when I did those triad movies," Jimmie said.

"Oh, that's right. I had forgotten about that, wasn't that Deep Cover?" Jane said, getting a surprised look from Rohini.

"If you ever see the blooper reel from that film, half the time I could hardly keep a straight face. We shot a lot more takes than the director would have liked. I had an easier time with the sequels, but that first one was tough. The director kept yelling at me the whole time. 'Come on, Jimmie, this isn't a damn comedy! Get your shit together!' It was rough."

"That's the one where you were an undercover cop who had infiltrated the triads right? So, you were an actor who was secretly in a triad playing a triad member who was secretly a cop. That had to be a bit confusing," Rohini replied.

"A little, but when you're an actor, you kind of always feel like you are playing a character. Sometimes it can be hard to switch back and forth, if you really get taken over by a role."

"Real spycraft isn't so different," Jane said. "It's easy to get lost in a cover if it lasts very long. It's something you always have to be wary of."

As they made their way towards Vancouver, they had plenty of time to catch Jimmie up on everything. Jimmie took quite an interest in Rohini, asking her all about herself. He was particularly interested in her passion for the environment.

"So, do you know much about permaculture?" Jimmie said.

"I do, as a matter of fact. I didn't know you were interested in that kind of thing. I would have thought you spent most of your time partying with the jet set," Rohini replied.

"I've gotten more interested in it in the last few years. I was into the whole celebrity lifestyle for a while, but that got old quickly. It can be quite stressful actually. I've come to value my time away from the limelight more. I spend a lot of time filming and doing publicity, so when I can, I like to spend time away from the hustle and bustle.

"I've bought some land up in Gansu actually, where I'm planning to build based on permaculture design. I always knew about my family's connection with the society, but it's only been in the last few years that I've become more involved with it myself. One of the things I heard about where the Guanzi lives is how sustainable the compound is. I find that very inspiring," Jimmie said.

"So, you've never met the Guanzi?" Rohini said.

"No. It will be my first time. I'm pretty excited about it. The society's inner circle is small, made up mainly of Daoist priests. They're the link between the Guanzi and the families who make up most of the society. Most ordinary members will never meet the Guanzi. It's quite an honor."

"Now you've got me excited. Is your land near there? I'd love to hear what you plan to do with it."

"Well, I've only got a rough idea so far. When I first bought it I had planned to simply build a home for myself—a place to get away—but later it occurred to me that I might be able to build something I can share with others, maybe even as an example of a sustainable community. Let me tell you about the site and maybe you can help me brainstorm."

They spent much of the rest of the flight to Vancouver chatting about permaculture and sustainability. Rohini told Jimmie about some of the sustainable communities she had visited over the years. In college, one of her courses had been an independent study, visiting and writing about several different ecovillages. She spent a summer semester on her project, writing a paper about the strengths and weaknesses of each and the possibilities she saw in them.

At times Jane and Guangming joined the conversation as well, but mostly they just listened or napped. Jimmie told Rohini how he had learned that living up to its Daoist roots, the society had always valued being in harmony with nature. This was usually thought of as a way to live one's own life as an individual, but in recent years the government and the general population had come to realize its importance for society as a whole.

In the years following the Cultural Revolution, there had been such a push to modernize and industrialize China that environmental concerns had been given short shrift. In its mad dash to catch up with Japan and the West, China's citizens and its environment had suffered greatly as runaway capitalism put profits over people and the planet. Eventually they realized their mistakes. When renewable energy production took off in the years following the Paris Agreement, China became one of the leaders in making the switch.

The country's Daoist Association had been one of the leading voices in the ecology movement in China, seeking to green their temples as well as encourage the country's move towards sustainability. As Daoism in China began to reestablish itself following its suppression and near extinction during the Cultural Revolution, it began to refocus on some of its traditional values, which promoted an ecological lifestyle.

Many of these ideas were incorporated into the modern renewal of Daoism as more and more temples followed the association's guidance to become officially designated 'Ecological Temples,' greening their daily operations and even including scriptural passages with an ecological bent into their daily prayers.

"I like how they are incorporating these ancient ideals into modern life," Rohini said. "Sometimes it seems like so many of our problems stem from our bad habit of throwing out our ancient wisdom in the pursuit of the newest shiny bauble. Before we had air conditioners and natural gas furnaces and all these things, humans found other ways to stay warm or cool that were not only low-tech, but also low-impact."

"That's right. Northwest China is actually a good example of that. In the past, much of the population lived in yaodong, or cave homes. Sometimes these are carved into the side of a hill and sometimes they are dug down around a sunken courtyard. Either way, they work the same. They maintain a more constant temperature than ordinary houses, staying warmer in the winter and cooler in the summer, and just as in much of the world, the rural population has a tiny carbon footprint compared to our modern urban lifestyles in the developed world. I mean look at me, jetting around the globe to make movies," Jimmie said.

"There is a thread there," Guangming interjected. "A connection between all these things. There is a reason Daoists have traditionally considered caves as sacred sites. We call these dongtian, or heavenly caves, and these traditions go back to Neolithic times. Caves are associated with xuan, or mystery. A word we also use to describe the Dao. There is a correspondence between these caves and cavities within the body. We think of them as being analogous to the place in our body where our primordial spirit dwells, but you can also think of them physically. A mother's womb is like a cave, so in a sense we were all born in a cave, the cave of the mother.

"Some of the heavenly caves in China have large caverns full of stalactites and stalagmites, different colored crystals, and shiny mineral deposits. The first time I saw the inside of a European cathedral that's what it reminded me of—a large cavern. The stained-glass windows like colorful mineral deposits and the columns like stalagmites. Aren't many of the cathedrals and the earlier sacred sites in Europe like Stonehenge supposed to be built on places where the energy lines on the Earth cross?"

"Yes, I think they call them ley lines," Rohini replied.

"This is remarkably similar to the dongtian fudi system Daoists developed in China. The dongtian are said to be connected by a network of channels we call dimai, or Earth channels. The Immortals are said to be able to travel through these. Sometimes people think of these as actual passageways but perhaps they are more of an energetic network like the network of acupuncture channels in the body. You know, the word xue, which we use to refer to acupuncture points on the body is another word for cave or tunnel. So, the dimai system links the sacred caves like the channels in the body link the acupuncture points," Guangming said.

"You said dongtian fudi. What's fudi?" Jane asked.

"Fudi are 'blessed lands,' like a kind of paradise. In the traditional system there are said to be ten major dongtian, thirty-six minor dongtian and seventy-two fudi."

"So, they're like the Garden of Eden, or a utopia?" Rohini asked.

"Yes, that's right. This is quite an ancient idea in China. There is a famous story by Tao Qian, called Peach Blossom Spring, about such a place. Peach Blossom Spring has become the term we use for utopia.

"The story is about a fisherman who found himself going along an unfamiliar river that winds through a forest entirely made of peach trees. When he reached the headwaters, he found that the river's source was a spring flowing out of a cave. He landed his boat, dragging it up onto the riverbank and proceeded into the cave, which turned out to be a tunnel. The tunnel became narrower and narrower until finally he reached a spot so tight he wasn't sure if he would be able to continue. Seeing that the cave appeared to widen again on the other side of the narrows, he pressed on, squeezing through. Before long, he began to see light at the other end of the tunnel. When he came out of the other end, he found himself in a small village.

"The villagers were surprised to see him, as they weren't used to visitors, but they were hospitable. They told the fisherman how their ancestors had fled to this place during an earlier time of civil unrest several hundred years before and had not had any contact with the outside world since. He stayed for a week, marveling at the way these villagers were able to provide for themselves, meeting all their needs without trading or bartering with the outside world. When he eventually left, he tried to remember the way to the village, telling his tale to others, but though many searched for the village, neither the fisherman nor anyone else were able to find the village of Peach Blossom Springs again."

"It almost sounds like you are describing a modern ecovillage, like the ones I visited. Although, I'm pretty sure I could find them again," Rohini said.

"If only that fisherman had had GPS," Jimmie quipped, eliciting a chuckle from the group.

"So, let me guess. Was this Tao Qian in the society too?" Jane said.

"No. He lived long before Zhongkui, but it is one of the most famous stories in Chinese literature. Tao Qian was a Daoist recluse, and he was said to be an Immortal by later Daoists. An interesting custom is said to come from him. Tao Qian was said to enjoy chrysanthemum wine a great deal. So much so that he is considered the god of chrysanthemums in folk custom. We have a festival, the Double Ninth Festival, on the ninth day of the ninth month of the Lunar calendar on which people traditionally enjoy climbing mountains and drinking chrysanthemum wine, among other things. It's an interesting story actually…"

The rest of the group shared an amused look as Guangming launched into his next tale.

"There was a man named Huan Jing whose parents died in a plague that was ravaging the countryside. He had almost succumbed to the illness as well. It was thought at the time that there was a demon responsible for causing the plague, so Huan Jing thought he would need some sort of magic or spiritual ability to defeat this demon and free the country from this plague. He had heard of an Immortal who lived near the Eastern Sea who he thought might be able to help, so he set off on a long journey to find this Immortal. After searching all over, he finally found the Immortal who took pity on him and taught him how to defeat the demon.

"The Immortal told Huan Jing that the demon would appear again on the ninth day of the ninth month and he told him the secret of how to defeat it. Huan returned home and told the villagers who were left to go into the mountains and to take with them some chrysan-themum wine and wear leaves of the plant Wu Zhu Yu, as a talisman against the demon. The story goes that when the demon crawled back out of the sea, the scent of the leaves and the chrysanthemum wine made it intoxicated and dizzy and Huan Jing was able to vanquish the demon, killing it with his sword. Ever since, climbing mountains and drinking chrysanthemum wine has been associated with the Double Ninth Festival."

"Guangming, I'd forgotten how time flies when you're around," Jimmie said. "We'll be starting our descent into Vancouver in just a few minutes."

# 27

Zhongkui sensed their approach long before they neared his cave. But while his mind registered the disturbance, his body remained perfectly still. After so long in retreat, he could stay immobile like this for hours on end.

He typically alternated between active and passive forms of meditation during the day, practicing his fighting forms every few hours to break up his sitting meditation. Ever the warrior, he kept his skills sharp even here in his retreat cave deep in the mountains.

After a few moments, Zhongkui uncrossed his legs and ended his meditation with a short routine of self-massage to get his circulation moving again. Then he rose and exited the cave. He grabbed his sword on the way. Zhongkui knew those approaching were no threat, but *old habits die hard,* he thought, *and I haven't practiced my sword forms yet today.* He estimated he would have time for a few rounds before his visitors entered the small valley below his cave.

Dayan and Jianhu wound their way along the faint path through the forested valley. Little more than a deer trail, it didn't appear anyone had been this way in quite some time. The Green Dragon Mountains formed the continental divide of the sole landmass which remained above sea level on the Elders' world. It ran like a sinuous spine from north to south, its northernmost peaks dropping precipitously down to the rocky cliffs above what was formerly known as the Northern Sea. Now there was only the Great Ocean in all directions.

The southern half of the range dropped more gradually, undulating its way from the high central ridge down to the tail of the dragon. Zhongkui's cave sat in a small valley near the head of the dragon in the far northwest. Dayan and Jianhu had traversed the dragon's spine from the New Capital, as it was still known, despite its great antiquity. The old capital city remained fresh in the Elders' collective consciousness, despite being abandoned after the Great War twelve thousand years before. Only a handful of Elders still lived from those times, most having chosen to return to the One.

Guanyin, his great love, had made that choice. Zhongkui had been tempted to follow suit, but she had already been ancient when they met, at least by Earth's standards. She'd lived through the Great War and become one of the first Immortals. Even now—being close to fifteen hundred years old himself—he found it hard to fathom. She'd often told him that he had saved her. She had considered returning to the One when they met, yet something about him had piqued her interest in a way she hadn't felt in centuries. She stayed with him until ten years ago, when time finally caught up with her again, and she had said goodbye. He'd been in the mountains ever since.

Zhongkui had returned from his last trip to Earth to find Guanyin even more quiet than usual. She had always been a peaceful soul. Having done and seen it all many times over would probably do that, he thought. But something had been different this time, and he'd sensed it immediately. In his absence she notified the Council she would be stepping down as Guide and they'd already appointed her replacement by the time Zhongkui returned, which made it feel all the more sudden to him.

At first, there had been reluctance from the council to let him enter retreat, but Zhongkui assured them his pupil, the Earth Guardian, was more than capable of performing her mission without further instruction from him. They agreed to let him go. Not that they really had much choice in the matter. He'd always been headstrong. Their permission had been a formality.

As Dayan and Jianhu approached, they heard Zhongkui before they saw him. His sword whistled through the air as he ducked and spun, leaped and stomped. As they cleared the trees and entered the meadow outside his cave, he finished the last few moves of his set, returning his sword to its scabbard, and stood in stillness.

*Zhongkui moves like a whirlwind,* Dayan thought. He found the intensity of his sudden stillness unnerving after the fury of his movement. When moving, he appeared as though he had always been in motion and his momentum would continue forever, like a great river flowing endlessly to the sea. Yet now, as he stood in stillness, he appeared immovable, like a mountain peak which had stood since the dawn of time.

Dayan knew Zhongkui only by reputation. His appointment as Speaker had come after Zhongkui had already left the capital. *It appears his reputation was well deserved.* Zhongkui's beard had grown wild, and his hair was unruly, even though pulled back into a topknot. The ferocity of his sword practice had shaken much of it loose. When Zhongkui opened his eyes, Dayan felt pierced by the fierceness of his gaze.

Jianhu, on the other hand, was no stranger to Zhongkui. She'd been his pupil during his tenure as Master of the House of Warriors. While other Earth Elders had trained there, some even becoming Trainers themselves, Zhongkui was, to this day, the only Earth Elder ever to be honored with the position of Master. A Master of the House of Warriors was universally recognized as one the greatest warriors alive.

Most who held the role occupied themselves with the administration of the House and the advanced instruction of the Trainers themselves. Zhongkui's tenure had been unusual in that regard. Then again, people had come to expect the unusual from Zhongkui. He had taken a much greater interest in his pupils, leaving much of the administration of the house to others.

Even after all these years, bureaucracy still left a bad taste in his mouth. While the legends of his early life on Earth were greatly exaggerated, like most legends, there was a grain of truth to them. He had been stripped of his degrees after passing the Imperial exams, not because of a physical ugliness, but the ugliness of his temper.

He'd always been a hothead growing up and despite the great level of dedication it took to study for the exams, he'd never completely conquered his negative emotions. He'd flown off the handle after a slight from a member of the court, in the presence of the Emperor himself. His offense could have resulted in his death, but he'd been fortunate. He was stripped of his titles and given an offer he couldn't refuse, death or military conscription.

By the time Jianhu met him his temper had cooled considerably, though not his intensity. As the two approached, they offered the traditional greeting on one knee. Masters of the House of Warriors were held with the same respect as members of the council, or the Guide herself.

"Greetings, Master Zhongkui," Jianhu said. "Our apologies for disturbing you."

"Rise, Jianhu, you are always welcome in my presence," Zhongkui said. "And who is this you've brought with you? He reeks of the council. They promised to leave me in peace."

"Greetings, Master Zhongkui. I am Dayan, the Speaker. The council sends their apologies for the intrusion, but under the circumstances, the Guide herself suggested we seek you out."

"Very well," Zhongkui said. "Let us discuss these 'circumstances' of yours over tea. Come," he said, already walking towards his retreat cave. Jianhu and Dayan followed.

They settled in to the cave and Zhongkui set to work preparing tea. While tea drinking on Earth had largely moved on from powdered tea, Zhongkui still preferred the ancient style. He poured hot water into three cups, whisking them until they were sufficiently mixed. While not identical to the *camelia sinensis* from Earth, he'd been able to find a native plant which was quite close. He'd never admit it, but he'd actually come to prefer it.

"Alright," he said after they'd had their first sips. "What is so important that the council felt the need to disturb my retreat?"

Despite being the Speaker, Dayan had deferred to Jianhu when she suggested that she handle things with Zhongkui. He was reluctant at first, as he was the official representative of the council, but after meeting Zhongkui, he was glad he had acquiesced. He'd let Jianhu handle this.

"Master, it's your pupil, the Earth Guardian, Sinéad—she's in danger, as is her mission," Jianhu said.

Zhongkui looked up from his tea at the mention of his student. He'd thought of her many times over the last ten years. Despite what he'd told the council, he'd second-guessed his decision to enter retreat many times. He hoped whatever danger she was in wasn't due to any shortcoming in her training. "Tell me."

"Much has happened in your absence. The plans the council had ten years ago have changed. We've had to accelerate things," Jianhu said.

"Have they not come to their senses yet? I was under the impression ten years ago that my fellow Earthlings were beginning to change their destructive ways?" Zhongkui said.

"They had, but they've been dragging their feet. Their greed has simply been too great, so it was felt that we would have to make ourselves known to the Earthlings in order to speed things up," Jianhu said.

Zhongkui was a bit shocked at this revelation. It had been the opinion of the council for as long as he could remember that they would remain hidden. Their policy of non-interference was one of their most deeply held beliefs. They had never yet revealed themselves to an entire planet. *Things must be dire indeed.*

"We went and spoke to their United Nations, and Dayan shared thoughts with their world leaders. We gave them the ability to change their technology to speed up the process of regeneration of their world. The council had even come up with a way to bring your pupil and her charge into the process. They were to be part of an ambassador program to come to our world to study our culture, that's where the trouble began. First, someone tried to abduct your pupil's charge, and then the entire group of ambassadors was attacked. Most of them were killed, as was one of Earth's leaders, the President of the United States."

That was a shock. While the United States was one of the newer countries on Earth, Zhongkui was aware of the powerful position they had come to hold on the global stage. "But Sinéad and her charge are safe?" he said.

"They are, for the time being," Jianhu said.

"Why didn't the council simply bring them here for training, if that's what they had decided? Why did they choose to reveal themselves to Earth?" Zhongkui asked.

"The council had another reason for such an unprecedented step," Jianhu replied. "Something which has shocked us all. We've received word from the Watchers—the Others are returning."

# 28

*Washington, DC*

SAC Edward R. Rooney's pulse quickened. *I knew that woman looked familiar*, he thought. When his agents brought him the CCTV footage from the Lincoln Memorial, the last thing he expected was to recognize one of the suspects, but there she was—Sinéad MacGowan. He hadn't thought about her much in the last few years, but early in his career, his hatred of her and their old instructor Burton Reynolds had been his fuel.

At the FBI Academy, it was all he could do to keep his temper in check. He knew if he gave in to their taunts and lost his cool, he'd never become an agent. In the field, he was determined to prove them all wrong.

Now Rooney had Sinéad in his sights, he knew that was the lead to follow. I always knew there was something off about her. I must have sensed deep down she was a traitor, even back then.

Sinéad McGowan was living under the alias Jane Smith. The CIA hadn't been entirely forthcoming at first. Several incidents over the years involving disputed jurisdiction had soured their working relationship with Rooney, but this was the kind of event which had all hands on deck. They grudgingly cooperated with his investigation, handing over Jane's file. When he learned of her past connection with the terrorists who claimed responsibility for the attack, he knew he was on the right track.

There was another interesting turn of events. Jane Smith had been spotted fleeing the scene with a half-Indian woman with an interesting connection to the president. *That can't be a coincidence. But what was her motivation?* She didn't appear to have any connections to the Middle-East, and her mother was Hindu, not Muslim. *She must have self-radicalized via the internet.* That had become the most common MO of terrorists in recent years. Then he discovered her involvement with several environmental and social justice groups. She even had a few arrests on her record from past protests. *She's an ecoterrorist—that explains it.*

Most people didn't see these groups as a threat. They had become more mainstream in recent years, and much of their agenda had become the common cause of both political parties in the Age of Climate Change. But Rooney knew better. He knew these people were just putting on a façade. He knew what they were *really* about. *These people are sick. If we left it up to them our women would all be lesbian witches in a generation. Our country would be unrecognizable.* As far as Rooney was concerned that was all the circumstantial evidence he needed to be her judge, jury and executioner.

Some people considered Edward R. Rooney a throwback, like a modern-day J. Edgar Hoover. While most people would take this as the insult it was meant to be, he wore the label like a badge of honor. Although history judged Hoover as a bigoted, paranoid zealot—with plenty of his own skeletons in the closet—Rooney was the kind of true believer who was able to overlook anything that didn't jibe with his view of reality. He was like the anti-Joe Friday—he never let facts get in his way.

Much like the way many modern conservatives practically deified Ronald Reagan, overlooking anything that conflicted with their idealized version of him, like raising taxes or pushing for gun control, Rooney had always idolized Hoover and the FBI. To Rooney he was the God of Justice and the same people whom Hoover held in contempt, Rooney did too. He knew who had ruined "his country"—the idealized 1950s *Leave it to Beaver* country which had never existed in reality, but only in the minds of those like him.

# 29

Zhongkui was speechless. *How could this be?* He'd thought the Others to be little more than a legend. He realized there were still a few Elders alive from the time of the Great War, but he assumed that such ancient history would remain just that: history. Were Jianhu an Earthling he'd think it was a joke, but the Elders' sense of humor was quite unlike that of Earthlings. They would never joke about something like this. "What do you mean, they are returning?"

"Apparently the Watchers have been aware of them for quite some time, but the Guide held off on telling the council until it became clear they were headed in our direction," Jianhu said. "The Others have continued their violent, rapacious ways. As our culture has progressed spiritually—becoming more and more harmonious over the centuries—theirs has only diverged all the more. We will have to speak to the Council to get the full picture. They've only given us the broad outlines, but the bottom line is that they are headed back this way. The Council felt we had no choice but to befriend the Earthlings and once we had their trust, inform them of our need."

"But how can the Earthlings help?" Zhongkui said. "Their weapons of war might prove sufficient to fight the Others, but they have no form of space travel to get here any time soon. We cannot bring their weapons back with us when we travel. How could they help?"

"The council is afraid our only hope may be to abandon our world before the Others arrive. We hoped that when we shared our knowledge with the Earthlings they might welcome us as refugees."

"I see. How soon are the Others expected to arrive?" Zhongkui said.

"That I don't know. We will have to speak to the council to learn more," Jianhu said. "What say you, Zhongkui? Will you come?"

"Let me pack my things."

# 30

*The White House*
*Washington, DC*

SAC Rooney had been in close contact with the White House during the investigation. The newly sworn-in President, Elizabeth Powers—feeling the tragic events more personally than most—wanted to stay apprised of the developing investigation. He had been to the Oval Office every few days to keep her up to date on the investigation's latest leads.

Rooney waited outside the Oval Office, relishing the news he was about to give the president. Not only did he have a major break in the case, but it was one of his old nemeses. He was already fantasizing about the day he'd be able to perp-walk Jane Smith into FBI headquarters—parading her in front of the cameras for the entire world to see—while he basked in the glory of her capture. *And if ever there was a time when a return to "harsh interrogation" was warranted, this is it.* He'd be happy to oversee that personally.

Rooney had to admit there had been some excesses in the intelligence community in the years following 9/11, but he thought the backlash that followed had swung too far in the other direction. *We've been coddling the terrorists lately. We've gotten soft with all this "eco-friendly-peace-and-love" crap.*

"President Powers will see you now."

Rooney thanked the president's assistant—he was always polite—and headed into the Oval Office.

"Ah, Rooney, what have you got for me today? Are you making any headway?" President Powers asked.

Rooney could hardly contain his glee as he relayed his great revelation. "We've had a huge break in the case, Madam President. We've identified some of the co-conspirators who helped the SOC from the inside," Rooney said. He took several 8x10 photos from a file folder.

"That's excellent, Rooney. Show me what you've got."

"This first photo is of a woman named Sinéad MacGowan, alias Jane Smith, a rogue CIA agent with past ties to the SOC. She was at the Lincoln Memorial that day and was caught on CCTV cameras fleeing the scene with her accomplices. She hasn't been seen since," he said, as he handed the first photo of Jane to the president.

"Are you kidding me? What is this, Rooney, some kind of joke? I know that agent. There's no way she's involved in this," President Powers said, her stern look giving Rooney pause.

"I'm sorry, Madam President, but I've confirmed her ties to the SOC with the CIA and she was seen leaving the scene with a foreign national and another woman with ties to the president," he said handing her the other photos. "This woman, Rohini Haakonsen, had close ties to President Johnson, which we believe allowed her to insinuate herself into the plot and get herself close to him. We believe she self-radicalized on the internet or perhaps was recruited by Jane Smith. Haakonsen has known ties to extremist environmental groups."

"Rooney, Jane Smith was on special assignment, working directly for President Johnson to train and protect Rohini Haakonsen—who, incidentally—was the victim of an attempted abduction by unknown perpetrators just blocks from the White House. I don't know how you got on this trail, but you're barking up the wrong tree, Rooney. These are good people."

"But, Madam President, I know this woman, we were at the academy together and I always knew there was something off about her. I know she is involved."

"Rooney, I'm starting to think there is something off about you. You will drop this line of investigation immediately. That's an order. I just hope in the time you've wasted pursuing these folks you haven't let the real perpetrators get away."

"With all due respect, Madam President, my orders come from FBI Director Marshall. If you have a problem with me, you'll have to take it up with him."

"You can bet I will, Rooney. Now get out of my sight."

Ed Rooney was beside himself with righteous indignation as he huffed out of the Oval Office. *How dare she!* Rooney knew he was right—despite what the president said—he felt it in his gut. President Powers had no idea what she was talking about. She had no law enforcement background. As far as Rooney was concerned she was just another clueless woman with no business in public office, let alone the Oval Office. It was an affront to his sensibilities. It was bad enough they'd been given the vote, now they wanted to run the show.

*Immigrants, minorities, women, they all played a role in the degeneration of this once great nation.* Rooney left the White House and headed for his car and driver waiting outside. He got in his vehicle and his driver informed him they'd been summoned to FBI headquarters. The director wanted to see him ASAP. *I'll get this straightened out. Surely the director will understand.*

He didn't. FBI Director Marshall had gotten an earful from President Powers by the time Rooney left the White House. Marshall had been afraid something like this might happen. *Rooney always did have a stick up his ass,* Marshall thought. *But what the hell was he thinking arguing with the President about this?* The director knew Rooney wasn't the brightest agent the FBI had ever fielded, but he was reliably diligent and about as straight-laced as they came. *Maybe too straight laced—wound up a little too tight.*

Marshall relieved Rooney of his command and took him off the case altogether. President Powers wanted him as far from the case as possible after his ridiculous blunder. He'd only compounded it with his obstinance in the Oval Office. Rooney had been indignant even with him, which made it all the easier for the director. Rooney would be headed to the Bureau's Minot, North Dakota Office, out of his hair for good, he hoped. *If Rooney ever works his way back into the good graces of the Bureau, it will be long after I've retired.*

President Powers was not at all pleased by Rooney's ridiculous behavior, but she was relieved to know that—by all appearances—Rohini and Jane were still alive. She'd spoken to Rohini's father the day of the attack and assured him they would do everything they could to find her once it became known that she was not among the dead or injured at the Lincoln Memorial. Her white blazer, and that of the Chinese Ambassador, Guangming, had been found near the scene but there were no remains so they had every reason to believe they were still alive. Once Rooney had come to her with the CCTV footage, that had been confirmed. After reading the riot act to FBI Director Marshall, she'd taken a few minutes to let Rohini's father know about this new information. She assured him that if Rohini was with Jane, she would be in good hands.

* * *

*Near Lanzhou*<br>*Gansu Province, China*

"Burt, what's the good word?" Jane said into the Gulfstream's satellite phone as they neared Lanzhou.

"'Good word' is an understatement, in this case. You guys are completely in the clear."

"What? That's great. Did they find the mole or something?"

"Not exactly, they still haven't tied any insiders to the attack—but I'll tell you about that in a minute. You'll never believe what that jackass Rooney did."

"I'm all ears."

"So, Rooney spotted you on the CCTV feeds—like you thought would happen—and got a bee in his bonnet. He was so excited about it that he took it straight to the president, which—it turns out—was the best thing he possibly could have done to help you guys out. President Powers knew you two had nothing to do with the bombing and let him know—in no uncertain terms—that he was to stop pursuing you as suspects immediately."

"Oh, that's great, Burt."

"Wait, you haven't heard the best part yet. Rooney—being the overzealous fool that he is—then proceeds to argue with President Powers," Burt said.

"Seriously?"

"I know, a real genius move, right? Anyway, after he leaves, she called Director Marshall and now Rooney is not only off the case, but is headed for Siberia."

"Oh, no. Really? He sent Rooney to North Dakota? I guess that's the last we'll hear of that pompous horse's ass. Couldn't have happened to a nicer guy."

"So, when are you guys coming in? The president wants you to go directly to her."

"Well, as great as that news is, we are way off the grid. It would be at least a couple days before we could get back anyways. Now that I know we can, I'll give President Powers a call, but we've got something we need to do before we can come in. We're actually on a bit of a pilgrimage of sorts. I think we need to see it through before we can come home."

"That's a bit cryptic. Mind filling me in? It sounds like you decided to walk the Camino de Santiago or something."

"Burt, buddy, there's actually quite a bit more going on here than you realize. Hell, there's more going on than anyone on Earth realizes. I promise I'll buy you a drink and fill you in when we get back, but for now just know we're safe and we hope to see you soon. We shouldn't be more than a week or two. Then again, the place we're headed might be a good place to lay low until the Elders return. We'll know more when we get there."

"This story sounds like it might take several rounds. But, I don't understand. Now that you've been cleared, shouldn't you just come in?" Burt said.

"You're probably right—but, like I said—it's a long story. Anyway, I'll feel more comfortable coming in after they're able to find the security breach. Whoever was responsible for getting the SOC that kind of access is in deep. I still can't believe they were able to pull this off."

"Fair enough. Well, take care of yourselves out there and keep in touch when you're able."

"Will do. And don't worry, we're definitely not roughing it out here," Jane said, smiling at her fellow Gulfstream passengers. "At least not yet."

Lanzhou was the final leg of their seemingly endless flight. From here they'd originally planned to take a train straight to Jinchang and then travel on to Zhangye, where they would head into the Qilian Mountains. Now that they felt a little less harried, as they were no longer considered suspects in the bombing, Jimmie thought they should take things a little slower, why not enjoy themselves and take in a few sights on the way?

Guangming suggested they go see the Baiyunguan, the White Cloud Temple in Lanzhou. While not as famous as its namesake in Beijing, the Baiyunguan in Lanzhou was the headquarters for the Daoist Association of Gansu. Jane and Rohini were game, having never been to China before, and Jimmie was always game for anything. So, after landing, they arranged for a driver to take them to the temple.

Situated on the eastern bank of the Leitan River where it meets the Yellow River, the temple was constructed in honor of Lu Dongbin, the most famous of the legendary Eight Immortals of Daoism. Though Daoist history was full of a myriad of Immortals, the Eight Immortals and Patriarch Lu, as he was also known, were the most famous. They learned all this from Guangming, their tour guide extraordinaire, whose knowledge of Daoist lore and Chinese history even impressed Jimmie.

"Does he have to be called Patriarch Lu?" Rohini asked. "That just rubs me wrong," she said grinning at Jane.

"Well, no actually. That was a more common translation of the term in the past. He can just as easily be called Ancestor Lu." Guangming said, smiling. "I see your point."

When their car pulled up to the curb to drop them off at the White Cloud Temple, they failed to notice the other car that had been trailing them from the airport. Jane was the only one who was giving much thought to security, or situational awareness, but she had failed to spot their tail. It was a harder skill to practice as a passenger. Had she been driving she might have noticed the car in her rearview mirrors.

Exiting the car and crossing the sidewalk, they walked past the pagoda-shaped incense burner in front of the temple and up the front steps. *What an imposing structure*, Rohini thought, the entry was perhaps fifty feet tall and made of gray stone, punctuated by three tall archways that led inside. Above the central arch a large plaque of golden Chinese characters on a blue background read *Bai yun guan*, right to left, in the ancient style. The archways held red lacquered wooden doorframes, the bottom of which were quite high off the ground—about a foot—requiring Rohini and her companions to step over them to enter the temple courtyard.

Much of the bright red paint was worn off the wood where countless shoes had scuffed them stepping into the temple. "It is a folk tradition meant to stop ghosts," Guangming explained. "It's a traditional belief that ghosts have no knees and are unable to step over things like this, so it keeps them out of the building." As they entered the temple and began to stroll around the grounds, Guangming continued his tale.

"One story goes that the Eight Immortals were once on their way to attend the birthday celebrations of Xi Wangmu, the Queen Mother of the West at Mt. Kunlun. During the festivities, there was a great banquet where they would get to partake of the magical peaches which bestow Immortality. On their way they encountered an ocean which they had to cross. Patriarch Lu suggested that they should each use their own unique magical powers to get across, which they did. A Chinese proverb evolved from this story, *'Ba xian guo hai, ge xian shen tong,'* 'The Eight Immortals cross the sea, each revealing their divine power.' This has come to mean that we all have our own unique contributions to make."

"There are only four of us, but I can see that saying applying to us," Rohini said. "We've all got unique backgrounds."

"It actually is more appropriate than you realize," Guangming said. "*Shentong*, or divine power, refers to the abilities Immortals develop through meditation, such as telepathy or the opening of the divine eye, the same sorts of powers that the Elders appear to possess."

"The Eight Immortals each had their own special skills and powers they were associated with and they each came from very different backgrounds; male and female, rich and poor, young and old. This, I think, is meant to demonstrate that the possibility of enlightenment or immortality is open to all."

"In the stories of the Eight Immortals, they all exhibit quite different personalities and have different symbols they are associated with. They each had a different magical tool or object which they could infuse with their spiritual power."

"Like a magic wand?" Rohini said.

"Yes. Something like that. They each have something they use to aid them in helping others or accomplishing tasks. For example, He Xiangu carries a lotus flower said to have the power to heal, both mentally and physically."

As they walked through the courtyard of the temple, passing the various halls, they eventually circled back to the hall in the front of the temple. Rohini was struck by how colorful it all was. It reminded her of the temples she'd visited with her aunt in Nepal, the architecture as well as all the brightly painted accents. There were even colorful flags strung overhead like the ubiquitous prayer flags of the Himalayas.

Unlike the Tibetan prayer flags she was familiar with, these were small triangular flags. But they shared the same colors, representing the five elements, and were emblazoned with the ubiquitous black and white *Taiji* diagram.

As Rohini recalled her time in Nepal with her aunt, Mt. Kailash came to mind, which sparked a thought. "Guangming, what was the name of the mountain Xi Wangmu lived on?"

"Mt. Kunlun. The Kunlun Mountains are thought by many to be the ancient source of many of the Daoist lineages. It is the mythological source of the Yellow River which has always been tied to the history and identity of the Chinese people, as well as home to Gods and Immortals."

"Who is Xi Wangmu?" Jane asked.

"It's fitting you should want to know more about her. She is the special patron of all women, and female Daoists in particular. It is said, 'In the three worlds and the ten directions, all women who aspire to immortality and attain the Dao are her dependents.' She was especially popular in the Tang Dynasty among women with a disregard for the strict societal norms of Confucian society; women who chose their own path in the world. They were expected to be submissive to the whims of their families—especially their male relatives—not to chart their own course in life. Of course, this is what leads many women to the Dao as well."

"I like her already," Jane said. "I had no idea there was an ancient Chinese patron saint of feminists."

"Well, Xi Wangmu was more famous in the past, in more recent times that would probably be Sun Buer. She was a Daoist cultivator who was quite beautiful. Thinking that her beauty would never allow her to avoid unwanted sexual attention from men, she purposely burned her face with hot oil so she could be left alone to meditate," Guangming said.

"Ouch!" Rohini said. "I appreciate the cojones that must have taken, but isn't it the men who need to learn some self-control, not the women? She shouldn't have needed to do that."

"That's true, though with these sorts of legends you never know which aspects of the stories truly happened," countered Guangming.

"Yes, but—true or not—the lesson being conveyed is that she needed to mutilate herself to avoid unwanted attention from men," Rohini said.

"I think that story actually comes from a popular folk novel," Guangming continued. "So, it may not be historically accurate. What is known for certain is that Sun Buer practiced her self-cultivation in a cave near Luoyang with another woman known as the Immortal Maiden Feng. It is said they kept men away by throwing rocks at them."

"I like that story better," Jane said.

"Me too," agreed Rohini.

By this time, they had circled around the courtyard to the hall dedicated to Ancestor Lu Dongbin. In front of the hall was a large incense burner as well as a long red kneeling bench for the faithful to use while saying prayers or making offerings to the Immortal. Following Guangming's lead they each took some incense and planted it in the censer, while Guangming and Jimmie both knelt and said a few quick prayers.

When Rohini and the others left the temple, Jimmie suggested they get some lunch. Guangming knew a good noodle shop that was in walking distance, so they let their driver know where they were headed and told him to meet them there. Walking to the shop along the waterfront, they had a nice view of the Yellow River and the green hills rising on the other side.

"Hey, everyone come here for a minute," Jane said. "Don't look now, but I think we've got company. There are a couple guys about a half block back I think followed us from the temple."

"What should we do?" Rohini said.

"Everyone stay close in case we have to run," Jane said. "Act natural and just keep heading towards the restaurant. We're going to have to find a way to lose them along the way. Guangming, you know this town best. Any ideas?"

"We could attempt to lose them over the footbridge. What if we send our driver around to meet us at the other end," Guangming replied.

"I like it. Give him a call."

# 31

"Gruber, what have you learned about our friends?"

"We tracked them to a small airfield south of DC where they flew out under assumed names two days ago."

"Both of them? Haakonsen and this Agent Smith?"

"Yes. They were traveling together, along with the other missing ambassador."

"That figures. Have you been able to find out where they went?"

"They flew out in a Gulfstream. Their flight plan had them initially headed for Vancouver, but it looks like the plane continued on to Hong Kong. I've contacted some assets there who have informed us they flew on to Gansu Province, to a city called Lanzhou. They are being monitored there."

"That's excellent, Gruber. Keep me informed. I don't want to let them slip away again."

"There's more, sir. They've been cleared of any involvement with the bombing, so we may expect them to return to the US sooner rather than later."

"Well, that's quicker than I would have expected. It was bound to happen eventually, I suppose. How are things proceeding on phase two?"

"The arrangements for the first action are being finalized as we speak. The second will follow a week later. We're right on schedule."

"Excellent. Proceed as planned and keep me apprised of any further developments."

Bartholomew Simms ended the call and sat back in his leather desk chair, his hands steepled at his chin as he contemplated the events of the coming days and weeks. The arrangements for the series of attacks on renewable energy infrastructure were coming along smoothly. Gruber's team had infiltrated all the targets and were proceeding with their plans.

The attacks would be carried out by members of SOC which Gruber's team had spirited into the country—jihadis who were ready to carry out suicide attacks at the solar installations, geothermal plants, and wind farms they planned to strike. Unlike the attack in DC which was carried out entirely by Gruber's team, it was time for the SOC to have some skin in the game. Gruber's team was also planning remote demolitions triggered to coincide with the suicide bombings, multiplying their impact.

Simms was surprised to find out that the SOC was practically defunct, down to a handful of members—who had for all intents and purposes degenerated into a social club—a bunch of washed up jihadis drinking mint tea and reminiscing about their glory days. But when they were approached with an opportunity to strike at the West, they jumped at the chance, especially when they realized that Gruber's team would be responsible for most of the work and most of the risk, while they got to claim responsibility—and more importantly the glory—for themselves. They wasted no time recruiting a new generation of bored, disaffected youth into their ranks, convincing them to martyr themselves for the cause.

That was one of the things Simms loved about the plan. Gruber's team could set up a trail leading straight back to the SOC while the terrorists also claimed responsibility for the attacks. It was like having willing patsies. And if the SOC leadership was taken out—brought to a sudden, unexpected martyrdom—all the better. Gruber's team could suspend their attacks and no one would ever suspect their involvement.

# 32

*Lanzhou*
*Gansu Province, China*

"The driver is on his way. He thinks it will take him about ten minutes," Guangming said.

"Great. Let's head out onto the bridge. When we get most of the way across, we'll look for the driver and try to give them the slip," Jane said.

"What if they've got someone else in a car too?" Rohini said.

"Yeah, I thought about that, but it's a chance we'll have to take," Jane replied. "If they do have a car they should be easy to spot leaving the bridge."

The group made their way onto the bridge, trying to pace themselves to get across in time to meet their driver, but also making a point to look nonchalant, stopping and looking over the railing occasionally at the roiling waters of the Yellow River below and the green slopes across the river, even stopping for photos which gave them a perfect opportunity to sneak glances behind them. Once they were sure their tails had followed them onto the bridge, Rohini's confidence in the plan started to grow.

When they were about three quarters of the way across Jane said, "Keep an eye out for our driver, he should be pulling up anytime now."

It was another couple of minutes before they spotted him. "There he is," Guangming said.

"When I say 'go,' run for the car, but try to stay together, we don't want to leave anyone behind," Jane said. "OK, go!"

They ran. Weaving through the other foot traffic on the bridge made it challenging to stay together. They almost got separated more than once. The upshot was that the traffic would also slow down their pursuers. It took less than a minute to reach the car, though it felt much longer, the stress of the moment seeming to stretch the bridge out ahead of them. Rohini thought she'd never get across, then all of a sudden they were there, jumping into the car and taking off down the street. They all kept a watch out the window, looking to see if a car might be following. They didn't see one, but as they hurtled down the street, they did see the two men on the curb looking down the street after them, one with a phone to his ear.

"We're going to have to switch rides. We've given them the slip for now, but they know this car, they'll be looking for it," Jane said. "Guangming, Jimmie, any thoughts?"

After a brief exchange in Chinese with Aiguo, the driver, Guangming turned back to Jane, "No problem. Aiguo will get us a new car. I know we were planning on taking the train to Jinchang, but do you still think that's wise?"

"Probably not. We've got to assume they'll be watching the station. Would Aiguo be willing to drive us?"

Guangming conferred with Aiguo again. "He can, at least to Jinchang, and then he's got to get back. But we can get someone from my family to take us from there.

# 33

*Jinchang City*
*Gansu Province, China*

After switching cars, they drove the four and a half hours to Jinchang, arriving in the early evening. As far as they could tell, they'd made it out of the city without being followed. Rohini was surprised to find a much larger city than she had anticipated from Guangming's description.

"I must admit it has changed significantly since my childhood," Guangming said. Like the rest of China's cities, it had grown quickly in the last half century as more people left the agricultural sector and joined the urban masses. The population had grown to over 200,000, but by Chinese standards it was still a relative backwater.

Guangming had been hesitant to let his family know they were coming, assuming that his parents would tell all his relatives in the area, but he realized being in the bosom of his family would keep them safe. Since most of his extended family was involved with the society, they understood the need to keep things quiet, but not too quiet.

Guangming's immediate family had taken them out, reserving a banquet room which seated twenty. It was at full capacity and then some as a few younger children where there too—cousins, nieces, and nephews of Guangming. The youngest ones spent most of the evening running around the table in circles when they weren't sitting on their parents' laps eating during the family-style dinner.

Most of them spoke little to no English, but they made sure Guangming's friends felt welcome. They all chatted with Rohini and Jane, with Guangming interpreting when necessary. The center of attention for most of the evening was Jimmie—which was un-derstandable—they did have a real live movie star in their midst, after all. She should have expected it, but over the past few days Rohini had stopped viewing Jimmie in that way. The close quarters of the Gulfstream and their long conversations brought him down to earth.

She had almost forgotten how she felt when she first saw him in the door of the jet until she saw the way Guangming's family treated him. They shared a look across the room more than once that evening, Jimmie surrounded by admirers, while Rohini sat chatting with a few of the younger women closer to her age. There were several teenage girls there. Most of them were quite taken with Jimmie's celebrity, but a few were more fascinated by Jane and Rohini, their eyes constantly on them throughout the dinner. She was beginning to feel a bit like a celebrity herself by the time they called it a night.

The next morning they woke early and headed on to Zhangye. They intended to get a driver from the society, but Guangming's uncle had insisted he take them in his mini-van. While not the most luxuri-ous ride—it was in dire need of a new suspension—it got them there in one piece.

"Don't worry, Rohini, this will get you ready for the horseback ride into the mountains," Jane joked.

"Well, if nothing else, it's definitely low-key. If anyone is still looking for us, I doubt they'll being looking for a beat-up old Mitsub-ishi mini-van."

Before taking them out of town, Guangming's uncle wanted to show them Jinchang's latest point of pride—a large complex of gar-dens recently built on the city's western foothills. It was becoming quite a tourist attraction for the city. Jane was resistant to taking the time to sightsee after the men following them in Lanzhou, but she'd quickly realized they had no choice but to humor Guangming's uncle. It helped that a few of Guangming's relatives were on the local police force and had agreed to escort them to the gardens and keep an eye on them until they were safely on the road.

As they arrived at the new gardens, Rohini saw row upon row of lavender stretching over the hillsides—a riot of purple flowers—gently swaying in the breeze. They spent a little while walking around, taking in the sights and smells as they followed the paths through the gardens. Rohini had always loved lavender fields. Purple was one of her favorite colors, which might have explained it, but there was something about the scent too which drew her to it.

As they strolled through the fields, Rohini rubbed some of the lavender flowers, releasing the essential oils, and held her fingertips to her nose, breathing in the scent. As was often the case, she almost felt like huffing it. Lavender is considered relaxing, but Rohini always found it also somewhat invigorating, almost like the way tea could make you feel calm but alert.

Guangming's uncle led them farther up the hillside to one of the newer sections of the gardens to show them the latest edition, an enormous taiji symbol made entirely of plants. It was surrounded by a group of symbols Rohini wasn't as familiar with—she only knew they were called bagua—made up of groups of solid and broken lines symbolizing yang and yin respectively, but that was about the extent of her knowledge. She asked Guangming to tell her more.

"They represent the forces of nature which make up the world and are considered auspicious in feng shui, the Chinese system of geomancy. The lines represent different combinations of yin and yang, almost like binary code. This is how the Yijing, the ancient book of divination, works as well. When these eight symbols are combined in all their possible combinations you get the sixty-four symbols of the Yijing.

"There are two different arrangements of the symbols meant to represent the energy patterns of the universe before it came into being, and one which represents the way energy works now when the universe is manifest through the seasonal cycles. These are referred to as Earlier Heaven and Later Heaven. This is the Earlier Heaven arrangement. On the south end where we are is qian, the symbol for heaven, and on the north is kun, the symbol for earth, forming a vertical axis.

The other symbols are also paired with their opposites across from them—mountain and lake, water and fire, and thunder and wind."

"Feng Shui is like the interior decorating thing, right?" Jane said.

"Not exactly. Traditional Feng Shui is much more complicated. It takes into account features of the landscape and the influence of timing, similar to astrology. The sort of Feng Shui you're thinking of is a modern simplification. It is a way of trying to bring balance into one's life by increasing harmony in one's home or office. Traditional Feng Shui practitioners might not give it much credence, but some of it is simply common sense—things like keeping your space unclut-tered—but it is really my uncle who should be telling you about this, he knows much more than I do."

Guangming and his uncle had a brief conversation in Chinese—ending with the two of them, as well as Jimmie, laughing at some-thing. Guangming turned back to Jane and Rohini.

"My uncle said he only knows a little bit about it and that he is sure I have explained it to you very well. He's just being modest. He's actually well-known as a Feng Shui expert around Gansu. He's quite in demand anytime someone with traditional sensibilities plans to build something. I think he's just anxious to get on the road. Let's head back to the van."

"What was so funny?" Rohini asked, as they walked back to the van.

"Oh, my uncle made a joke. I told him he was just being mod-est, trying to be a *zhan long*, a hidden dragon, and he said, "No, I am simply a useless old tree."

"It must lose something in translation," Jane said.

"Yes, I suppose so. *Wuo hu zhan long* is a Chinese idiom you are probably familiar with, it means crouching tiger, hidden dragon."

"Oh, like the movie," Rohini replied.

"Yes, it refers to people having hidden talents—you never know what skills or expertise someone might have—the most humble, un-presuming people are often the most surprising," Guangming said. "There is a similar idea among Daoists. We value humility as a virtue, especially when it comes to knowledge or spiritual attainments."

"I have three treasures which I hold dear. The first is compassion. The second is frugality. The third is humility," Rohini said, recalling the passage from the Daode Jing. "But what about the useless tree, is that another idiom?"

"In a way. It's not as common perhaps, but it comes from a well-known story from the Book of Zhuangzi. The story goes that one day, Zhuangzi and his friend Hui Shi were having a philosophical discussion, as they often did. Hui Shi said to Zhuangzi, "I have a large tree. The trunk of this tree is so gnarled that it can't be measured, and no good boards could be cut from it. Likewise, its branches are all too twisted for a straight cut or a square piece of wood to be gotten from it. If it were next to a road in plain sight, any self-respecting carpenter would walk right by without giving it a second thought. Your philosophy is the same, vast but useless. People pay it no mind." To which Zhuangzi replied, "You shouldn't try to fit this tree of yours into a preconceived notion of what is useful. Accepting it just as it is, you could rest in its shade, sleep beneath its branches, or simply admire its natural beauty. Instead of trying to find a use for this tree of yours, you should follow its example. A useless tree like that will live a long peaceful life. No axe will ever chop it down and no harm will come to it. If you can be useless, no one will ever trouble you."

"So it was really a bit of a humble brag, then. Good one, Uncle," Rohini said, smiling at the old man who smiled back, a twinkle in his eye.

Piling back into the van, they headed for the highway that would take them on to Zhangye, where they would meet with their guide and begin their journey into the Qilian Mountains for their meeting with the Guanzi.

# 34

The eastern sky glowed with the first light of dawn, yet the sun wouldn't appear over the mountains for another hour or so. They each rode their own horses, while their guide rode his horse and led another loaded with most of their supplies. The ride through the mountains to the Guanzi's compound would take two and a half days. While Jane and Guangming were experienced riders, Rohini and Jimmie were not.

Rohini had gone on one of those horseback rides as a kid where some old, slow nag—who was content to just follow the horse in front of him—was led in a loop around a ranch for an hour, but that was it. Jimmie had been on a horse for a few days for a period piece he once starred in, but it was mainly for stationery close-ups, his stunt double did most of the real riding. It didn't take long for Jane's joke about chafing to come to mind.

The trip could be done quicker by more experienced riders, but with the challenging terrain and their novice status, they planned to take it easy—even planning to walk, leading their horses at times—both to give their backsides a break, and to help navigate some of the more challenging terrain.

Guangming had a general idea of the route, though he, like the rest of the group, had never been to see the Guanzi. His interactions with the Guanzi had always been through intermediaries—the Daoist priests who made up the society's inner circle. He told Rohini and the others a bit about the trip the night before, but he left out some of the more notable features of the landscape, letting them remain a surprise. He knew what to expect along the way, but seeing it in person would be a thrill.

But most of all, he was anticipating meeting the Guanzi. The Guanzi's wisdom was legendary and those who had been in the Guanzi's presence said it was quite an experience. Rohini could imagine that perhaps it would be like when she had met President Johnson, or the way her aunt Shanti had described meeting the Dalai Lama in Dharamsala. *The Guanzi must have that kind of gravitas.*

They met their guide at the outskirts of the city. He was a jovial fellow with the sun-burnished cheeks of a life spent mostly outside. His most remarkable feature was a rough leather gauntlet on his left wrist. On it sat a large raven, as if it was a hunting falcon. As they prepared to mount their horses to leave, Rohini watched the guide release the raven, which flew off to the west towards the mountains. As it flew, disappearing into the distance, something didn't seem quite right about it.

"Weird. I could have sworn that raven had three legs," Rohini said. "What's with the raven anyway?"

"It's a messenger. The society uses them like carrier pigeons to deliver messages. He is just letting the Guanzi know we are on our way. The ravens carry a small tube in which the messages are carried. That must be what you saw hanging down," Guangming said.

"Unless the bird is just well-endowed," Jimmie said, eliciting a mix of groans and rolled eyes from Jane and Rohini.

Rohini gave him a shove. "What are you, five years old?" She said. *He can be a bit juvenile from time to time, but he can also be quite charming.*

Their ride began on a dirt road. The first several miles were well-used. It was a less frequented route to the first of the geographic features they would be encountering on their journey—and the one part of the trip Guangming was familiar with from past experience—the Rainbow Desert.

As the foothills of the Qilian Mountains rose gradually from the outskirts of the city, the road passed through a ridge cut, after which they caught their first sight of it. It immediately reminded Rohini of the redrock country around Jemez Pueblo in New Mexico she'd visited with her uncle.

Jemez was north of Albuquerque on the long way to Santa Fe. Past the pueblo, the road followed the Jemez River up a long canyon before climbing to Valles Caldera, a long-extinct volcano which was like a small world unto itself.

The caldera contained vast meadows and grasslands, and was home to thousands of elk, as well as some of the best trout streams in New Mexico, according to her uncle. The area was sacred to the Pueblo people, many of whom made pilgrimages to the sacred sites on its slopes. Rohini had never ventured into the caldera herself, she and her uncle had simply stopped off at the scenic overlooks along the highway before continuing past Los Alamos to Santa Fe, but it had been a striking sight.

The caldera itself, formed around a million years ago, was about a dozen miles wide with Redondo Peak in the center, sticking out like the hub of a wheel. Redondo Peak in turn, had been formed by a dome of magma after the collapse of the caldera itself. Several smaller domes had formed along the northern half of the caldera, but Redondo Peak was the most prominent of them, especially from the south.

The thought hadn't occurred to her at the time, but now as she recalled the caldera in her mind's eye from the back of her horse in the far reaches of northwest China, the structure of the caldera reminded her of a massive mandala, the symbolic representations of the cosmos used in India and the Himalayas. She'd been introduced to them by her aunt Shanti in Nepal.

Her aunt was a practitioner of Vajrayana, the Buddhism of Nepal and Tibet. On their trips around Nepal installing and teaching about solar technology, they'd often stopped off at temples and shrines along the way, where she would follow her aunt's lead, circumambulating the stupas and spinning the ubiquitous prayer wheels. She also recalled the earlier conversation she'd had with Guangming about sacred mountains.

Buddhists and Hindus consider certain mountains to be natural mandalas— like Mt. Kailash in western Tibet—taking pilgrimages to circumambulate the sacred peak. Her aunt made the pilgrimage the year before Rohini's visit. They spent many nights discussing it that summer. Hindus saw the mountain as the abode of Shiva; Buddhists viewed it as the home of the Buddha Chakrasamvara. *What sort of great being might call Valles Caldera home?* she wondered.

As her thoughts returned to the present, her awareness was brought back to the rhythmic sway of the saddle under her, and the spectacular shades of red, yellow, and orange in the folds of the foothills around them. *The Rainbow Desert certainly lives up to its name.*

"Pretty amazing, isn't it?" Jimmie said.

"Yeah, it reminds me a lot of New Mexico where my uncle lives, though it's not this colorful," she replied. "Have you ever been?"

"No, but I've heard great things," Jimmie said. "People in New York and LA always rave about Santa Fe. I was afraid it had become overrun with celebrities and billionaires, but if this reminds you of it, that must not be the case. It's so desolate out here, but beautiful in its own way."

"The landscape is a lot like this, even down to the cave homes," Rohini said. "The traditional houses there are made of adobe mud brick and plaster. The indigenous people there, the Pueblo, often made cave homes like the people here."

As they continued through the surreal landscape of the Rainbow Desert, Rohini continued to marvel at the terrain. The hills were basically striped, with distinct bands of color cutting across the rolling ridges—the result of different minerals in the sediment which made up the layers of sandstone—before the tectonic uplift that formed the mountains pushed them up into their current state.

Before long the dirt road they traveled came to an end. They took the opportunity to dismount and take a break for a few minutes, resting the horses as well as their backsides. At the end of the road a simple wooden guardrail prevented vehicles from continuing past into the hills, but a narrower trail around one side was clearly visible ascending up the gentle slope before disappearing over the next ridge.

Rohini noticed the landscape beginning to change as they gradually gained elevation. First, more grasses and small plants appeared, followed by scrubby brush. The morning passed quickly as they continued to climb deeper into the mountains. Later, small gnarled evergreens began to appear as they followed the meandering trail, sporadically at first, on the shadier sides of ridges, then becoming more numerous as they continued to climb.

They chatted occasionally as they rode, but also spent long stretches in silence, taking in the peace and beauty of the mountain scenery around them. The foothills past the Rainbow Desert had been brown and barren, but once they had crossed a few higher ridges and ventured deeper into the mountain range, the distinctive character of the Qilian Mountain's ecology began to reveal itself.

Forming the northeastern rim of the Qinghai-Tibetan Plateau, the Qilian Mountains share much of its characteristic flora and fauna. As they continued their journey they passed through small alpine meadows, ringed by small patches of conifer forest, mainly on the north-facing slopes. As they wound their way through the ridges and valleys, the green of the vegetation often gave way to scree-covered slopes that pushed ever higher past the tree line.

Rohini continued to be struck by how similar it was to the mountains of New Mexico, even sharing some of the same flora. She suspected they might be similar species, not necessarily identical, but there was one flowering shrub she thought looked exactly the same, with small buttercup-like yellow flowers and pale green foliage. *Shrubby Cinquefoil?* There were also some willows along a few of the small creeks they passed, fed by the glacial snow melt.

They stopped often, allowing the horses to rest and drink, taking the opportunity to stretch their legs. By the first night, they were feeling the ride, just as they had expected. At one such stop, Rohini saw a large pile of stones festooned with prayer flags marking the pass which led out of the far end of the small alpine valley they found themselves in. They reminded her of the stupa she used to visit in

Santa Fe which sat next to an ancient cottonwood tree festooned with many layers of prayer flags. She recalled the epic New Mexican sunset she'd caught as she was leaving the stupa that day, the sky ablaze in various shades of red, orange, and yellow, with some purple in the clouds. The colors were more saturated, more intense to her in the thin air of the high desert. She'd stood in the gravel parking lot of the stupa until the sun had completely set.

She was brought back from her memory by the crunch of gravel. At first, she thought she was still in New Mexico enjoying the sunset in the gravel parking lot until she realized it was Jane walking over to her across the gravelly bank of the small creek they'd stopped at, deep in the Qilian Mountains. Much of the creek bed was dry, but it was apparent that it would be a much bigger stream when the spring thaw turned the gentle creek into a raging torrent.

"We're getting ready to saddle up," Jane said.

"OK, let me fill up my canteen really quick," she replied.

She took her canteen off her belt, unscrewed the cap and submerged it into the stream. The water looked slightly milky from the grinding of the bedrock by glaciers over the millennia, forming a fine silty powder which became suspended in the water. She took a quick swig from her canteen and remounted her horse, following the rest of her party as they headed up the valley toward the pass.

That night they camped in another valley near a similar stream. They brought tents, but the beauty of the stars kept them out late into the night. They sat around the campfire chatting, learning more about each other, including their guide, Tenzin. He spoke little English, so Guangming interpreted for them.

Tenzin was Tibetan, hailing from *Qinghai*, to the south of the Qilian Range, where he'd grown up in one of the nomadic clans which still roamed the high plateau. Though Tibetan, when the topic of conversation turned to horses, he became much more animated.

Through Guangming, he told them his family traced itself back to the *Xiongnu* culture which had lived in the Qilian mountains before being driven out by the Chinese over two thousand years ago during the *Xiongnu-Han* Wars. He was proud of their heritage as horsemen, mentioning the *Shandan* Horse Ranch, saying that much of their original breeding stock had come from the *Xiongnu* horse native to the Qilian region.

"Isn't that the ranch you told us about before, Guangming, the one started by that general?" Jane said.

"Yes, that's right, General *Huo Qubing*."

Tenzin muttered something in Chinese and spat. He and Guangming had a short conversation before Guangming filled the others in.

"Tenzin does not think too highly of the general, as you might have guessed. Huo Qubing was the general who defeated the *Xiongnu* and drove them from the Qilian Mountains. Although he is held in high-esteem as a famous war hero in Chinese history, he wasn't held in particularly high regard during his lifetime. He had a reputation as a very hard man. He was the nephew of Empress *Wei Zifu*, wife of Emperor *Wu* of the Han Dynasty.

"There are many interesting stories about him. *Jiuquan*, a city to the north of here, owes its name to an episode from his life. The story goes that one day after defeating the *Xiongnu* in battle Emperor *Wu* rewarded him with a vat of a famous rare wine to celebrate his victory. The general ordered the wine poured into the spring so his troops who were downstream could get a taste of the wine in the now-flavored water. The name *Jiuquan* means wine spring."

"That doesn't sound so bad," Jane said. "I like a commander who looks after his troops, but I understand Tenzin's sentiment. History is always written by the victors."

"Yes, in the eyes of the Han, it was necessary to drive the *Xiongnu* out after their raids into Han territory became too frequent to be ignored. At least that was their rationale for the war. In the eyes of others, it could have been seen as a war of expansion as the territory held by the Han grew immensely from their victory," Guangming explained.

"So why did you say he had a bad reputation?" Rohini asked.

"Well, despite the story of wine springs there are other stories which paint a different picture about how he treated his men. It was said that he received special rations which he would not share with his men and that he would order them to engage in *cuju* games for his entertainment, even when they were short on rations. *Cuju* is like a type of ancient soccer. But much of it stems from another incident. There was a man named *Li Gan* who was under the command of *Huo Qubing's* uncle, *Wei Qing*, another general who fought in the campaigns against the *Xiongnu*.

*Li Gan* apparently assaulted his commander, *Wei Qing*. He was forgiven by *Wei Qing*, but *Huo Qubing* wouldn't stand for this slight to his uncle, and killed *Li Gan* during a hunting trip. The Emperor apparently covered for *Huo Qubing* telling everyone that *Li Gan* had been killed by a deer."

"Whoa, sounds like he pulled a Cheney on him," Jane said, eliciting a laugh from Rohini. Guangming and the others failed to get the joke. "We once had a vice president who shot his friend in the face during a hunting accident. There's no indication it was intentional, but this vice president wasn't well liked, so people always questioned whether maybe his friend had crossed him somehow," Jane said.

By this time the fire had burned down to glowing coals. Despite being late summer there was a chill in the high mountain air. They decided to turn in finally, knowing they had another long day ahead of them, climbing into the two tents they had brought, the three men in one, Jane and Rohini in the other. Rohini was the last to go, lingering at the fire alone for a few minutes, wanting to soak in the beauty of the night sky for as long as she could.

The next day passed much as the first, except they found themselves coming across more wildlife the deeper into the mountains they ventured. The first day they mainly caught sight of birds. Vultures circled high above and a few geese flew overhead. There was hawk being harried by some ravens, a familiar sight anywhere, but something about it struck Rohini as strange. The hawk had flown over them several times before the ravens had finally chased it away for good. *Persistent,* she thought, *the ravens must have a nest in this valley.*

There were many smaller birds. Rohini wasn't so good with small birds. She wasn't sure if she knew her finches from her swallows or her nuthatches from her chickadees. She knew cardinals and blue jays, and woodpeckers were easy, but a lot of the little birds blended together. She was lost in thought trying to remember her small birds when a sudden shrill noise and a flurry of flapping wings shook her back to her surroundings. They had flushed some Tibetan eared pheasants, which had suddenly flown out of the grass ahead. The horses remained stoic, but their riders, especially Rohini, were quite startled by the unexpected sight.

The second day they first heard and then saw a few marmots standing in the rocks above, their high piercing chirp carrying quite far in the high thin air. Rohini couldn't resist the urge to wave as they passed through what must be the marmots' territory.

"Don't mind us, we're just passing through," she said, smiling at the furry critters.

The second day also brought them glimpses of some of the larger animals of the range. White-lipped deer fled their appearance as they entered one valley, and what must have been gazelle jumped quickly out of sight in another.

Guangming said snow leopards—the major predator of the plateau—were still known to roam the mountains, though seeing them was increasingly rare as their numbers had dwindled over the years. Their numbers had rebounded slightly as demand for their pelts dropped after the Dalai Lama and several other prominent Buddhist Lamas called for the practice of wearing their furs to stop. Apparently faux snow leopard fur was now all the rage across the Qinghai-Tibetan Plateau. *PETA would be so pleased.*

When they set up camp, Rohini was filled with anticipation for their arrival the following day. The closer they got, the more her curiosity about this mysterious figure, the Guanzi, grew. As they sat around the fire that night, Rohini began to pick Guangming's brain about him.

"So tell me more about the Guanzi. I know you said you've never met him, but what have you heard, what is he like?"

"Well, to begin with, the current Guanzi is a woman, not a man," Guangming replied.

"Really? Wow, somehow I assumed the Guanzi was a man. Maybe because you always say 'the Guanzi' which could refer to either gender," Rohini said.

"You know what happens when you assume," Jane joked, leaving the rest unsaid.

"I always liked the one from that movie better," Jimmie said, joining in. "Do you know what happens when you make an assumption? You make an ass outa you and umption. Such a classic."

"*The Long Kiss Goodnight*. There were a lot of great lines in that film," Rohini said, smiling at her friends in the firelight. "So, what else, Guangming?"

"Well, I actually don't know what else to tell you about this particular Guanzi. I know more about the position than the person. I am as curious as you are to meet her. It's quite a rare privilege, as it's usually only the inner circle of the society that interacts with her personally. Throughout our history the Guanzi usually spend a great deal of time in retreat.

They spend much of their time studying the lore and history of the society and Daoist scriptures. Although the society is secret, the core of the society, as well as the Guanzi, are also ordained Daoist priests, so much of their time is spent in self-cultivation. What I will be most curious to learn, is what the Guanzi thinks about the Elders, and whether the scrolls from Dunhuang shed any light on them and their possible connection to the society."

"From the story you told us, I assumed you knew all about those old texts." Rohini said.

"There you go making assumptions again," Jimmie said, eliciting more smiles in the firelight.

"I only know about them in the most general terms, not much more than what I told you about before, that the chest was full of old writings from the early years of the society, and of course the Jade Scepter."

"What Jade Scepter?" Jane asked.

"Yeah, I don't think you mentioned that before," added Rohini.

"Oh? Well, in the chest found by Priest Wang, with the manuscripts was a Jade Scepter wrapped in a scroll. As the story was told to me, it looked like it was simply a rolled up hanging scroll, but when Wang unrolled it, he realized that what he thought was simply the roller stick from a hanging scroll was actually the Jade Scepter. The scroll it was wrapped in contained information about what it was. It is said to be kept by the Guanzi as a symbol of authority. That's all my mentor ever told me about it."

"Well, as my uncle Ragnar likes to say, I guess we can get it straight from the horse's mouth tomorrow," Rohini said.

Tenzin's ears perked up at "horse." Turning to Guangming in Chinese, he asked what had been said. After a brief exchange, he nodded. "*Hao hao. Zhe shi yige hen hao de yanyu.*"

"Tenzin said this is a very good saying."

Later that night, Rohini was again the last one into her tent, although this time Jimmie sat with her by the fire. They chatted late into the night, watching the stars. They even saw some shooting stars. First one, followed by another, then a handful more. Judging by the time of year, Rohini guessed it must be the Perseids or else the Leonids. She could never remember which, but she knew one of the meteor showers usually fell in the late summer.

The first time she had seen them was still clear in her memory all these years later. She'd taken a canoeing trip to the Boundary Waters with her parents one summer when she was ten. *It was about this same time of year.* They had been prepared for the worst, the mosquitos that time of year being legendary—Minnesotans jokingly called them the state bird—but they hadn't been bad at all.

It had been quite cool that summer, so perhaps the early cold had suppressed them that year. The climate in northern Minnesota being quite temperamental that time of year—you could have eighty-degree days or an early frost—you never knew from one year to the next. The entire trip had been memorable, paddling through the Boundary Waters for a week, camping out on the banks every night. That had been the first and only time she'd seen a moose in the wild. They'd even seen a mother black bear with two cubs. What stuck with her was how the wildlife hadn't paid them much mind as they silently glided by in their canoe. It was different than hiking where wildlife, hearing you coming from a long way off, gave you a wider berth.

But it had been the spectacle of the night sky that had formed her most vivid memories from that trip. They caught the tail end of the meteor shower over the first few nights. Living most of her life in the city, where the night sky was obscured by so much light pollution, she hadn't realized before that trip how solidly packed with stars the night sky was. She didn't realize you could see the Milky Way in a band across the sky.

The end of their trip had been just as memorable. A strong solar storm began during their last night which provided the fuel for an amazing display of the *Aurora Borealis*, the Northern Lights. She remembered it scaring her at first, seeing a giant green ribbon of light suddenly snaking across the sky, followed by occasional flashes of yellow and pink. She was terrified until her father had explained what it was. After she lost her fear, she found it fascinating. To think that she could see the electro-magnetic field of the Earth still blew her away.

But tonight, she was seeing sparks of a different kind. After she and Jimmie had both gone to their respective tents, she still lay awake thinking. She was beginning to feel really comfortable with Jimmie. She could tell something was brewing between them. Thinking back, she realized she felt something between them from the first moment she got on the Gulfstream. She had chalked it up to being a bit starstruck at the time, but now she realized it was something else. They had a connection.

# 35

As the party approached Qilian Shan the next day, they dismounted and bid farewell to their guide, Tenzin. He would be returning to his home in a nearby valley on the Qinghai side of the range, less than a day's ride to the south. When they were ready for the return trip to Zhangye, he could be summoned by raven and be ready to go on a day's notice.

Shouldering their gear, they began the hike onto the mountain. Qilian Shan lends its name to the entire mountain range, but Guangming told the group this particular mountain was also known by that name, as well as *Xigui Shan*, Western Turtle Mountain.

They trudged along the single track across the scree-covered slopes, angling ever upward toward the craggy peaks above. As their route took them to the north side of the mountain, they began to see more patches of snow, some of the last remnants of the previous winter slowly melting in the late summer sun. At one point, Rohini thought she heard a faint rumbling. Being in the mountains, her first thought worried her. "That's not an avalanche, is it?" she asked.

"That's what I was thinking," Jane said. "Or a rockslide."

"No, but it is a sign that we're getting close," Guangming said, enigmatically. "That is the *Rou Shui*."

"The *Rou Shui* River?" Jimmie said. "The lazy river that passes through the Hexi Corridor?"

"Yes, the same *Rou Shui* that irrigates the corridor before disappearing into the sands of the Gobi Desert," Guangming explained. "The headwaters flow from the slopes of Qilian Shan. Closer to its source it is known as the *Hei He*, the Black River. It is not as gentle as it cascades through the mountains. We should be able to see it shortly."

Sure enough, after a few minutes they turned a corner and the river came into view, first below them, cascading down into a narrow canyon carved out over eons, then directly ahead where the source of the *Rou Shui* appeared to be a waterfall plunging down into a series of cataracts. It was a beautiful sight. But what was most remarkable about the waterfall was the rock formation from which it flowed. Its appearance was unmistakable. In a quirk of nature, the rock had eroded such that the falls appeared to be flowing over the rear half of a turtle's shell, complete with an overhang which looked uncannily like two legs and a tail.

The trail brought them right next to the falls where they paused for a moment, taking in the view. Raising his voice to be heard over the roar of the falls, Guangming said, "This is called Turtle Tail Falls. The river flows out of a cave above called Turtle Tail Pass. This is thought to be the origin of the name Western Turtle Mountain."

They continued to take in the natural beauty of the scene for a few more minutes, enjoying the falls as well as the vast panoramic view their vantage point afforded of the cascades churning down the mountainside, and the row upon row of ridgelines which gradually gave way to the lowlands far below.

After a few minutes enjoying the expanse, they resumed their climb. The trail skirted the left side of the turtle shell in a series of steps carved into the rock. As they stood on the upper banks of the river above the falls, Rohini noticed something in the water, something familiar. She wasn't sure what it was at first until it suddenly struck her. Under the water on the back of the turtle shell which formed the riverbed, was the *Bagua*, the same design they had seen in the gardens in Jinchang. "Look," she said, pointing into the water.

"Fascinating, isn't it?" Guangming said. "No one knows if it is naturally occurring or carved by man. In the society there are some that say this is the true source of the *Bagua*. It is usually thought to have originated in the Yellow River Valley to the east. This could have been carved later, once the turtle rock was found, but no one knows."

The cave which had been hidden from their lower vantage point was now visible, though it could easily have been mistaken for a shadow on the rocky cliff were it not for the river flowing from it. The mouth of the cave was about fifteen feet wide, the river taking up much of that, with a bank of stone about three feet wide leading into the cave. *Perhaps that explains the name Black River,* Rohini thought. The cave was certainly black up here, as was the stone it was formed from. She thought it might be basalt, though it had been awhile since she'd been in a geology class. As they walked into the cave she let her hand trail along the black stone. It felt cool under her fingertips.

The grotto grew darker as they continued walking deeper into the mountain, the path along the rocky bank narrowing as they progressed. Guangming warned them to watch their step. A plunge into the river here would mean a quick trip over the falls. Following Guangming's warning they kept a hand on the wall as the cave grew increasingly dark and the path continued to narrow.

When the cave appeared to reach its narrowest point, Guangming drew their attention to a chain attached to the wall of the cave. "Grab this. We'll need to turn sideways and hang onto the chain to get past this narrow section."

Following Guangming's lead, they each grabbed the chain in turn, shuffling sideways for about ten feet, their packs hanging out over the water behind them. The cave was almost pitch-black at this point, the only light the glimmering reflections from the rippling surface of the river. After passing the narrows, the tunnel turned abruptly to the left as the trail began to widen again and the way ahead brightened.

When they approached the end of the tunnel, the light outside shone so brightly it was difficult to make things out, but as their eyes adjusted to the light, they began to see what lay on the other side.

Rohini's breath caught as she scanned their surroundings. The tunnel exited into a verdant hanging valley. They couldn't help but be momentarily dumbfounded by the sight.

"*Zhe wuyi shi yige fudi,*" Guangming whispered.

"What did you say, Guangming?" Rohini asked.

"He said this is definitely a *fudi*, a blessed place," Jimmie explained.

"It's like Shangri-La up here," Jane said.

"This is just the kind of place those myths come from," Rohini said. "In Tibet they call these kinds of places 'hidden lands.' My aunt told me about the legends of Shangri-La and Shambhala. Those stories were probably based on real places like this, beautiful lush valleys tucked away in the Himalayas. She told me of one called Pemako where many of the Tibetans fled in the 1950s, hoping to avoid having to leave the country altogether. It's somewhere around the border of Nepal and Bhutan. They are supposed to be places which have a potent spiritual energy or allow for easier spiritual cultivation because of their ideal surroundings."

"Yes, that is like the idea of *fudi*," Guangming said.

One of the first things they noticed was a small lake, which appeared to be about a third of the way up the valley, its color a vibrant azure blue, its appearance so similar to the sky above, Rohini wondered if it was simply reflecting it like a mirror. The river they followed into the valley appeared to flow from there. Along the right side of the valley was a narrow, rocky ridgeline which rimmed the western side of the valley.

She could see that the trail leading out of the cave forked as it neared the lake, one branch leading around the lake to what looked like a small village on the far side. Some of the structures were free standing, but many appeared attached to the slope below the ridgeline. The other branch turned towards the ridgeline before the lake. Scanning the ridgeline with her eyes, it looked like the trail must follow the ridgeline, leading into the mist-shrouded peaks at the southern end of the valley.

They followed the path as it worked its way through an alpine meadow, keeping left towards the village when it split. As they ventured farther, Rohini began to notice other things. The path leading to the ridgeline crossed the river over a small wooden bridge. Just upstream from the bridge was a waterwheel on the other side of the creek. It was also wooden and appeared quite old, but showed signs of more recent repairs. Some of the wood was obviously newer, the difference in color apparent even from a distance. The water wheel was connected to a small building which looked as though it was made of adobe, again reminding her of New Mexico.

They passed the small lake—Rohini realized, to her surprise, it was that azure blue color—and headed up towards the village. Downslope from the village there appeared to be a few larger and smaller cultivated fields, though from a distance it was hard to tell what the crops might be. *I'll have to spend some time here later*, she thought, curious to see what they grew. There were a few figures in the fields, focused on their work. They hadn't yet noticed their new visitors. As they followed the path farther up the gradual slope towards the village, some heads turned their way, and a few hands waved in greeting.

Past the fields were groves of trees on either side of the trail. These weren't evergreens, so Rohini wondered what they might be at this elevation. There was some variation in the color of the leaves and some were shinier as well, glittering as they fluttered in the gentle breeze blowing through the valley.

They reminded her of the orchards at her uncle's farm in New Mexico, something she certainly wasn't expecting here. But then she recalled the Colorado peaches she'd come to love while staying with her uncle and realized they could well be orchards after all, even at this high altitude. As they grew closer, she noticed the peaches first. They were on one side of the path, while there were apples on the other, and beyond these were dark purple plums as well as what she guessed were Asian pears.

Passing through the orchards they met a man walking down the path towards them. He greeted them in Chinese first, *"Wuliang shou fu. Huanying. Women yizhi zai deng ni."* Then in English. "May you be blessed with endless happiness and longevity. Welcome. We've been expecting you," he said, bowing in greeting, his hands clasped in an unfamiliar way. Rohini was more used to the traditional style of greeting in India and the Himalayas—*or the ubiquitous yoga studios on practically every corner in New York,* she thought, smirking to herself—the hands pressed palm to palm in front of the heart. But this was something different, the man's palms faced inward and his hands overlapped, the thumb of one hand tucked inside the other fist. Guangming and Jimmie returned the gesture, while Jane and Rohini simply bowed slightly, unsure of the appropriate protocol.

"Greetings Long Daozhang," Guangming said. "It is so good to see you, it has been too long."

"This must be Rohini, Jane, and Jimmie. It is a great pleasure to meet you all," said Long Daozhang.

"This is Long Daozhang," Guangming said. "He is the abbot of the temple here. He is also my mentor. I knew him as a child when he was a priest at the local temple in Jinchang."

Abbot Long was an older bespectacled gentleman. He had a long beard that had not quite turned fully gray, and he wore the work clothes of a Daoist priest which were quite different than what Rohini would have expected. In her mind, monks, nuns, and priests wore robes like the Buddhist lamas she was more accustomed to.

This priest wore dark blue pants with long white socks or leggings which came up to the knees. They reminded Rohini of uniforms she had seen in old photos of World War I infantrymen. *The doughboys,* she thought, remembering their nickname. He also wore a matching dark blue jacket-like robe which came to just above the knees, and a black hat which had a hole in the top through which his long black hair, tied into a topknot, protruded.

Long Daozhang led the party up the path, past the orchards to the group of buildings they'd seen from across the valley. What Rohini had taken as a village from a distance, now appeared more like a combination of a monastery and a farm with several outbuildings. To the right, she saw chickens scratching and pecking in the yard in front of their coop. On the left, a corral was attached to a small barn, containing a few of the sheep typical of the region. She saw one ram with its long spiraling horns, and several ewes with shorter ones.

"What kind of sheep are these? Rohini asked. "They're quite different than the ones I know from my uncle's farm."

"These are called Gansu Alpine Finewool. They are quite well-adapted to this environment, but also have high quality wool," Long Daozhang replied.

"They're beautiful. Do you have the sheep just for wool or do you use them to make cheese?"

"We make cheese too, which is unusual for this area. Cheese is certainly not typical of the Chinese diet, though it is more common among the nomads. They were bred for their wool, but since we try to live sustainably here, we realized it made sense to try this several years ago."

"Sheep are a good choice. Their milk has a lot more solids than cow or goat milk. You can get twice as much cheese from it," Rohini said, enjoying the farm talk. She hadn't realized how much she missed it.

As they continued towards the monastery proper, passing a few more outbuildings, Rohini noticed that the larger buildings had solar panels on their roofs. There was something that seemed strange about them.

Rohini looked to the sky, then back at the panels; she realized they were all pointed in the direction of the afternoon sun, not due south, as she would have expected this far north. They must be set up to track the sun across the sky for greater efficiency. It was a pretty sophisticated system. They had to be off grid so far into the mountains, so judging by the number of panels they had, they must also have placed a battery storage system somewhere.

*These put our installations in Nepal to shame.* The solar systems she and her aunt Shanti installed had been quite basic in comparison, but they had still been highly appreciated by their new owners, giving them access to a small amount of electricity in areas which had previously had none.

"Do you have batteries for your solar panels, or do you only use power when the sun shines?"

"Oh yes, we have quite a large storage system. We also have other sources of power, so we have no shortage in the evenings. Did you see the waterwheel on your way up the valley? It was originally built for grinding grain long ago, but we've converted it to produce electricity. It gives us a steady source of power twenty-four hours a day, although we don't need a great deal of electricity here.

"If we couldn't get this much power in a sustainable way, we would find other ways to meet our needs without it. Humans receive all we need from *Dadi Muqin*, the Great Earth Mother. It is unnecessary to resort to the destructive excesses of the past."

"So, you limit your consumption of resources then. We will all have to follow your lead if we're going to be able to avoid the worst consequences of climate change, Elders or not," Jane said.

"You are right, of course," Abbot Long replied. "But we go one step further here. We have tried to find ways to go beyond simply minimizing our damage, to actually regenerating the Earth. As it was said by *Tai Shang Lao Jun*, The Most High Laozi, 'Returning is the movement of Dao.' In ancient times, farmers in China understood this. They placed great emphasis on returning vitality and nutrients to the soil, using the various constituents and processes of the farm to complement each other.

"Much of this knowledge was lost in the last century during the Great Leap Forward. In our rush to modernize we threw out the wisdom that allowed farmers to grow intensively and continuously on the same land for thousands of years without destroying the soil. Modern industrial agriculture follows a strictly extractive model, destroying the soil that supports us and all other beings. Nothing else in nature works this way, so there is no reason we should have expected it to work."

"But things are changing in China, as they are in the rest of the world. I remember hearing about the regeneration of the Loess Plateau several years ago," Rohini said.

"Yes, precisely. That is a perfect example of what needs to be done everywhere," Long Daozhang said. "They showed what a difference could be made. I have been to that area, both before and after, and seen the transformation with my own eyes. In the years before the restoration project, the Loess Plateau—the heart of Chinese civilization—had degenerated into a veritable desert, nothing would grow and the hillsides were being swept away by erosion. By reverting to traditional techniques with modern adaptations, they have returned the area to its past glory, it is once again bursting with vitality. The *Gu Shen*, the Valley Spirit, has returned."

"The Valley Spirit is also from the *Daode Jing*, isn't it?" Rohini asked.

"Quite so. *Tai Shang Lao Jun* described this attribute of the Dao as the 'Valley Spirit' and the 'Mysterious Feminine'; all beings draw upon it continuously, and yet it never runs out, its creative power of transformation is endless. This refers to the cyclical patterns found in nature. If we follow the example of nature, it will provide for us indefinitely, but if we draw upon it without the movement of return, without thinking about regeneration, we will wither and die."

"We certainly will," Jane replied. "I saw it first-hand in the Middle East. That's one of the sources of instability in the region getting little attention. At the heart of the Syrian Civil War and the refugee crisis was a long-term drought—brought on by climate change—in an already extremely dry region."

"Yes, but it was also their farming practices which set up the perfect storm for their agricultural sector to collapse, from what I understand," said Jimmie, joining in the conversation. "They pumped their aquifers dry and overgrazed the land which left them in a much more precarious position when the droughts came."

They continued to the monastery grounds, entering through the front gate. Seeing the monastery's sign above the archway, Rohini asked the Abbot the name of the temple. He replied that it was called *Huanyuan Guan*, 'Return to the Source Hermitage.' *How appropriate*, she thought, even the name of the monastery pointed towards the idea of regeneration.

The monastery's layout was quite irregular, appearing to follow the natural contours of the landscape. The main gate and front wall were straight, but upon entering the grounds it was clear that the rear of the monastery was anything but. The right side was much smaller, being closer to the rocky slope above, while the left side was much deeper with most of the monastery's buildings located there.

"This is so different from the temple in Lanzhou," Rohini said. "I imagine it's quite a bit older, other than the solar panels."

"Yes, the farm as it exists now is fairly recent, but the monastery itself is quite ancient. No one is sure how old it is," Abbot Long said. "It was originally built around a grotto where an Immortal was said to reside. It is still there in the heart of the grounds. It is said that the grotto leads to the Abode of the Guanzi, but if there was a tunnel, there is no sign of it now. Perhaps there was a cave-in at some point in the past."

"The Abode of the Guanzi? But I thought the Guanzi lived here. Isn't that why we came, to see the Guanzi?" Rohini asked.

"Yes, the Guanzi is here, but not in this temple. The Abode of the Guanzi lies farther up the mountain. You will go there soon enough. First you should rest. You must be tired from your journey. You can rest and relax here for the time being. You will be summoned when the Guanzi is ready for you. I will show you to the guesthouse."

As they walked through the grounds towards the guesthouse, they were struck by the natural beauty of the place. All the various structures of the hermitage were interspersed with different kinds of fruit trees as well as small gardens and fishponds. Rohini felt like she was in a botanical garden as they passed through round moon gates into hidden courtyards and up stone steps past small pavilions.

Through one courtyard, a small group of monks and nuns were practicing martial arts of some kind, while an older monk, presumably their instructor, looked on, his hands clasped behind his back. It reminded Rohini of Tai Chi, but not any she had seen before. The priests moved in a slow flowing manner like Tai Chi, but it was much more intricate than forms she was familiar with. The forms the monks and nuns were practicing had much lower stances and more dynamic movements.

"Long Daozhang, is that Tai Chi they are practicing?" Rohini asked.

"It is. This is *Wudang Taijiquan*. The monks from the *Wudang* Mountains preserved many of the traditional styles of Daoist martial arts when Daoism and the rest of traditional Chinese culture were suppressed in the last century. The teacher you see there grew up in *Wudang*, but eventually found his way here when he was practicing as a wandering Daoist. As Daoists we believe it is important to practice

VOICE OF THE ELDERS                                    183

these arts for health preservation, but also as a moving meditation, and spiritual cultivation. It is a good way to bring the clarity and stillness of meditation into our daily lives off the cushion. As members of the society we also try to keep up our fighting skills should we ever need them to fight against injustice, or defend others. In this modern era this is rarely needed. The society usually works to influence events behind the scenes in a more systemic way."

After showing them to the guesthouse, the Abbot left them to settle in to the simple accommodations. There was a central sitting room which led to six bedrooms, three on either side of a short hallway, as well as a bathroom at the end of the hall. There were two chairs and a couch around a table which held a vase of flowers, as well as a few extra ottoman type seats in the corner, and a bench under one of the room's two windows. After choosing their rooms and freshening up a bit, Rohini ran into Jane as she came out of the bathroom.

"I feel right at home. They've even got a composting toilet in there," Rohini said.

"You mean like one of those chemical toilets?" Jane said.

"No, these are much simpler. It's basically like an outhouse toilet you might find in a National Forest in the US, but instead of being built over a pit, they usually open from the outside to be emptied or else the entire bottom pulls out like a cart. Sometimes, they'll have peat or something like that to sprinkle over the top to keep the smell down. Here they use sawdust, but it works surprisingly well for something so simple. Just sprinkle a layer of sawdust over your business when you're done and voila. I imagine they probably use the composted night soil in the fields."

"Well, it sure beats digging a hole," Jane said, after she came out. "Thanks for the heads up on the sawdust—I'm not so sure I would have figured that one out right away."

A short time later a monk retrieved them and led them to the dining hall. Once there, they sat with the other residents of the monastery and enjoyed the simple fare offered for dinner. There were plentiful vegetable dishes, which Rohini learned later was typical of the monastic diet. Daoist monks, like their Buddhist counterparts in

China, typically eat a vegetarian diet and often avoid the so-called 'five strong-flavored foods' from the allium family: onions, scallions, shallots, leeks, and garlic. Rohini's aunt practiced this tradition as well, which is where Rohini had first heard about it.

It came as a bit of a shock to Rohini. She had grown up eating Indian food as well as developing a love of Mexican and Italian food. Onions, garlic, and strong flavors were an integral part of her diet. There were few things she liked better than a nice rustic *fettunta* or a good garlic *naan*. Yet the dishes offered here didn't follow the usual monastic diet, they were quite flavorful—a few even a bit spicy—and along with some tofu, they were using the sheep's milk cheese in a few of the dishes. It was treated much like Indian paneer, diced and lightly fried.

Guangming had been a bit surprised, expecting typical monastic fare, but this was not a typical monastery, in more ways than one. The meal concluded with a prayer, after which it was acceptable to speak. Rohini had hoped for a chance to explore the grounds a bit more, but the sun had gone down and having spent a few days in the fresh mountain air, exerting themselves on their journey, she was more than ready for an early night's sleep in an actual bed.

She noticed on the way back to the guesthouse that although the monastery had electric lights, they were just sufficient to allow for navigating the grounds, and there was little light pollution. The lighting along the various paths and courtyards was small and low key, and hooded to prevent the lights from shining up into the night sky. Rohini wondered if this was to make the monastery less visible or just in keeping with the sustainability and frugality of the place.

Regardless, she was highly appreciative of it, as it left the view of the night sky in all its vast, dark glory. One of the small gazebo-like structures was on their way back to their quarters, up a flight of stairs on a natural rocky prominence incorporated into the design of the temple grounds. There was a large boulder embedded into the railing of the structure, inscribed with characters.

"What does this say, Guangming?" Rohini asked.

"It's the name of this place, 'Waiting for the Immortals Terrace,'" Guangming said.

"How appropriate," she said, stopping to admire the stars.

Living in the city, she had forgotten how much she liked to stare into the night sky, but the last few nights around the campfire had reminded her. She thought the others had all gone on to the guesthouse, but after a few moments she realized Jimmie had lingered as well.

"I hope you don't mind the company," he said.

"Not at all."

They were quiet for a few minutes, taking in the stars, but Rohini could sense the tension between them. She was attracted to Jimmie and knew the feeling was mutual. They stood side by side, their hands resting on the railing as they looked at the stars, or at least pretended to. She reached out and covered his hand with hers, noticing his surprise, and smiled. The thought of inviting Jimmie to her room occurred to her, yet it seemed wrong somehow, given their current surroundings. *How ironic*, she thought, *here I am falling for a movie star in the middle of a monastery*. Jimmie reached over and brushed the hair back from her face and slowly leaned in, kissing her softly, her lips rising to meet his.

They lingered on the terrace for a while before walking back to their quarters holding hands, but when the guesthouse came into view, Rohini let Jimmie's hand go.

"Let's keep this to ourselves for now, OK?" she said.

"That's fine, I understand. We're in no rush here. We'll have plenty of time to see if this is going anywhere when we get back to the real world," Jimmie replied.

When they arrived, Jane was in the sitting room. "There you are. I was about to come looking for you. We probably can't get much more low-key than this place, but you're still my responsibility," she said, looking back and forth between Rohini and Jimmie.

"I'm fine. Besides, I had Jimmie to look out for me," Rohini replied, trying somewhat unsuccessfully to hide the grin threatening to break out across her face. "It's getting late," she said, faking a yawn. "I think I'll head to bed. I'll see you in the morning, Jimmie."

"Goodnight."

# 36

*Green Dragon Mountains*
*The Elders' World*

They left as soon as Zhongkui had packed his things. While the Elders could travel energetically within a world as well as between planets, there were limitations. For one, they were limited in what they could bring with them, which basically amounted to the clothes on their backs. And not just any clothes. They had to be made of natural materials.

The Elders over the centuries had perfected materials which worked best for this as well as for their everyday needs. Another constraint was that it took some practice to reform the clothing correctly when rematerializing. It usually took many hours of meditation until one could come to identify with the clothing sufficiently. It needed to become like a second skin if they wanted to be able to reform it without a great conscious effort after traveling. During training, it wasn't unusual for neophytes to reappear from some of their initial attempts stark naked.

While Zhongkui could have left his weapons and other belongings in his retreat cave—had he been sure he would return—it was customary for warriors, especially a master warrior such as himself, to be armed. There had been no wars on their world in thousands of years, but despite that fact—or perhaps because of it—the custom had persisted.

Crime, like that which he had known on Earth, was virtually unheard of here. The only people who stole were children, or those with mental problems, both of which were rare in the Elders' society. The usual motivations for theft simply didn't exist. Everyone had access to all the basic necessities of life. Food, water, clothing, and shelter—these were all taken for granted.

The Elders had long moved beyond the acquisition of wealth as a primary motivation and were more concerned with self-cultivation. For some, this meant meditation and spiritual cultivation. For others, it meant becoming highly skilled in the various arts and crafts of their culture. Builders were afforded the same respect as swordsmiths. Scholars or chefs, bards, or brewers—all were shown equal respect on their world.

Only members of the council and the masters of the two houses—the House of Scholars and the House of Warriors—were perhaps afforded a greater amount of respect, but this was in recognition of their wisdom and skill, not their position. For any member of the twelve clans to be elevated to councilor or master meant they were universally respected.

The trip back over the Dragon's Spine to the New Capital would take more than a day. Speaking with the Council and preparing for traveling to Earth would take the next, Zhongkui estimated. He should be on Earth the day after next. *Hopefully that will be in time.* While it didn't sound as though his pupil Sinéad and her charge were in immediate danger, he'd feel better knowing firsthand.

Zhongkui had every confidence in Sinéad's abilities, despite her lack of training in the House of Warriors. After all, he'd trained her himself. Because she was an Earth Elder, the council wasn't willing to bring her to their world for training. It was felt that Zhongkui, being one of the greatest warriors in memory, and being originally from Earth, was especially suited to mentor her on Earth. He only hoped it had been enough.

*If they are harmed due to a lack of instruction on my part, I'll never forgive myself. I'll have to go back into retreat.* Zhongkui chuckled to himself as the thought occurred to him, drawing strange looks from his companions.

*Well, he is an Earthling, after all*, Dayan thought. *They always retain a peculiar sense of humor, no matter how long they've been here.* While he would never display a breach in etiquette—a quality which served him well as Speaker—Dayan had never quite been able to see off-worlders as equals. He'd always looked slightly down his nose at them. Even those of the bloodline from Earth, such as Zhongkui, who had proved themselves every bit as capable as natural-born Elders.

They spoke little as they trekked, Elders were generally not big on small talk. Unlike Earthlings, they outgrew the need to fill a void during their long lives. But when they stopped to camp that night there were story and song as was customary. Elders always remained curious despite their great longevity. When they stopped being curious, it was seen as a sign they were ready to return to the One.

As they sat around a small campfire that evening, Jianhu spoke first. "Master, do you still have that stringed instrument you used to play? Would you honor us with a song?"

"The *guqin*? It's a little bulky to travel with," Zhongkui said. "I only have a flute, I'm afraid, but I'd be happy to play a song." Retrieving a flute from his pack, he returned to his seat on a fallen log and began to play. It was a sparse melody, with a haunting quality, different than the musical styles of the Elders which tended to be more upbeat. This was a song of loss.

"That was beautiful, master," Jianhu said, when it was finished. "Thank you."

"It was quite unusual," Dayan said. "Is that a typical song of Earth?"

"That style of flute playing comes from the country of my birth, China. As you know, Earth's cultures are many. There is just as much variety in their musical styles. Most cultures have music for happier times—celebrations and the like—which you would find similar to the music of this world. Music on Earth tends to express the full range of human emotions which tend to have higher highs and lower lows than this world."

"So, this was a song of sorrow then?" Dayan said.

"Indeed. Leaving retreat to see the Guide and the Council, I can't help but be reminded of my great love, Guanyin," Zhongkui said. "I am also worried about my pupil and this song seemed a fitting expression of my mood."

"I see," Dayan said.

"Elder culture was more diverse before the Great War, was it not? I would imagine the music must have been as well. I must admit as harmonious as society is here, I sometimes miss the sheer variety of life on Earth," Zhongkui said.

"But doesn't that diversity lead to the discord which is responsible for the dire situation they find themselves in?" Dayan said.

"Perhaps. I think it has more to do with negative emotions and delusion than an honest difference of opinion, however. It is possible to disagree without being disagreeable—the council is a prime example of this. Earth's problems have only changed by degree, it seems. The self-centeredness, the avarice, and lust for power which have fueled most wars on Earth have not really changed. The difference now is that human society has become so much more intertwined," Zhongkui said.

"When major disruptions, whether in a society or the environment, happen today, the ripples are felt around the world. Not so long ago, people on one side of the globe could live their entire lives completely ignorant of other countries and cultures. When I was a child growing up in China, I knew nothing of the outside world. This is becoming less and less possible, although there are always those willing to lead small lives, oblivious of the greater world around them."

"Maybe one of the benefits of learning of the existence of worlds beyond their own will be a newfound sense of unity among the Earthlings," Jianhu said. "That would be a natural reaction to such a revelation."

"That is my hope as well," Zhongkui said. "Although, knowing my fellow Earthlings as I do, it is just as likely that they will turn on each other. They may react to the unknown with fear and suspicion. If, as you told me, someone on Earth is trying to sabotage our two worlds working together, I fear that—at least for some of them—that is the case."

"Master Zhongkui, is it true what I've heard, that you have become a mythic figure on Earth?" Dayan said, "That some view you as a God?"

"Yes. For better or worse, it is true. Many legends and superstitions have grown up about me. Some are based in truth, others are purely fantasy," Zhongkui said.

"What is it they call you, the Ghost Hunter?" Jianhu said smiling, enjoying the rare opportunity to tease her former teacher.

"Ghosts? You mean you have disembodied spirits roaming the Earth?" Dayan said.

"Some would say so," Zhongkui said. "The culture of China where I was born and raised developed quite an extensive knowledge of these things. They categorized ghosts and spirits into dozens of different kinds. Don't the Watchers say there are entire worlds like this in the universe? On Earth, people tend to either believe in these types of spirits, or else they discount them completely as purely imaginary."

"And what do you say?" Dayan asked.

"Well, there is a third way to view these phenomena, much in the way the Elders deal with mental illness. These phenomena can be viewed as existing, just not in the way they appear," Zhongkui replied. "As energetic phenomena, they have an existence of a sort, but they are inextricably tied to the viewer, like all phenomena in the universe. Sometimes these phenomena are given life by the viewer. They are literally willed into being—intentionally or otherwise. At other times, outside energetic phenomena seem to actually exist independently and affect the viewer, and in many cases the origins are not clear."

"So, how did you acquire this legendary status, if I may ask?" Dayan said.

"Well, as a Daoist priest I was trained in rituals and methods to deal with these cases," Zhongkui said. "Sometimes all that was needed was a ritual occasion to help someone deal with whatever had brought about the phenomena. This was the case when the issue was more psychological in nature. I was also trained to deal with less benign energetic phenomena such as the incident which cemented my legend.

"After I had become an Elder, I returned to Earth many times. On one of these trips I became aware that a malevolent energy was causing the leader of my country, the Emperor Xuanzong, to fall ill. None of the royal physicians were able to heal him, so I traveled energetically to his sleeping quarters one night to see if I might be able to help. Emperor Xuanzong slept fitfully, and awoke in a feverish state as I was removing this pernicious energy from him. I explained that I was an Immortal and that I was curing him. In his feverish state his dreams mixed with reality. The next morning, he awoke healed and my legend was born. Of course, the legend is much more colorful than the reality."

"I'm not sure that's true, master. Didn't you once tell me that in the popular stories it was said you were thrown out of government service because you were too ugly?" Jianhu said, smiling.

Dayan couldn't help but chuckle, until Zhongkui fixed him with a glare.

"Go ahead, have your fun," Zhongkui said. "Obviously it wasn't a physical ugliness," he said, a grin slowly spreading across his face. "But a meanness of spirit. As a young man I had quite a temper. Conquering my rage was essential to my self-cultivation. There is a great deal of energy in anger. When transformed it becomes a powerful fuel which can be used for good, but when it burns out of control it can consume you."

As Zhongkui spoke, the campfire flared up suddenly, startling Dayan and Jianhu. With an eyebrow raised, Dayan shot Jianhu a questioning look. She simply shrugged in reply. While it was said that some Elders had these types of abilities—especially among the older ones—displays such as this were rarely seen. Most could travel as they had to Earth, and many had some degree of telepathy as Dayan and Jianhu did, but telekinetic powers were infrequent enough to be the stuff of legend, even on the Elders' world. *Perhaps it was just a coincidence*, Dayan thought, until he noticed the grin on Zhongkui's face as he warmed his hands over the fire.

"Ah, that's better," Zhongkui said. "These mountain nights can get a bit chilly."

# 37

*Qilian Mountains*
*Gansu Province, China*

After dropping his party at the base of Qilian Shan, Tenzin had been riding for about an hour when he spotted them—two men were hiding in the rocks a few hundred yards ahead. They lay in wait on the uphill side of the trail he followed. He'd spotted them quickly, his eyes accustomed to taking in the wide-open spaces of the mountains with his peripheral vision. The stillness of the mountains made even the subtlest movement glaringly obvious.

He continued down the trail, giving no indication he noticed them, but his hand slowly slid into his *chuba*. He made sure his weapon was accessible and the safety was off. He would avoid bloodshed if possible, but if left with no alternative, he was prepared for that as well.

The nomads of Qinghai, the former Tibetan Provinces of Amdo and Kham, were no strangers to violence, despite being followers of the Buddha. They had put up the fiercest resistance to the Chinese Army when they moved into Tibet in the last century and, though rare, it wasn't unheard of for feuds between clans to be settled with bloodshed if no understanding could be reached to address a dispute.

The traditional Kham-style knife he carried on his belt was really more of a short sword, its blade over a foot long. It had a handle of nickel-silver, matching the elaborately carved scabbard. But this was no ceremonial or ornamental weapon, its steel blade was razor sharp, despite being used as an all-purpose tool for the horseman. There was a dragon carved on the handle, with another eight on the scabbard. His knife hung on his left side, while the right side held a traveling cutlery set of chopsticks and a small knife in a similarly designed scabbard, decorated with the eight auspicious symbols of Tibetan Buddhism, a common design motif in the region.

As he neared the boulder, he stopped his horses about ten feet away and dismounted. He feigned checking on his horses, one eye on the boulder behind which the men hid. They would have to come to him. He positioned himself amongst the horses and just as he expected, they stepped out onto the trail when they thought their presence would be least noticed.

"Don't move," one of the men said in Chinese.

As he came around the front of his horse, taking them in at a moment's glance, he registered the two handguns trained on him. He waved his right hand in front of him as he pleaded, "Please don't shoot," while his left hand was already drawing his knife in a reverse grip. In one smooth motion he slashed the gun hand of the man nearest him. The other man fired, his shot going wide as Tenzin spun away, positioning himself on the other side of the man he had slashed, now doubled over holding his arm.

While the shot missed Tenzin, an awful groan told him one of his horses hadn't been so lucky. His free hand found his own pistol in his *chuba* as he completed his turn, drawing and firing in a flash. The second assailant fell, an angry red eye appearing in the once pristine flesh of his forehead. Tenzin cursed, and clocked the injured man with the butt of his gun, knocking him unconscious. Wiping his knife on the man's pants before sheathing it, he turned to his injured horse, which had fallen where it stood, still tethered to the others.

Though his horse still lived, he could tell by its labored breathing and the blood-flecked foam around its nostrils that it wasn't long for this world. Kneeling next to it, he put a hand on its neck, stroking it tenderly and whispering into its ear to calm it. Then he fired the fatal shot, ending its pain. He began to recite the *Mani* mantra, said to liberate beings from rebirth in the six realms of existence, continuing as he focused his awareness on the man he had killed. Even his enemies deserved his compassion.

He took a moment to calm the other horses before he returned his attention to the unconscious man. Sitting him up, he grabbed him under the arms from behind and dragged him towards one of the horses. When he got close he heaved him upright, until he could bend down and grab him around the waist, then he pushed him onto one of the horses, before binding his wrists and ankles.

Returning to the dead man, he searched the body, checking his pockets. He didn't find anything of interest until he pulled up his left sleeve. On the inside of his left wrist was a tell-tale tattoo. It was unmistakable, the Hawk of Quraish with crossed swords, the symbol of the Soldiers of the Caliphate. Though tattoos were usually considered taboo amongst devout Muslims, members of the SOC broke with tradition and marked themselves with the would-be country's symbol.

He dragged the body back behind the boulder, and began piling stones over it from the scree-covered slopes. He'd notify the *rogyap-as*, the body-breakers, of the location of the corpse when he returned to his village. They would dispose of the corpse through sky burial, leaving it in pieces to be picked clean by the vultures. He kicked dust over the blood left on the trail, and prepared to depart. He would hurry to his village and leave the captive with members of the society before returning with one of his clan to deal with his horse, if the scavengers didn't beat him to it.

# 38

*Huanyuan Guan*
*Qilian Mountains, China*

The next morning the group awoke and joined the community for breakfast. The morning meal was again somewhat unusual for a typical Daoist monastery as eggs were available. That made sense with the chickens they'd seen outside. Thinking about it, Rohini hadn't heard a rooster that morning. She could have slept through it, or perhaps their sleeping quarters were far enough away from the coop not to hear the rooster crow. The meal was again eaten in silence followed by a group prayer.

After breakfast Rohini noticed Guangming in conversation with the Abbot, so she walked over to join them.

"Sorry, I didn't mean to interrupt," she said.

"No, please join us," the Abbot replied.

"Long Daozhang was just telling me we've been summoned, so we'll need to head up to the Guanzi's abode this afternoon," Guangming told her.

"Does that mean we might still have time for a quick tour of the farm? I'd love to see what you're growing and experimenting with here," she said.

I would be happy to show you around, Rohini," the Abbot replied. "I just have a few duties to attend to first. I will come fetch you shortly."

They headed back to the guesthouse to wait for the Abbot. When they arrived Guangming had other news. "Long Daozhang had some worrying news for me this morning," he said. "It appears we were followed from Zhangye."

"Oh crap. That's not good," Jane said, rising from her seat. "Are they here in the valley?"

"No. Fortunately, they were intercepted outside the valley. As far as we can tell they didn't get close enough to follow us here."

"Who intercepted them, someone from the society?" Jane said.

"Yes. It was Tenzin, actually. He spotted two men on his way back to his village after dropping us off and took care of them," Guangming said.

"Tenzin? Really? Did he kill them?" Rohini said.

"Unfortunately, he did have to kill one of them. He was able to subdue the other one. He took him back to his village where he's being questioned," Guangming said.

"Tenzin seemed like such a sweetheart," Rohini said, "I wouldn't have guessed he had it in him."

"Don't let his jovial personality fool you," Jimmie said, "The nomads from Kham and Amdo are a hardy bunch. I'm sure you must have noticed his knife. Those aren't just for show. Many of the men carry guns as well."

"I didn't realize this was the Wild West out here," Jane said. "Did the Abbot tell you anything about the men?"

"He said they were SOC. They had the Hawk and Swords tattoo on their wrists," Guangming replied.

"That makes no sense," Jane said. "There's no way they would have the connections to track us here."

"You said there was no way they should have been able to pull off the attack in DC either, remember?" Rohini said.

"That's true. We've got to find out who they're working with. We've got to let the White House know about this. I'd better fill in President Powers while you take your tour," Jane said.

Jane went to her room to retrieve her satellite phone, then headed outside to make her call. Before calling the White House, she put in a quick call to her old friend Burt to give him a heads-up as well.

"Burt, it's Jane," she said, after he picked up.

"Jane, what's up? Are you guys still doing OK out there? Wherever 'out there' is?" he replied.

"Yeah. We're fine for the time being. Listen, I've got some intel. I'm about to call the White House with this as well, but I wanted to keep you up to speed," Jane said. "Somehow we were tracked by the SOC. One of our local contacts was able to take them out—most likely keep them from gleaning our location—but somehow, they tracked us most of the way here. Listen, Burt, we're in the middle of nowhere, way out in the mountains in Gansu, China—there's no way the SOC could have tracked us to China, let alone way out here."

"Gansu! You are way out there. But you're right. They must have had help, or someone else is calling the shots for them. Even state-sponsored assets would've been hard-pressed to track you there. Unless the SOC reconstituted themselves in China. There is a significant Muslim population in that part of China, isn't there?" Burt speculated.

"It's possible, but I think it's highly unlikely. If you recall these guys weren't just fundamentalists like other Wahhabis, they were also Arab Nationalists. I know there were indications that Wahhabism spread into China, but the SOC never had much tolerance, even for non-Arab Muslims. I think these guys were sent to follow us by whoever their current paymasters are. Our contacts managed to take one of them alive, so perhaps we'll know more soon. I haven't heard anything further yet," Jane said.

"Who have you got watching your back out there, anyway? Are they locals or agency people?" Burt asked.

"Definitely locals. Alright, look, I'll let you in on part of that long story I was telling you about. Our hosts here are from a Chinese secret society," Jane said.

"You mean the Triads? How they hell did you get tangled up with them? Are you sure you can trust them?" Burt responded.

"They're not quite like the triads you and I know, Burt. Think more like the historical predecessors to the current day gangsters.

These guys apparently go way back for over a thousand years and are more religiously and ethically motivated. They're more like do-good-er vigilantes than mobsters," Jane said.

"Well, I'll be damned. Who knew?" Burt said. "I guess I shouldn't be surprised. You always had a knack for stumbling into some weird stuff, Jane."

"Yeah, well, it's only going to get weirder, old buddy. But I'm afraid the rest of the story will have to wait. I'd better get on the horn with the president. Take care Burt. We should see you in a few weeks, at the outside."

Jane ended the call and placed another to the White House. The president called her back a short time later with some interesting news of her own. In their absence, another attack had occurred in the United States.

# 39

Jane was still on her call with President Powers when the Abbot came for Rohini, so she stayed behind while the others went on a tour of the grounds. The Abbot gave them a little history about the valley and the monastery as they made their way out toward the orchards and fields beyond.

The monastery had originally sprung up around a shadowy figure known as *Tianyinzi*, the Master of Heavenly Seclusion, who lived in the small cave located at what was now the rear of the monastery grounds. The monastery itself hadn't been built until several centuries had passed, the early history of the original community gathered there lost until the discovery of the society's texts at Dunhuang by Wang Yuanlu. As it turned out, *Tianyinzi* was none other than Zhongkui himself, according to what the Guanzi had told the Abbot.

As they walked past the chicken coop, Rohini noticed something she hadn't seen on the way in the previous day, there was another building beyond, to which the Abbot now led them. Opening the door and turning on the lights, they saw rows and rows of shelves. At first Rohini thought the Abbot had taken them into a storeroom until she realized what she was looking at. It was a mushroom growhouse.

Many of the shelves held trays full of a composted growth medium, while others held small logs which had been inoculated with spores. There was quite a variety. She thought she recognized a few, like shiitakes and maitakes, though she only knew them by their Japanese names. But there were others she was less familiar with, so she asked the Abbot about them.

"Actually, several of these are shiitake. We grow three different kinds here, *Donggu*, *Xianggu*, and *Huagu*. They each have slightly different characteristics. The shiitakes and maitakes are usually considered food mushrooms though they are quite good for one's health. We also grow several types of mushrooms which are considered more medicinal like *Lingzhi* and *Yunzhi*," Abbot Long explained.

"I think we have these in the states too, but we call them Turkey Tail mushrooms," Rohini said. "What does the Chinese name mean?"

"*Yunzhi* means 'cloud mushroom,'" Guangming said. "But we don't have turkeys in China."

"Well, maybe just the one, anyway," Rohini said, pointing a thumb at Jimmie standing next to her.

"Hey, I heard that," he said, smiling.

They left the mushroom shed and continued their tour of the grounds, making their way through the orchards and out to the fields. The Abbot showed them the garden of medicinal herbs first, most of them unfamiliar to Rohini, though some she recognized as common ornamental plants in the US, like balloon flower. The Abbot called it *Jie Geng*, and said its root was used to open up the lungs and treat cough. Rohini recognized most of the vegetables in the next field. They were fairly common varieties, with the exception of a few, like bitter melon, *Gai lan* or Chinese broccoli, and burdock, which she certainly didn't expect to see.

When her family visited her grandparent's farm as a child, their golden retriever always got covered in burrs from the burdock which grew along the fencerows around the farm. She never expected to see someone growing it on purpose, but Guangming explained that burdock root was a common vegetable dish in much of East Asia. She didn't recognize the crops in the next field either, though they looked familiar.

In the first field were tall grassy plants with large red plumes which reminded her a bit of the ornamental plant cockscomb.

"What are those, are they just weeds or a cover crop of some kind?" She asked.

"These are some grains we are experimenting with. They grow well at this high-altitude and are quite prolific," the Abbot said. "This first field is quinoa and the field beyond is amaranth."

She only remembered amaranth as a weed from her uncle's farm in New Mexico, but as they walked closer, she realized it was indeed the same plant. This looked like a variety that had gone through some degree of selection though. The seed heads looked much heavier than the weeds she remembered from her uncle's fields.

As they walked around the farm, Rohini was struck at how much it reminded her of the ecovillages she had visited in the past. It sounded like they used the farm in much the same way, both as a source of self-sustainability for the monastery and also as an education and research facility—albeit an unofficial one—passing their knowledge on to the outside world. Rohini recalled how she'd felt at the UN the day after the Elders had appeared. She was reminded once again that the people of Earth already had much of the wisdom and knowledge necessary for avoiding the worst catastrophes of climate change. We had simply lacked the political will—or just the maturity—to make the necessary changes. Then again, she realized, that was not entirely the case. Much of the problem lay with the forces in the world that were actively fighting against the necessary changes.

There were people who had gotten filthy rich by keeping us complacent, corporations which had known about the disastrous effects of climate change for decades, yet kept it hidden from the public. It was much like the smoking lobby before them. They'd tried to hide the science on how destructive cigarette smoking was for years. In fact, she thought she remembered learning once that many of the very same PR firms were responsible for both charades.

They had taken the same strategy of 'muddying the waters' they'd used with tobacco companies and applied it to climate change. The science was still unsettled, they'd said, years after a scientific consensus had been reached. Though much of the public hadn't been fooled by this, enough were that business as usual was accepted long after we should have begun to clean up our act. She was glad the tide finally seemed to be turning.

They finished their tour of the farm and were headed back to their quarters a different way than they had come before, passing by two small structures set off by themselves in the northwest corner of the grounds. Walking past, Rohini caught a glimpse of a statue inside the open doors and stopped.

"Long Daozhang, what is this building?" Rohini asked. "I hadn't noticed it before. May we go inside?"

"Please. It is called the *Shengxia yuan*, the Hall of Ascension, or the *Qianhua yuan*, the Hall of Transformation," the Abbot said.

They stepped inside where they were able to get a better view of the statue which had caught her eye as they passed. It was an image of a Daoist in seated meditation—like a Buddha statue—but with one unusual exception. Its left hand pointed into the sky above.

"Why is he pointing to the sky like that?" she asked.

"The Hall of Ascension is where monks and nuns come who are preparing to leave their bodies. You might think of it like a spiritual hospice," the Abbot explained. "The monk is pointing to the sky in a gesture known as 'ascending to emptiness,' indicating that he is returning to the source, returning to the Dao. The building next door is the Hall of Incense where we hold funerals and memorial services."

"It looks like he is pointing to the stars," Rohini said.

"That could be the case," the Abbot said, pointing above himself. "Look." There on the ceiling was a diagram of the Big Dipper. "The Immortal realms are sometimes said to be located in the Stars of the Northern Dipper where *Doumu*, the Cosmic Mother, rules over the Nine Heavens, represented by the nine stars of the dipper."

"Nine stars? I thought there were only seven stars in the dipper?" Jimmie said.

"There are two hidden stars, along the handle of the dipper, called 'the Attendents,'" Guangming added.

"The Stars of the Northern Dipper are like a string of pearls in the night sky," the Abbot said. "As it turns throughout the year it always points to *Beiji*, the Polestar. It serves as a reminder that one should always maintain an awareness of the Dao's presence at the center of our being."

"I can't help thinking of the Elders," Rohini said, as she looked at the constellation. "I wonder where their world is?"

# 40

*Green Dragon Mountains*
*The Elders' World*

The next morning when Dayan awoke, he rolled over and propped himself onto an elbow. Zhongkui was already up, practicing with his sword in the small meadow in which they'd camped the night before. It had been a fascinating evening. Zhongkui had been quite a surprise. While Dayan had expected a gruff barbarian, from the stories he'd heard, the man had been quite different.

Dayan suspected that Zhongkui might have lived up to his reputation had he met him a thousand years ago. *Perhaps that's the impression he gave when he initially came to our world.* Of course, all Earthlings seemed a bit barbaric to Dayan. Despite his apparent mellowing, there was still an intense quality to Zhongkui which most would probably find intimidating. Being honest with himself, Dayan had to admit that he did as well, especially after Zhongkui's trick with the fire. But he was also intrigued. *What other tricks does he have up his sleeve?*

"Ah, you're awake. Greetings, Dayan. May the sun shine upon you," Jianhu said.

"And may it shine upon you, Jianhu. Has he been at it long?" he said, nodding toward Zhongkui.

"He was up before the sun, I think. Certainly before I was," Jianhu said.

Before long, Zhongkui had finished his practice and Dayan had returned from his morning ablutions at the nearby creek. They shared a simple meal of nuts and dried fruit. Zhongkui prepared tea for them all and Dayan had to admit, this beverage was growing on him. While the plant Zhongkui used was from the Elders' world, it wasn't a plant they had traditionally used in this way. Dayan enjoyed the subtle energizing effect it carried, and its warmth was certainly a welcome addition in the cool morning air.

While the Elders would build a fire for cooking or warmth, their culture didn't really drink warm beverages, at least not since the Great War. Before that time parts of their world had been much colder, especially the far northern and southern climes near the poles. Much of the lands of the lost continents had been covered in ice and snow, or so the histories said. *Hard to imagine,* Dayan thought.

Once the icecaps and glaciers had all melted, and the oceans had risen, those lands were soon forgotten. For his entire lifetime the Elders' world had been green and lush, with a mild climate. Neither too hot, nor too cold. The planet had cooled somewhat over his lifetime, but not enough to change things much. It might take thousands of years for the glaciers to be seen again, if they ever returned. *Unless we are forced to leave. There may be no one left to see that day if the Others do return.*

After breakfast they packed up their things and set off, nearing the capital by mid-afternoon. Dayan had always enjoyed that first glimpse of the capitol city from a distance. Unlike the ancient cities of their world which had been built in a haphazard fashion, most of which were now sleeping quietly on the ocean floor, the New Capitol had been built after the Great War, its design consciously planned to reflect the new-found harmony of Elder society.

The heart of the capitol was made up of the council buildings, which included the council chambers themselves, as well as the living quarters of the Guide and the council members representing the twelve clans. They were arrayed in a circle around a courtyard where the grand ceremonies which marked the changing of the seasons were held throughout the year.

As they came down out of the mountains, they passed between the two foothills known as the Legs of the Dragon. The Northern Ridge was home to the House of Warriors, where Zhongkui had once been Master. Generations had studied the way of the fist, honing their martial skills, and refining themselves through the body. The Southern Ridge held the House of Scholars. Here students followed the way of the heart, practicing meditation and studying the sacred texts passed down through the generations.

"Do you miss it, master?" Jianhu asked as they passed the fork in the trail which led up to the Northern Ridge.

"I don't miss the formality or the bureaucracy, but I do miss teaching. It was a joy to watch our students' progress over time," Zhongkui replied.

"You must have spent time studying the way of the fist, Dayan. How did you find your time there?" Zhongkui.

"Yes, I spent time training in both Houses, as is customary for service to the council. I must say I preferred my time in the House of Scholars. Of course, my time in the Houses was during your absence as Master. Had you still been there perhaps my experience would have been different," Dayan replied.

"I'd wager you'd have liked it even less," Jianhu said, smiling. "Master Zhongkui is a truly gifted teacher, yet his training can leave one feeling like a sword in the forge. I'd never really felt the truth of the ancient saying 'caught between the hammer and the anvil' until I'd experienced Master Zhongkui's instruction. Yet, like a finely crafted blade, I came out of the process both stronger and more flexible. I will forever be grateful for the experience."

"True transformation is never an easy process," Zhongkui said. "Simple, yes, but never easy."

Dayan had not grown up in the capital himself. He had been raised in the village of the Horse Clan in the South. Many of his clan had a reputation for their skill in communications and negotiations, and were sometimes derided as silver-tongued devils by the other clans. There had been many Speakers from the Horse Clan over the years. Dayan had only come to the capitol when he entered the Houses to prepare for service to the council.

They entered the city and made their way around the Central District of the council buildings which could only be entered from the east, passing into the Trade District. It had been ten years since Zhongkui had been immersed in the sights, sounds, and smells of the city.

Traders hawked their wares in the marketplace as Elders from all twelve clans strolled among the stalls, identified by the different totem animals they wore either embroidered on their clothing or as jewelry. Barring that, the color of their cloaks often told of their clan affiliation. The smells of fresh fish and street food filled his nostrils, reminding him of the distant past and the first time he had accompanied his father to a city market in the China of his childhood. It still amazed him that he could be visited by such a vivid memory after more than a millennium walking through two different worlds.

"Ah, good. She's still here. I must make a quick stop before we go to the council," Zhongkui said. Walking past a few more stalls he stopped at the next, where a woman was selling small skewers of roasted mushrooms of various kinds. Mushrooms had been a staple of the Elders' diet since the Great War. The woman wore a dark yellow cloak, and a silver ring dangling from her septum further identified her as a member of the Ox Clan.

"Master Zhongkui," the woman said, her eyes lighting up. "It has been too long."

"Indeed, it has, Chushi. I'm glad to see you are still here." Zhongkui said. Turning to his companions he said, "Chushi's mushroom skewers have always reminded me of the flavors of my youth. I could smell them a mile away."

They purchased several skewers for each of them and began to eat, standing at the counter attached to Chushi's stall. "I can see why you are so fond of these," Dayan said after he'd finished his skewers. "These are quite extraordinary, and I dare say I could drink a mug of this sauce."

"I'm honored by your words, Speaker," Chushi said. "That can certainly be arranged," she said, with a gentle laugh.

"Perhaps another time, Chushi. I'm afraid we're expected by the council," Dayan said. "Master Zhongkui, we really should be on our way."

"Very well. Until such time, Chushi," Zhongkui said.

"Until such time, Master Zhongkui. Speaker. Guardian," she said, bidding the three goodbye.

# 41

*Qilian Mountains*
*Gansu Province, China*

Rohini, Jimmie, and Guangming returned to their quarters to retrieve Jane and get their gear together for the hike to the Abode of the Guanzi, in the peaks above. Jane had finished her call with President Powers when they returned, and told them about the most recent attack. Fortunately, it was nothing as dramatic or deadly as the bombing of the Lincoln Memorial. An attack had been carried out on the energy sector—they had bombed a community solar project in Nebraska. No one was killed in the attack, except the bomber, but a five-hundred-kilowatt solar installation was completely destroyed.

"That seems kind of random, doesn't it?" Rohini said. "I mean, why solar panels of all things?"

"It's a strange choice," Jane said. "Then again, it's definitely a soft target. Facilities like that have virtually no security. Maybe it was simply a target of opportunity? But, you're right, it seems especially random coming from the SOC. They've traditionally gone in for more deadly attacks. The bombing of the Lincoln Memorial was much more their style. This seems out of place."

"We'll have to leave that to someone else to figure out for now," Guangming said. "We'd better get going."

"I'm all set," Jane said.

"I'll just be a minute," Jimmie said.

"Oh, Jimmie, sorry," Guangming said. "I forgot to mention it earlier after hearing about the SOC men, but the Guanzi only summoned the three of us. You'll have to wait here."

"Oh, OK. Only the green-eyed devils, huh?" Jimmie joked. "That's OK. I'll hold down the fort," he said, attempting to downplay his disappointment.

He and Rohini shared a long meaningful look as they left. He'd walked them out to the gate, then waved until they reached the orchards, at which point Rohini lost sight of him. Just as things might be going somewhere between them, they would be put on hold. *It's probably for the best*, she thought. A little distance might give her some perspective; a little time to think things over before she got too swept up in this budding romance.

It didn't take them long to make it back down the valley to the fork in the trail—perhaps an hour—and only about twenty minutes to cross the bridge over the river near the waterwheel and make it up to the ridgeline. She could see the trail more clearly from this higher vantage point, and could make out more of the path ahead than the previous day. *Had it really only been a day?* It felt like they had been there much longer.

The traverse along the ridgeline took a couple more hours. It was mostly easy going, the trail gaining in elevation very gradually, with the exception of a narrow pass about halfway along the ridge which required them to scramble over some boulders and squeeze through a tight gap. At the far end of the ridge they climbed through another narrow pass. It wasn't as tight a squeeze, but Rohini found it fascinating. The rocky walls on either side were streaked in veins of jade. Once through the pass, they found themselves among the peaks which rose to form the southern end of the mountain. They had been shrouded in mist the previous day, but the clouds had blown away overnight. She could make out nine peaks rising above. The trail, which was well marked and easy to follow, led them between the peaks to a central summit which appeared to be the highest of the nine. It was also the location of the Abode of the Guanzi.

As they neared the central peak, the trail ahead began to climb, turning into a series of steps cut into the rocky slope. The mossy steps appeared quite ancient, showing signs of weathering and wear from the many feet which had trod this path before. They wound around a few blind turns until the view ahead opened up to reveal a small valley which led to what appeared to be a cave at the far end. As they grew closer, they could make out a doorframe built into the cave, which had been hidden in shadow. The door opened as they approached and at the entrance was a woman dressed in Daoist robes holding a small lantern.

"Welcome," she said, greeting them. "I am Jingyi, the Guanzi's attendant. Please, follow me and I'll take you to her."

As they passed inside, the cave went a short distance before widening into a large central cavern with several doors along two sides. While the cavern itself appeared naturally occurring, it was clear that the doorways had been carved out, as well as the many niches which lined the walls. Some held beeswax candles, while others held small statues of various saints, sages, and Immortals. There was a large table here as well, with benches on either side and at the far end of the cavern was an altar much like the ones Rohini had seen at the monastery.

There were two large statues here which appeared to have been carved from the cave wall itself, a fierce-looking male figure with a sword, and a more feminine figure holding a vase and a lotus flower. Above were three small figures of bearded men sitting on thrones, and below was a table which held offerings.

"These must be Zhongkui and Guanyin," Rohini said. "But who are the three figures above?"

"Those are the Three Pure Ones," Guangming explained. "They represent many different things—the three main groups of scriptures in the Daoist Canon and the three main energy centers in the human body, for instance."

"You may leave your things in these rooms," the woman said, pointing them towards the doors. "Then I will take you to the Guanzi."

After stowing their packs, they followed the Guanzi's attendant through the last doorway on the right. It led down a short passageway, then up a flight of stone steps, circling to the left as they ascended. Being in the cave, it was hard to tell how far around they had circled, but Rohini guessed they were probably somewhere above the main cavern. Reaching the top of the steps, they came to a curtain outside, where the attendant paused briefly, as though listening, before pulling back the curtain for the three of them.

"The Guanzi will see you now."

They entered the next chamber, which was similar in shape to the cavern below, though smaller. Its walls were lined with wooden cabinets and a few open shelves full of books and scrolls. On a low dais at the far end sat an old woman in Daoist robes on a small meditation cushion, holding what looked like a cane across her lap. Her gray hair was in a topknot, secured with a jade hairpin. Her eyes twinkled behind her crow's feet. Though she appeared quite old, she looked healthy and vigorous. She exuded an air of peace and calm. On the floor in front of the dais were three cushions on a long rug which covered most of the floor of the chamber. There were no candles lit in the room, yet natural light seemed to be coming in from behind the Guanzi somewhere. *There must be a window of some kind*, Rohini thought.

The three approached, following Guangming's lead. He bowed like he had to the Abbot, Long Daozhang, the previous day, but he sank onto his knees and bowed all the way to the floor, before rising again. Jane and Rohini simply bowed from the waist.

"Please, have a seat," the Guanzi said in a warm voice.

"I am so pleased you could come to us," she said, smiling. "This is a very special time. I assume Guangming has told you some of the history of our society?"

"Yes," Guangming replied. "At least what little I know."

"He is much too modest. Guangming is actually quite bright," the Guanzi said, bursting into laughter.

Her laughter was contagious and soon the three of them joined her, before Guangming explained the joke, 'bright' being the meaning of his name.

"We have much to discuss," the Guanzi said. "But first, we must have some tea."

As soon as she spoke, her attendant returned with a tray and five cups of tea. She handed one to the Guanzi before passing the others out, leaving one for herself. She set the tray down before taking a seat on an empty cushion to one side of the Guanzi. The Guanzi began by recounting a brief history of the society. It was similar to what Guangming had told them in DC, but the Guanzi filled in some of the gaps, being privy to more of the story. What the Abbot had told them was correct, Zhongkui had indeed become the Daoist recluse known as Tianyinzi, the Master of Heavenly Seclusion, and lived in the cave in the valley below.

The story passed down in the society was that one day, during his meditation, Zhongkui had a vision of Guanyin who led him to this very cave which was now known as the Abode of the Guanzi. The cave was actually a complex, containing several other chambers besides the ones they had seen so far.

The Guanzi explained that the grottoes above where they now sat were special. They were known as the Lower, Middle, and Upper Guanyin grottoes. While the society had known about the caverns—the previous Guanzis always living there once they assumed the role—their true nature had not been known until the society's lost archives had been found at Dunhuang.

"The archives told a slightly different story," the Guanzi said. "In that story, Guanyin had not been simply a vision, but flesh and blood. She and Zhongkui had met and fell in love and lived together here in the mountains for several years. One day, Guanyin revealed to Zhongkui that she was an Immortal and that she would have to return to the Celestial Realms eventually. She brought Zhongkui to this place because she knew that to stay together, he would have to become an Immortal and gain the ability to follow her when she left this world. He did—achieving the Pure Yang Spirit—and ascended into the heavens with Guanyin."

"So, Guanyin was an Elder?" Rohini said.

"I believe so. We have always interpreted the stories through the lens of our own culture, but once the Elders made themselves known, the implications became clear. Many of our traditions will have to be reexamined in this new light," the Guanzi explained.

"In deep meditation I have had the ability to travel in spirit, my awareness leaving my body. I have been able to view distant places on Earth, but I had not yet been able to leave this earthly realm until the Elders appeared. When the Elders appeared at the United Nations I was aware of their presence, as they were aware of mine. In my meditation one of them spoke to me and told me to follow them when they left. I attempted to follow bodily, traveling as they do, but was only able to follow them in spirit. I saw their world, and have been able to see it several times since, but have not been able to achieve the Pure Yang Spirit, the body of light, allowing me to travel to their world bodily."

"Is that how they travel," Guangming asked, "the light body?"

"Yes, it would appear so. They are able to transform themselves into pure energy which allows them to travel from world to world. They remain immortal because when they return to corporeal form, they return to whatever age they see themselves as—their ideal self. They only age if they choose to stop traveling."

"That jibes with what my mentor told me," Jane said. "Although at the time it didn't all make sense to me. Learning what I have from Guangming about some of the traditional Daoist worldview has actually filled in some of the gaps for me."

"How so?" Rohini asked.

Jane thought back to when her mentor tried to explain how the Elders traveled. The memory of it was now crystal clear, much more so than it had been in the past. She almost felt like she could hear his words. He had told her how the structure of the universe resembles the neural pathways of the human brain. *Innerspace is contained within the mind. This structure is like a holographic microcosm of the universe*, he said. *While it seems to be small, isolated, and cut off from the rest of the universe, in truth it contains the universe within it, or at least an individual's experience of the universe. For all we can know, all we can experience, is through the lens of the mind.* Coming back to the present, she tried to express some of what she remembered.

"Well, the energy networks through the earth for one thing," Jane said. "My mentor told me how the universe was all linked together through a vast network of energy which was like the structure of the brain. He said the structure of the universe was similar at every level. It didn't make a lot of sense to me at the time, but the ideas you've told me about, that Daoists see humans, the earth, and the Dao as all being different levels of microcosm and macrocosm, seem like they are referring to the same idea."

"Yes, this is much like what the Elders communicated to me when they spoke to me in meditation," the Guanzi began. "They said each solar system is like a neural cluster. The energetic pathways are much stronger between planets within a solar system and especially between planets and their sun. They told me that some of our traditions on earth point to this connection, but that we didn't fully understand the implications of this connection or how to use it. According to them, these connections also exist between solar systems, though they are not as strong, and between galaxies as well, though they are even more subtle."

"Yes, that's right," Jane said, as she remembered more. "My mentor explained that there are gaps or gateways which open in the earth's electromagnetic field and that these gaps are the openings through which they travel. He said they can only enter or leave when these gaps are open, but apparently they happen quite frequently."

"That sounds like you're describing solar breaches," Rohini said. "I remember reading about them a few years ago. They're a relatively new discovery, from what I remember. NASA had a satellite called THEMIS which first discovered the gaps. They allow solar plasma into the outer layers of the magnetosphere."

"It reminds me a lot of our conversation on the plane about the acupuncture points too," Jane said.

"Yes, the xue," Guangming said. "These gaps or gateways could be like the acupuncture points of the earth's electromagnetic field."

"This certainly sounds like a rational explanation for the Elders' method of travel, but of course accomplishing it is another matter," the Guanzi said. "The gap between theoretical knowledge and actually putting something into practice can be great indeed.

"The Elders also gave me a warning when I attempted to follow them. They said that if I succeeded in traveling with my body, I could only become corporeal again on planets which have similar conditions to Earth, such as their own world. They said I would be able to travel with my consciousness anywhere—the sun for instance, or a gaseous planet, or even worlds with quite different lifeforms—yet the moment I tried to become corporeal there I would die."

# 42

"Gruber, what news have you got for me?"

"We've lost contact with our operatives in China. We think they must have been taken out."

"I thought they were going to be more careful after being made in Lanzhou?" Simms said.

"They were, as far as we know, but they must have been discovered anyway. I've taken the liberty of having the area around their last known location searched with a drone. There is only one place they could have gone based on the trail they were following."

"Tell me about it. I want to know what they're up to."

"Well, it's odd. They've gone to what appears to be a monastery in the mountains. We've checked the entire area and haven't found heat signatures anywhere else."

"That doesn't seem so strange in that part of the world. It's not that populated a region, from what I understand," Simms said.

"That's what we thought at first, until we checked the satellite footage of the area. The monastery is blurred out on the satellites. Someone is trying to keep it a secret, but from what we could tell from the drone there was nothing special about it other than a lot of solar panels, which was a little strange."

"It's not a government facility, is it?" Simms said.

"No, we haven't found any government or military links to it."

"Alright. I want those people found, Gruber. Either bring them in or neutralize them."

"Yes, Mr. Simms. I've already got a strike team standing by. We can be there in twelve hours."

*Excellent,* Simms thought. He'd prefer they be captured, to find out what they were up to, but barring that he'd be content to have them out of the picture.

# 43

"Thank you for coming, Master Zhongkui. I know the council had agreed to leave you in peace, but I'm sure you realize the urgency of the situation," the Guide said.

"Yes, Grandmother. I appreciate your concern," Zhongkui said. I will gladly seek out my former pupil, the Earth Guardian and her charge. The Speaker and Jianhu have told me of the situation on Earth. But, please, tell me more of what the Watchers say. Is it true that the Others are returning? Forgive me, but I thought after so many thousands of years they would have died off or found a new planet to inhabit."

"Unfortunately, it is so. The Watchers first noticed them shortly after you entered retreat—not very long into my tenure as Guide, as you may recall. At first, we thought it was of no concern, simply an interesting discovery that they were still alive. But as the Watchers investigated further, they discovered some of what had transpired over these many years. The Watchers discovered the path of destruction that the Others had left in their wake. It appears the Others' single-minded pursuit of technology has led them down a dark path."

"How so, Grandmother? What has everyone so spooked?" Zhongkui said.

"Instead of settling on a new planet, it appears the Others' reliance on energy-intensive technologies has required a strategy of continual conquest to supply the resources required. In many ways they've pursued a path similar to ours, in that they've achieved a sort of immortality through technological means, but the costs have been great. Let me show you what I mean, Master Zhongkui. Let me share what the Watchers shared with me."

Zhongkui had always been uncomfortable with the sharing of thoughts. His mind was strong enough that he was invulnerable to the skill. No Elder could force their thoughts on him, unlike the weak-minded guards at the UN that Jianhu had scared into submission. The Guide had warned Dayan about it. Ordinarily Dayan would have simply shown his message to Zhongkui when they reached his retreat cave, but the Guide had counseled against it, and Jianhu had echoed the warning. He wouldn't be able to force his way into Zhongkui's mind, and any attempt to do so would likely only irritate him.

But Zhongkui trusted the Guide's judgment, and time was of the essence if things were as dire as they were being portrayed. "If you think this is the best way, I will allow it," Zhongkui said. "Please, go ahead."

The Guide closed her eyes, as did Zhongkui. It only took a few moments, despite the great amount of information being conveyed. While Earth remained obsessed with the puzzle of faster than light travel, the Elders had long ago discovered the speed of thought was far greater.

The images flooded Zhongkui's mind. So much information at once could be difficult to take, but his mind was up to the task. In an instant in the material world around them, their two minds joined for what felt like hours. There was so much to tell; so many worlds destroyed by the Others, and so many beings enslaved to fill the ranks of their conquering army. And now, as Zhongkui saw what the Watchers had shown the Guide, he understood. As he opened his eyes again, a tear rolled down his cheek. "So much death and destruction," Zhongkui said. "I must prepare for my journey to earth at once."

"Go now, Master Zhongkui with our blessing," the Guide said. "A meditation cell has already been prepared for you. Until such time,"

Zhongkui put his fist over his heart and gave a quick bow, then turned and strode from the council chamber.

# 44

*Abode of the Guanzi*
*Qilian Mountains, China*

That night they ate a meal together with the Guanzi and her attendant, along with two old monks who also stayed in the cave complex. They sat around the large communal table in the main cavern. The meal was much like those they'd had at the monastery in the valley, eaten in silence followed by a closing prayer.

The Guanzi returned to her chambers after the meal, her attendant telling Rohini and her companions that she would see them in the morning. They spoke with the two old monks who lived there, learning that they were longtime residents. They were part of the group that formed the inner core of the society, which consisted of Daoist monks and nuns from all over the country. Many of them held positions of authority in other monasteries—these two were retired abbots themselves, who now spent most of their time in self-cultivation.

The following day after the morning meal, they sat with the Guanzi once again in her chamber. "Today I would like to present the basic teachings on self-cultivation we use in the society," she began. "Guangming, you may already be familiar with them, but I would also like to relate them to the experiences I had with the Elders. Jane, you may also be able to help in this process from the teachings you received from your mentor. I believe this will lead us more quickly down the path towards discovering the Elders' methods.

"In our society, we follow the general path laid down by *Tiany-inzi* which describes Daoist self-cultivation, and an eventual return to the Dao, as a five-stage process. The system begins with the first stage called Fasting and Abstention. This stage refers to the basics of building a good foundation conducive for self-cultivation. Fasting and Abstention refers to cleansing the body and emptying the mind. This has often been interpreted in moralistic terms, but it basically refers to engaging in a healthy balanced lifestyle, as well as abstaining from things which may lead one's mind astray or become a distraction to one's inner work.

"Instead of prescribed moralistic behaviors, I want you to think of this in terms of mental states or negative emotions which can cause us turmoil in our lives and prevent us from seeing reality clearly. We can think of negative thoughts and emotional states as mud stirred up in the mind. As it says in the *Daode Jing*, 'Can you wait quietly while your mud settles?' Just as muddy water will become clear when the sediment is allowed to settle to the bottom, the spirit or consciousness becomes clear when we learn to sit in stillness.

"The second stage is Seclusion, or withdrawing deep into the meditation chamber. This can be a physical seclusion, especially in the beginning stages of practice, when removing oneself from the many distractions of normal daily life can be beneficial, but it can also refer to a mental seclusion, a withdrawal from the emotional turmoil in our everyday lives which can pull us under, like a riptide at the seashore."

The Guanzi turned to Rohini. "That is why I asked your boyfriend to stay behind at the monastery, Rohini, he might be too much of a distraction for you." Rohini blushed as the Guanzi chuckled before continuing, "Just as we need to keep our meditation chamber free of clutter and dust, sweeping it often, so we must keep the heart free of distractions and worries. As it says in the *Huangting Jing, The Yellow Court Classic*, 'The spirit hut must be kept orderly and regulated.'

"Once we have developed some healthy lifestyle habits and begun the process of withdrawing from the drama of everyday life, we can begin to develop the third stage, called Visualization and Imagination. This refers to taming the mind and recovering our inner nature through meditation. First, we develop some degree of stability and concentration, and then we can turn that concentration towards the mind itself.

"When we have developed this stage sufficiently we move on to the fourth stage, Sitting in Oblivion. This is the quintessential form of Daoist meditation referred to as far back as the *Zhuangzi*. Sitting in Oblivion refers to letting go of the ego and the personal body and completely forgetting oneself in meditation.

"This leads us to the fifth and final stage; Spiritual Liberation, the spiritual pervasion of all existence, or returning to the Dao. These final two stages I believe are what lead to the abilities of the Elders. Forgetting the self as this distinct body, and allowing the consciousness to roam freely is a necessary step in being able to view distant realms, including the Elders' world. Once we can pervade existence, we are no longer strictly identified with this physical form. This is the transformation which leads to becoming a Pure Yang Spirit. As it says in the *Tianyinzi*, 'Those who pervade all existence are called Spiritual Immortals.' It seems this would also be an apt description of the Elders.

"In Daoism, we have two concepts that may shed light on the abilities of the Elders; alignment and returning. In our practice we attempt to align ourselves with the Dao, and align our bodies in meditation. We also speak of 'returning to the Dao.' But this returning refers not only to returning to the Dao, it also refers to returning to life from the Dao—Being returns to Non-Being, and Non-Being returns to Being in an endless cycle. We can see this clearly in the seasons.

"At the winter solstice for instance, we can see how the bright yang energy of the sun is at its weakest point, yet this is the time of its return, the time when it begins to grow again."

Hearing this, Rohini recalled another line from the *Daode Jing*,
All things spontaneously arise together
Residing in the world they must return
The Celestial Dao cycles round and round
Everything returns to its root

Returning to the root is tranquility.

"Very good, my dear, *Tai Shang Laojun* expressed this idea many times in the *Daode Jing*," the Guanzi said. "We also use this idea in meditation when we speak of the waterwheel or the celestial circulation. When the vital energy in the body rises up the spine, it also returns again to the lower abdomen in a cyclical motion. Often people make the mistake of attempting to force this movement, yet if we are aligned and tranquil, it will occur naturally. It grows, moving up the spine, or what we call 'traversing the narrow ridge,' until it reaches the Jade Palace among the nine peaks of the head.

"We often used the symbolic language of internal alchemy to describe these things. We may speak of creating the 'Elixir of Immortality' by 'setting up the cauldron and stoking the furnace,' or we speak of 'the green dragon and the white tiger.' But we will keep things simple. I will just teach you a simple formula, what we call the four alignments.

"The four alignments are the body, the four limbs, the breath, and the mind. As it says in the *Neiye*, 'Align the four limbs and keep your circulation and breathing tranquil. Unify your awareness and concentrate your mind, and your eyes and ears will not be over-stimulated. Do this and even the far-off will seem close at hand.'"

"Traditionally we have interpreted this phrase, 'the far-off' to refer to the Dao, but we might also think of it in terms of traveling as the Elders do," the Guanzi continued. "After all, it also says in the *Neiye* that, 'The vital essence of the universe gives life to all beings below and connects the stars above. When flowing freely between heaven and earth we call them ghosts and spirits, those who can store it within we call sages.' It also says, 'Ghosts and spirits pervade the universe not through their own power, but due to the ultimate refinement of the vital essence.'"

"It's striking how similar that is to what my mentor said of these things," Jane said.

"There is also an instruction from *He Xiangu* which is very similar to the warning the Elders gave me in my meditation," the Guanzi said.

"*He Xiangu*, the woman from the Eight Immortals?" Rohini said.

"That's right. In the *Nugong Zhengfa*, a text on self-cultivation written especially for women, she said, 'When the training is complete and the light is perfected, Earth Thunder resounds and the gates of heaven will open naturally. The Yang spirit may now leave and return. Initially it stays close at hand before venturing far-off, but one must take great care against getting lost at this stage. When the Yang Spirit is able to travel easily, visiting all the heavens, the true master comes, leading to final transformation as an Immortal. This is transcendence of the world.'"

Rohini was struck by how closely these lines from an ancient text seemed to mirror what she knew of the Elders. Her mind was starting to swim a little with all of this new information.

"I can see this has been enough for you to digest for the moment," the Guanzi said. We will talk more later."

They took a break from the Guanzi's teachings while Jingyi, the Guanzi's assistant, showed them around the rest of the cave complex. Some of the chambers were wholly natural, full of stalactites and stalagmites, while others had obviously been shaped and expanded by human hands. After lunch they met again with the Guanzi, Jingyi once again escorting them to her chamber and bringing tea as they began.

"This afternoon I would like to give you a brief teaching and then guide you through a meditation," the Guanzi began. She held up the stick she had been holding across her lap. "Do you know what this is?" she asked.

"The Jade Scepter," Guangming said.

"Yes," the Guanzi said, "but do you know what it is?"

"Only that it is a symbol of your authority as head of our society," Guangming replied.

"It is, yet it is also so much more," the Guanzi said. "It is true that since it was recovered from Dunhuang it has been handed down by my predecessors, but it is more than a symbol, it is also a guide. It was left to us by Guanyin and Zhongkui. The head appears to be common jade, yet there is something special about it. I don't know if it came from the Elders' world or if it has simply been imbued somehow with power, but it is no ordinary piece of stone. It has an inscription in ancient seal script, which describes a meditation practice which I will guide you through. But there is something more. This stone has a peculiar energetic quality which I have been able to sense. I believe it is because of the Elders' bloodline, which the four of us carry. What we call the bloodline of Zhongkui in our society.

"The inscription itself describes a method which sounds very much like the celestial circulation practice I mentioned before. It is quite concise. The first words—usually considered a title—say *Xingqi*, which we have taken to mean 'to circulate the vital breath' as this is how it is commonly used in later Daoist texts. The rest of the text goes on to describe this process. It says:

Circulating the Vital Breath
Breathe deeply, so that it will collect.
When it collects, then it expands.
When it expands, then it will descend.
When it descends, then it stabilizes.
When it stabilizes, then it will solidify.
When it solidifies, then it sprouts.
When it sprouts, then it will grow.
When it grows, it returns.
When it returns, it becomes heavenly.
The movement of Heaven is revealed in ascending.
The movement of Earth is revealed in descending.
Follow this method and live.
Go against this method and die.

"So, as you can see, it sounds very much like the celestial circulation. We breathe in and retain the breath, descending it to the abdomen, the lower dantian, and when we build a stable base, the qi ascends up the spine toward heaven with the inhalation, and then the qi descends from the head back down to the lower dantian with the exhalation. Following this method leads to health and longevity, breathing poorly and shallowly leads to ill health and premature death. This is how we would usually interpret these instructions, and it is quite true, as the experience of many Daoists has shown throughout history.

"But there is another way this inscription can be read—and, in light of the Elders' existence—I believe it is quite illuminating. The title for instance, could also be read as 'To Travel Energetically.'

"You mean it describes how to travel as the Elders do?" Jane said.

"Yes, I believe so. But I also believe that this method will not work for everyone, or at least not without many years of self-cultivation. As I said, I believe this stone itself holds a key. After the first time I followed the Elders in spirit to their world, I had trouble finding it again initially. In my meditations that followed, I was able to travel around the earth again, as I had before, but couldn't manage to find my way beyond.

"Then, in a flash of insight, I recalled the Jade Scepter, and a line of verse from an old legend of the Jade Maiden, who is sometimes associated with Guanyin. It reads,

> Flying high above
> I wander over rocks and clouds;
> The heavenly sprout grows without nourishment
> And its great virtue lasts forever.
> Immortals do not descend to earth for nothing,
> But to help humans according to their fate.

"The heavenly sprout reminded me of the Jade inscription and the rocks and clouds sounded like she could have been referring to different types of planets. I had not read the Jade inscription for quite some time, but as I read it again in this new light, its meaning changed completely. It was then that I sensed that the stone itself might also be part of the key.

"In my next meditation I sat with the scepter and held the jade in my hands. I sensed an energy there, subtly at first, with a different quality than I had ever felt before. I began my meditation and I left my body much more quickly and effortlessly than I ever had before. I was immediately drawn in a direction and when I followed that pull, I traveled immediately to the Elders' world. So, in addition to the method described by the inscription, I believe the energy of the stone acts as an aid to accomplishing the pure Yang spirit—and traveling as the Elders do—perhaps even directing the consciousness to their world like a homing device."

The Jade Scepter took on a new significance to Rohini. It seemed to shine brighter in her eyes. What before she had simply thought of as a cane topped with a jade knob now appeared almost like a magic wand. *It's amazing how much our perception shapes our reality.* The thought reminded her of a story her aunt Shanti told her.

One day in India, a man was walking home in the twilight when he saw a snake crossing the path ahead of him. Thinking it might be venomous, he jerked back suddenly. His heart began to race as adrenaline surged through his body, his senses now on full alert. He noticed the snake was not moving, so curious, he stepped closer. Looking around, he found a stick and used it to poke at the snake. Maybe it is dead, he thought to himself. As he poked at the snake, he realized it was just a piece of rope. He breathed a great sigh of relief and laughed at his own foolishness, then continued down the path toward his home.

But in this case the rope is actually a snake, Rohini thought.

"Yes, Rohini," the Guanzi said. The sound of her name brought Rohini's attention back to the present. "We also have a saying like this. We say, 'Bitten by a snake one morning, afraid of the rope by the well for ten years.'"

Rohini sat up straight. She could hardly believe her own ears. "But, how could you know what I was thinking?" she said.

"The Dao is mysterious," the Guanzi replied. "Come, let us begin."

They stood and followed the Guanzi to another doorway, on the opposite side of the room from the one they had come in. Her assistant Jingyi held the curtain open for them as they left the chamber, before following behind.

"Where are we going?" Rohini said as they began their ascent up another flight of stone steps.

"The Guanzi is taking us to the Guanyin Grottos to meditate," Guangming replied. Reaching the top of the stairs, they entered another chamber. It was much smaller than the Guanzi's chamber, slightly larger than the rooms they each stayed in below. A single candle set into a niche in the wall, provided the only light in the cave. As her eyes adjusted to the dimly-lit chamber, Rohini realized what she had initially taken for a table was actually a stalagmite rising from the floor of the grotto. Instead of coming to a point, the top formed a basin about a foot across, which was full of water. The floor of the chamber was highly irregular, with a pathway through it, curving around the basin. The basin was located in the center of the chamber, surrounded by smooth mineral deposits which were worn smooth on top from the many generations which had sat and meditated here before them. As she looked around the chamber in the flickering candlelight, she noticed what appeared to be ancient petroglyphs carved into the walls. In the dim light they were hard to make out completely, but they looked like faces or masks, and geometric patterns. There were also images of animals. In the dancing candlelight they almost appeared to be moving.

"Please, be seated," the Guanzi said, taking a seat. The rest followed suit with the exception of Jingyi, who remained standing near the entrance to the chamber, as there was only room for the four of them to sit. "As you can see, this place has been visited since ancient times. The prehistoric peoples of this area must have sensed its sacred character long before the Nine Scions of the Dragon ever existed, and even before the time of Laozi and Zhuangzi.

"This is called the Lower Guanyin Grotto. The other two chambers are above, each progressively smaller. We will begin our practice here. Please make yourselves comfortable, take a few deep breaths, and begin to relax your body and mind. Breathe in slowly and smoothly. Use your intention to guide the breath deep into the abdomen to the lower dantian, below the navel. Try to sense something there. The dantian can absorb energy continuously, it will never fill up, but eventually it will spread throughout the rest of your system. Keep the breath slow and smooth and keep the intention focused on the lower dantian."

They sat this way for quite some time before the Guanzi spoke again. "In the Daoist tradition we often speak of meditation in terms of setting up the cauldron and stoking the furnace. The cauldron refers to the lower dantian. Stoking the furnace can be as simple as turning the mind's intent toward the lower dantian, or it can be an elaborate visualization. The symbolism refers to turning the yang fire of the mind's intent associated with the heart and the middle dantian, combined with the breath to cook the elixir in the cauldron of the lower dantian associated with the water element. When you practice this for a while you will begin to feel a heat building up in the body and a sensation of movement. We compare this to steam rising from the cauldron, or say that jing is being refined or transformed into qi.

"I told you before that this chamber and those above are special, that is because they act as an external representation of what we visualize happening inside ourselves. I believe it may be due to the electromagnetic field here. The walls of the chamber contain a great deal of magnetite. We believe this allows for a certain degree of resonance between ourselves and the chamber. The water you see in the stalagmite is heated from below. The same is true of the lake below in the valley, although it only remains warm enough to prevent it from freezing in the winter.

"The mountain is still geologically active? Is there any danger it will erupt?" Jane asked, always ready to assess the potential risks in any situation.

"I suppose there is always that chance, dear," the Guanzi said, smiling. "But I don't believe it will happen anytime soon. While the valley below was formed by an old caldera, it is becoming less active as the years pass, not more. There used to be many vents which released gases in the past, but most no longer do. There has not been an eruption of any kind for several thousand years. Perhaps we are due? Wouldn't that be exciting!" she said laughing.

Rohini had to hand it to her; the Guanzi certainly knew how to keep a sense of humor. She had a way of making everything feel light and easy, like she just flowed through life in an effortless way. The Guanzi resumed her instruction.

"Now we will return to our meditation, but this time we will focus on becoming aware of the celestial circulation. Now, if we are successful in our meditations, we will be able to see it reflected in our surroundings.

"Close your eyes and return to your meditation. This time imagine your lower dantian like a cauldron of water. Imagine there is a flame below, which grows ever so slightly as you inhale. Just like a real fire, you must not blow on it too strongly, or too weakly. Let the breath be smooth and even in order to stoke the flames."

They sat with this image for several minutes, breathing quietly, before she spoke again, "Now I would like you to imagine that the water in the cauldron is starting to steam. It is not boiling, or even simmering, just imagine a steady vapor rising from the water. Imagine it rising up the spine as you inhale, up to the top of the head. As you exhale, imagine the energy falls down the front of the body. Each time it passes the lower dantian some of it gathers there before resuming the circulation."

They continued like this for quite some time. Rohini had lost all sense of time in the chamber. It was hard to tell whether it had been five minutes or an hour. At some point Rohini began to feel warm, then hot. Soon a light sweat began to bead on her skin. Then the Guanzi spoke again, "Open your eyes."

When she opened her eyes, Rohini saw steam rising from the water in the stalagmite. "It appears you were successful," the Guanzi said. "Did any of you feel a stirring, a movement in your lower abdomens? This is laying the foundation."

# 45

Later that evening after dinner, Rohini, Jane and Guangming sat at the large table in the lower chamber. "That was weird today, wasn't it?" Rohini said.

"You mean the Guanyin Grotto?" Jane said.

"Yes, do you think we really made the water hot or do you think the mountain just heats it up enough to steam every so often, like the geysers at Yellowstone?" Rohini said.

"I don't think the Guanzi would try to trick us that way," Guangming said. "And compared to what the Elders can do, heating up some water through meditation doesn't seem so far-fetched."

"I suppose you're right," Rohini replied, laughing. "It's amazing how much our expectations can change. How do you suppose it worked? How could we have interacted with the cave like that?"

"I was wondering that myself. The Guanzi said it contained a large amount of magnetite, didn't she? Do you guys know how birds are able to navigate?" Jane said.

"I would assume they use the sun and stars, just like we do, or else they learn by following their parents or other birds, why?" Guangming said.

"That may be partly right," Jane said. "But it's more complicated than that. Scientists made an interesting discovery years ago. They realized that birds could navigate in cloudy conditions as well, when neither the stars at night, nor the sun during the day were visible. They discovered that birds had an inborn compass, an ability to sense the electromagnetic field of the earth. This compass in their heads contains magnetite."

"So, we have magnets in our heads?" Guangming said skeptically.

"Not exactly, but they've since found that many other animals have some magnetite in their bodies as well, from bacteria all the way up to humans," Jane said. "The bacteria actually line up and move along the lines of the earth's electromagnetic field. Humans don't have the same types of structures as either birds or bacteria. From what I remember the magnetite is much more diffusely distributed throughout the brain, and potentially throughout the body. I don't think they know yet."

"I wonder if the magnetite helps form our body's electromagnetic field," Rohini said.

"It might, maybe that's what allowed us to resonate with the magnetite in the cave," Jane said.

"The shape of the grotto may play a role as well," Guangming said. "The human electromagnetic field and the electromagnetic field of the earth both form a torus. If the cave has its own field, I think it was probably toroidal as well."

"Isn't our field just like a big sphere?" Rohini said.

"Almost," Guangming said. "A torus is like a sphere which has collapsed in on itself, forming a channel through the center. Earth's electromagnetic field forms this shape. At the North Pole, it flows into the earth, and at the South Pole it flows outwards. The human field is the same; the top of the head is like the South Pole and the base of the spine is like the North Pole. The toroidal forms continue throughout the universe. The earth's field is embedded in the sun's electromagnetic field, the heliosphere, which is also toroidal and the heliosphere is in turn embedded in the larger field of the Milky Way Galaxy. Even the taiji symbol can be thought of this way, if we think of it three-dimensionally. If you imagine a channel connecting the two dots and the circle being a sphere, you get a torus."

"There we go with the microcosm and macrocosm again," Rohini said. "Maybe that's part of the idea of alignment the Guanzi was talking about. Maybe when the central channel of our field aligns with a larger one we can somehow level up to the next field? It's a bit mind-boggling. It's kind of making my head spin a little actually; I think I'll call it a night."

\* \* \*

The next day they met with the Guanzi in her chamber, where they sat sipping tea which Jingyi had graciously brought them again.

"Does anyone have any questions before we begin?" the Guanzi asked.

"We were wondering last night about the shape of the human energy field," Guangming began. "Isn't it spherical, and if so shouldn't we visualize the energy flowing more three dimensionally, instead of just in a circle?"

"Yes, it would be fair to say that is true, and one could certainly practice that way. We start with the Du and Ren, the energy channels on the front and back of the body because they form the major energy reservoir in the body, they in turn fill the rest of the body with energy. We want to make sure the body is replete with energy as a foundation. Once we have built the foundation by aligning the body, the breath, and the mind, and learn to dwell in stillness, the next stage of transformation can occur.

"When we begin the process of heating the cauldron, the steam we create rises up the central channel to the middle dantian, the Crimson Palace. This is the stage of refining jing into qi. Just as you felt a stirring in your lower dantian yesterday, today you may feel a stirring rising farther up your body. Today you will be meditating in the Middle Guanyin Grotto. This chamber is smaller than the lower grotto, so I will not be sitting with you, the three of you will fill the chamber.

"What I want you to focus on today is the sprouting that we mentioned from the inscription on the Jade Scepter. If you recall we spoke of the qi expanding, then descending, becoming stable and solid. Then it is said to sprout and grow. This is the stage we are focused on. I don't want you to try to force this process, but simply allow it to happen. After you begin to feel a stirring in the lower dantian, you should feel it begin to rise toward the middle dantian. It is possible you may feel uncomfortable during this process. You may feel nauseous or feel as though you have a knot in your stomach. If this happens simply place one hand on the area, keeping the other hand on the lower dantian, and allow the energy to find its way. Between your heritage of the bloodline and the meditation chamber itself, you should have no problems. We can discuss your experiences afterwards. If you have no further questions, Jingyi will take you now."

They followed Jingyi, taking the same route as the previous day, passing through the Lower Guanyin Grotto, where another flight of steps took them up to the middle grotto, which the Guanzi had referred to as the Crimson Palace. Rohini could see why. The walls of the middle grotto were the color of blood. She might have thought it was paint had it not been for the slight variations in the streaks of color where it was clear the minerals had precipitated down the walls. There were stalagmites and stalactites here as well, indicating the naturally occurring character of the chamber.

There were smooth areas similar to the lower grotto where it was clear others had sat before. The three took their places, crossing their legs on the rock seats. The Guanzi had been right, there was little space left after they sat, although the chamber didn't feel cramped. As she began to relax and follow her breath, Rohini felt a sense of spaciousness in the chamber, as though it were quite large, instead of being barely big enough to hold Rohini and her companions.

They began their meditation. Rohini focused on breathing deeply and smoothly into her lower dantian, and removing any extra tension from her body. As her breathing became more relaxed and smooth, it eventually became very fine. She turned her attention to the celestial circulation, allowing the energy to flow up her back on the inhalation and fall down the front of her body on the exhalation, passing by the lower dantian and energizing it with each pass. When she was ready, she turned her focus to her lower dantian and felt a stirring. She kept one hand on her lower dantian and placed the other above the navel, where she felt the stirring. After some time the stirring seemed to calm itself. But then she noticed it again. It had risen higher, closer to her solar plexus. It felt slightly uncomfortable at first, almost like heartburn or nausea as the Guanzi had mentioned. She placed her hand on the area and within a short time the sensation dissipated.

Soon after, a sensation began to arise again, higher still, in the area the Guanzi had described as the middle dantian, between her breasts. If the previous sensation had been akin to nausea, this was more like a panic attack. She began to feel like her heart was going to beat out of her chest, yet at the same time there was a stifling sensation like she couldn't breathe, but she realized she could; it was more of a mental or emotional sensation than a physical one. It was then that she realized what the sensation felt like, it was grief. Deep, heart-wrenching, grief. The pressure began to build and build until she felt like she would implode. Then she remembered the Guanzi's instruction again, and moved her hand up to her heart. Instead of dissipating, the pressure continued to build until she almost felt like crying out, then suddenly in a rush, she felt as though her heart exploded out of her chest. Where moments before she had felt an intense knot of pressure, she now felt as though her chest was empty and open; hollow like the crimson cave they sat in. A flood of tears began to pour down her cheeks as she sat silently crying, yet they were tears of joy. She felt a great sense of relief and a lightness of spirit she had never known before.

After an unknown period of time, Rohini opened her eyes as she sensed a brighter light in the cavern. Jingyi had returned to escort them back to their chambers. As she looked at her companions she saw her own experience reflected in their tear-streaked faces.

# 46

They didn't discuss their experiences of the Middle Guanyin Grotto that night. Rohini and her friends each seemed to be processing what had occurred, and the emotions which had been released. For Rohini, the experience had brought with it the recognition of a lot of unexpressed grief which she had unknowingly been holding on to for the last several years, ever since her mother had died, while Rohini was away at school, her freshman year of college.

She remembered it like it was yesterday. She had been sitting in her Psychology 101 class in a large lecture hall when she had felt her phone vibrate. She checked the display out of habit and saw that it was her dad's cell. She figured he'd leave a message, and he had. But he'd also immediately left a text, "Please call ASAP." Something was definitely up. She gathered her things and headed for the exit, whispering apologies as she made her way past the knees and backpacks of her classmates. Once out in the hallway, she had called her father and gotten the dreadful news.

Her mother had died suddenly. They weren't sure if it was a stroke or a heart attack. *Not that it mattered.* All she knew was that her mother was gone. She'd gone home immediately and packed a quick bag. Her father had already bought a plane ticket for her, which was waiting at the airport. She took the quick flight back to New York that night, arriving at LaGuardia ninety minutes later.

Her father picked her up at the curb. She'd just brought a carry-on, so she hadn't needed to wait for her bags. When he pulled up, he threw the car in park and jumped out, coming around to the passenger side and embracing her. The tears had flowed freely as they stood there, a pocket of shared grief amidst a flurry of activity as others came and went, each wrapped up in their own lives, oblivious to their pain.

They hadn't said much on the ride into the city. What was there to say? Her mother was gone. *She may as well have been abducted by aliens*, Rohini had thought. *She was snatched from us so suddenly.* Lying in her bed in the Abode of the Guanzi that night, the irony hadn't been lost on her. Rohini couldn't help smiling through her tears. In hindsight, she realized she hadn't cried about it since that day at the airport.

The next few days had been a blur. She'd helped her dad arrange the funeral and helped her aunt Priya make food for the wake. People had brought food as well, but they had felt the need to be good hosts. It had been a welcome distraction at the time, a way to avoid thinking about the reality of the situation. Yet cooking in her family's kitchen with her aunt hadn't been the best way to avoid it. There were many moments that reminded her of all the time she'd spent cooking with her mother in that very kitchen.

The next day after breakfast, the three followed Jingyi once more to the Guanzi's chambers. After their tea was served, they began the day's teaching. "I can see you all have experienced the Crimson Palace. When we begin to purify our energy and purify the heart, many old memories and unprocessed emotions will reveal themselves to us. For some, there is simply an energetic release, for others, we may be confronted by our own demons. These may take the form of regrets from our past or suppressed memories of traumatic events. As painful as it can be, it is a crucial step in the process of self-cultivation. I can see you all understand," she said looking at each of them in turn, her deep compassion evident in her expression.

Rohini looked from the Guanzi to the faces of her companions. They each exchanged a knowing glance. Perhaps one day they would be ready to talk about their experiences.

"Today we will be going to the Upper Guanyin Grotto, also known as the Jade Palace. This chamber corresponds to the upper dantian in the human body. It is often called the Third Eye and is thought of as the seat of wisdom, as well as where the spirit is refined leading eventually to a return to the Dao. This process first leads to the formation of the Pure Yang Spirit and the ability of the awareness to leave the body, and eventually I believe to the ability to travel as the Elders do. Since I myself haven't been able to accomplish this last part yet," she said with a twinkle in her eye. "I don't necessarily expect any of you to master this in such a short time. This is simply to help you awaken this process in your body and energy field.

"It would seem the Elders do not expect you to be able to travel yourselves when they return, which must mean they have the ability to take you with them. I wonder about this ability, especially as I wasn't able to follow them before. Perhaps being in bodily contact with them is the key. Alas, I fear I will have to proceed from my own accomplishment," she said, chuckling. "The Upper Grotto is even smaller than the Crimson Palace; only one person at a time will practice there. That is how we will proceed today. Each of you will spend a period of time in the chamber and when you have each finished we will meet again.

"The process you follow today will be similar to the last two. You will begin with the celestial circulation, energizing the lower dantian first. Then when you feel the stirring in the abdomen you will allow the energy to rise to the middle dantian in the chest. Eventually you will feel the energy continue to rise further. Follow the technique I told you about yesterday; placing a hand on the area to assist the energy in moving higher. Eventually, if you succeed in moving your awareness to the upper dantian and are able to hold your awareness there, you may feel a sense of spaciousness arise. You may lose awareness of yourself as an embodied being, falling into a state of oblivion. Alternatively, you may find yourself leaving your body behind, roaming freely around the earth. If this is the case remember the warnings of *He Xiangu* and do not wander too far. You will have many opportunities to explore this world and the realms beyond in the future. For now, just stay close.

"I am sure Guangming knows this story, but I'm guessing that you two have not heard it before," the Guanzi said, turning towards Rohini and Jane. "Like *He Xiangu, Li Tieguai* was another of the Eight Immortals. He is associated with healing as he carries a drinking gourd full of medicine, but it is also said that he descends to earth to fight for the oppressed and the needy. He is said to appear in the form of an old beggar who walks with the aid of an iron crutch, which is the meaning of his name—*Tieguai* means iron crutch.

"Li was originally known as Li Yuan and was considered quite handsome, before becoming an Immortal. One day he was traveling outside his body in meditation and intended to travel to heaven to meet with the Immortals. He told his apprentice, Li Qing to guard over his body for seven days and that if he had not returned in that time, that he should dispose of his body, as he would have ascended to heaven.

"Five days had passed when the apprentice received word that his mother was on her deathbed and wanted to see her only son, before she died. Li Qing was beside himself, not knowing what to do. He wanted to fulfill his mother's wishes, but he was afraid to leave his master's body unattended. He waited one more day, figuring that if his master didn't return on the sixth day, he wouldn't return at all. On the sixth day the apprentice cremated his master's body and hurried home to see his dying mother.

"Later that day the master Li Yuan returned from his spirit travel. His spirit searched for his body, but could find no sign of it, other than an urn full of ashes the apprentice had left in the master's meditation hut. Searching nearby, all the master's spirit could find was an old crippled beggar with an iron crutch, who was slowly dying of starvation. Li's spirit lingered nearby and as soon as the beggar died, Li's spirit entered his body. He was thereafter known as Iron Crutch Li. So, I suppose the moral of the story is that if you roam too far, we'll use your body for kindling!" the Guanzi said, laughing.

"But, in all seriousness," she said. "Please try not to wander far. From my own experience I can say that it is harder to return to your body the longer you are away. It takes a great deal of practice and requires gradually lengthening your journeys. As you will have to go to the chamber one at a time, Rohini you will be first. Take this," she said, handing Rohini the Jade Scepter. "Hold it in your hand during your meditation and try to sense its energy. Jingyi will escort you to the Jade Palace."

# 47

Rohini followed Jingyi. The first day hadn't been particularly troubling. It had actually been quite exciting. But after yesterday's experience in the Middle Grotto, she was feeling a bit more trepidation. The previous day had been quite intense and emotional. She hoped today would be gentler. She had thought people trying to kidnap her and blow her up were intense, but compared to her experience in the Crimson Palace, those events felt like something she'd seen in a movie. There had been so much water under the bridge in such a short period of time that those events were beginning to feel like distant memories.

Jingyi led her once more through the Lower Grotto, up the stairs to the Middle Grotto where they again passed through and out the other side. The passage to the Upper Grotto, the Jade Palace, was similar to the lower passages which connected the other grottos with the exception that the passage was much narrower, and the stairs much steeper. Jingyi left her at the Middle Grotto, handing her a candle.

She took the candle and ventured on ahead. As she entered the chamber she could understand why Jingyi had stopped when she had. The stairway led right into the small chamber, which consisted of a low shelf of rock to sit on like the lower chambers, but little other room. The walls of the chamber contrasted with the Crimson Palace. Instead of the streaked red walls which almost appeared to be covered in the blood of the earth itself, this chamber was streaked in shades of green and white. The mineral formations in the chamber—the stalagmites and stalactites—were all connected, forming small jade columns. She set the candle down on a small flat spot in front of her which showed traces of wax from meditators who had entered the chamber before her, and settled in. She set the Jade Scepter across her lap, holding the jade knob in her hand.

She began as she had the previous days, relaxing her body and mind, before beginning the celestial circulation exercise. She followed her energy around her body, up the back and down the front of her body. It felt different somehow today. She wasn't sure how at first, until she realized that the qi flow felt like it was just rotating around a sphere or an egg. If she thought about it, she could feel her body, yet if she let her mind just dwell, her sense of her body in space became fuzzy.

Letting her awareness rest on the sensation, she began to feel as though she were a sphere of energy. She began to feel the telltale stirring in her lower abdomen, or what she would have thought of as her lower abdomen, now it was just somewhere in the lower half of the sphere of energy she perceived herself as. The energy began to rise, first to her solar plexus, then to her heart.

She felt a brief moment of panic, afraid of experiencing the same overwhelming emotions of the previous day's meditation, and for a moment it felt as though the experience would repeat itself. Then, just as suddenly the feeling subsided and she realized the energetic stirring had passed the heart and was moving closer to her throat. She moved a hand up to the area to help it along. *How strange, I still have hands, but I don't feel like I have a body.*

After some time, she felt a pressure begin to build. This time it was at the base of her throat. She felt like she was gagging on something. It was almost as though her throat was in danger of closing, like she was having an anaphylactic reaction, yet her airway remained open. She realized it was more of an energetic or emotional sensation than a physical one, as with her experience the previous day. At first, she thought it was just the fear of gagging or not being able to breathe, but soon the sensation grew. She continued to breathe and allowed her energy to continue circulating, but the sensation grew.

It was fear; fear of conflict, fear of speaking her mind, fear of hurting others. She had always kept to herself emotionally, usually choosing to think things through herself rather than talk things out with other people. She had always chalked it up to being introverted, but now she realized she had been hiding, afraid to expose herself. She also realized this too was connected to her mother's death.

She began to remember what she'd been like when she was younger, when her mother was still alive, and realized this habit of emotional isolation had only been a tendency before her death, but had become a habit and a coping mechanism since. As these threads of her psyche continued to unravel, she had other insights into her personality, as well as a new level of understanding about many of her relationships with others.

She realized the sense of closeness she had felt with Jane, whom she had begun to think of as the older sister she had never had, was deeper than that. Being honest with herself, she had almost come to rely on her like a mother. She trusted Jane to protect her. As she began to focus her thoughts on Jane a sense of relief and safety flooded through her and then something unexpected happened.

It was like she had suddenly noticed something that was always right in front of her. She slipped into a dreamlike vision. She saw herself in a hallway which she knew represented her mind. It felt familiar, like she had walked down this hallway many times but there was a door there which she'd never noticed before. *I wonder what's behind that door*. Then a new sensation began.

It was a deep dread. The realization made her senses come alive as a shudder passed through her, every nerve ending tingling. She felt like a child afraid to leave her bed for fear that the monster lurking underneath would reach out and grab her ankle as soon as her foot touched the floor. The more she thought about the door, the more her terror grew. But she had to know. *What is behind that door?* In her mind she reached for the door, grasping the knob. The sensation grew in intensity until she felt as though she was screaming silently inside, or had she actually screamed? She couldn't be sure. As soon as she opened the door, the sensation began to pass.

The room was dark. She didn't recognize it at first, but she knew she'd seen it before. Then it all came flooding back. It was one of the blank pages in her mind. One of the nights she'd lost. But now she remembered. She remembered it all.

She'd been at a party. She'd gotten drunk. Then the memories she'd lost, the parts she'd hidden away—even from herself—returned. She had gone to a bedroom and passed out. At some point she had stirred, and realized she wasn't alone. Someone was pulling her clothes off. She had struggled to regain consciousness, but kept slipping in and out. She tried to move, tried to stop him but she could hardly move. She'd tried to say something, tried to scream, but the most she could muster was a mumble. He'd gotten her naked and his hands had been all over her. A feeling of revulsion swept over her as she felt the sensations all over again. Then the room suddenly flooded with light as the door burst open, a figure silhouetted in the open doorway. She couldn't see the figure's features clearly, but she realized she knew who it was. It was Jane.

"Get away from her now!" she heard Jane say.

"Get the fuck out of here, this is none of your business," he'd snarled.

Jane immediately walked over and decked him. He got back up on wobbly legs and tried to grab Jane. They grappled, crashing into a dresser and then the wall, before Jane was able to land a quick kick to the crotch, doubling him over. Jane took advantage of the opening that left her and grabbed him around the head with both hands in a clinch, bringing his head down as she drove a knee into his face. That finished it. He fell to the floor and didn't move again, at least not while they were there. Rohini could remember the aftermath clearly now. She had continued to drift in and out of consciousness, but Jane had somehow gotten her dressed and gotten her home. The next morning she'd woken up none the wiser.

Jane had said she'd been guarding her, but she'd had no idea. The morning after had been the day that Rohini had realized she had to stop her self-destructive behavior. Although she couldn't remember what had happened, it had still impacted her. *It was Jane that was there for me, years before I even knew she existed.*

Eventually these new memories and insights passed. There were tears on her cheeks, but her mouth had formed a beatific smile. She felt light and free. Free of the doubt; free of the unknown possibilities that had haunted her. She was so deep into her meditation that through it all she hadn't moved a muscle. Soon her awareness returned to her energy. It now felt as though it had passed into the center of her skull. She felt as though she herself were inside her own skull. At first it was like a soft light filtered through an opaque surface, like frosted glass. Then the light began to flicker and brighten, slowly at first, then progressively faster until the light once again appeared constant. As the light continued to brighten, her sense of space changed.

First, she felt as though the sphere she inhabited was the size of her head and that the tiny spark of her awareness was her true self. Then this sphere expanded. Slowly at first, then gradually accelerating until it seemed like infinite space in all directions. Then in a flash, a new sense of space emerged, and with it an image. She saw a flickering light like a candle flame and a figure sitting in a stone chamber. It felt familiar somehow. Then she realized she was seeing herself— her own body sitting in the Jade Palace.

Her sense of self was subtle, fuzzy, almost non-existent. She felt as though she were seeing the chamber from multiple angles, multiple vantage points all at once, unless she focused on something in particular. Then she felt more definite, more distinct, if only slightly. The thought occurred to her that it was almost like the electron shell in an atom. *Maybe this is what non-locality is like. But if I'm non-local, I'm not tied to my present location.* As the realization hit her, it became true; she was free!

She felt a sense of joy and freedom, but also peace like she had never known. In an instant her awareness had expanded out of the cave and she found herself in the sky, flying high about the Abode of the Guanzi. She was aware of the mountain peaks, and saw the valley below, then the entire Qilian Range. She recalled the route they had taken through the mountains, and just as suddenly she was there, soaring above it back towards the Rainbow Desert and Zhangye.

*Amazing! This must be what the Guanzi described.* But thinking of the Guanzi she was also reminded of the Guanzi's warning. *I'd better not wander too far.* Then she heard it, although she wasn't sure her hearing was accurate. It was like a thought in her mind.

"Rohini, there is danger. You must return to your body."

She saw an indistinct shape glowing in the sky in front of her. At first, she took it for a small cloud catching the light of the sun, but as she focused on it, it began to change, becoming more distinct. She saw a face begin to form, then a body. The figure pointed to the valley below. "Look."

She turned her awareness from the cloud-like apparition to the temple below. What was she seeing? It was hard to tell at first. There were figures moving in the valley below. They were in a semi-circle around the temple, moving closer. The thought hit her that it was like a noose tightening around it. *I need a closer look.* Then she *was* closer and the realization of what she was seeing dawned on her. The dozen or so figures were dressed in black—like the men who'd tried to kidnap her—armed with assault rifles and closing in on the temple.

It was then she understood the warning. As her thoughts returned to the apparition it was there in front of her again. "Yes," she heard in her mind. "Go now." She simply thought of her body in the cave and she was there again. She saw her body seated in the cave, and then she was back in her body.

Her body felt heavy and solid, like a statue. Then she realized someone was gently shaking her on the shoulder. She opened her eyes to the dimly lit chamber. It was Jingyi. "Come!" she said, somewhat breathlessly. "He has returned!"

"Who?" Rohini said, confused. "Who's returned?"

"Zhongkui!" Jingyi said.

Rohini was fully alert now. She uncrossed her legs and stepped down off her seat, following Jingyi back down the steps through the Guanyin Grottos until at last they were back in the Guanzi's chamber. She saw Jane, Guangming, and the Guanzi who was standing with them, along with a fourth person whom she didn't recognize, yet he seemed familiar. They looked up at her approach and when she saw his eyes, she knew. He was the apparition she'd seen in the clouds.

# 48

Jane, Guangming, and Jingyi were sitting with the Guanzi sipping tea and chatting. They were curious to see what Rohini would experience in the Upper Grotto. The Guanzi told them that it would probably be unlike anything they had experienced before.

"We should probably retrieve her before too long," the Guanzi was saying, when suddenly Jingyi spit out her tea, startling them all. They all looked at her wondering what had happened, then realized she was staring at something across the chamber. They all turned to see a man standing there; from his dress he appeared to be an Elder.

"Hello Sinéad, it's been too long," he said, looking at Jane. She leapt up and crossed the chamber, embracing him in a hug.

"Where have you been for so long? I was afraid you weren't coming back," Jane said. Then turning to the others, she said, "It's my mentor, he's back!"

"Zhongkui?" the Guanzi said. "Is it really you?"

"Yes, I am Zhongkui. My apologies, Daozhang," he said bowing. "Are you the Abbess here? Have the grottos become a temple?"

"Yes, you could say that. It's quite a long story, I'm afraid," the Guanzi said. "So, then it is true, you are an Elder."

"I was an earthling once, but yes, I am known as an Earth Elder, having become Immortal many centuries ago," Zhongkui replied.

"I encountered your charge on my way here, Sinéad. She has made remarkable progress in her self-cultivation. Is she in the upper grotto?" Zhongkui said.

"Oh, Rohini! Jingyi, can you please fetch her?" the Guanzi said. Jingyi left the chamber to summon Rohini from her meditation.

"I also saw danger," Zhongkui said. "There is a temple in the valley below, there were soldiers approaching it. We must warn them. If they use the tunnel they should be able to escape in time."

"You mean the tunnel from Tianyinzi's cave?" the Guanzi said. "I'm afraid it is no longer there, or if it is no one knows how to access it."

"I can show you the way," Zhongkui said. "Can you contact the monastery to warn them? If they can make their way to the cave, we can get them into the tunnel."

"I can," she said. "One moment." The Guanzi stepped behind the screen on the dais, from where the light seemed to emanate. "Please, Guangming, give me a hand, would you?"

As Guangming followed the Guanzi he saw there was a perch with a raven tied on a tether behind the screen, as well as a window which had been mounted into a hole in the cave wall. The Guanzi bent over a small table and wrote off a quick message which she rolled up and placed in the small tube attached to the raven. "Please open the window, would you, Guangming?" she said. She gave the raven a gentle pat on the head and said, "Go quickly, my little one!" and let it go.

Guangming closed the window and they returned to the others as Jingyi and Rohini entered the chamber.

"It was you in the sky, wasn't it?" Rohini said. "You're Zhongkui."

"Yes, Rohini. I was surprised to encounter you out of body. Your progress is quite remarkable," Zhongkui said. "But now we must hurry if we are to help those at the temple. Do you have any weapons here, a sword perhaps?"

"I've got a handgun in my pack downstairs," Jane said.

"We have swords, staffs, and guandao. No firearms, I'm afraid, we've never had a need for them," the Guanzi said. "One of the chambers downstairs is a small armory. But where is the tunnel?"

"Come, I'll show you," Zhongkui said.

They started down the stairs, Zhongkui leading the way. As they entered the main chamber, Zhongkui did a double take as they passed the altar, before continuing past. There were more vital matters to attend to. "Which room is the armory?" he asked.

"That one," the Guanzi said, pointing.

"Grab whatever you feel most comfortable using," Zhongkui said as they entered the armory. "An unfamiliar weapon could be more of a liability than an asset."

"Sounds like someone else I know," Rohini said, nudging Jane with her elbow.

There were racks against the walls holding an assortment of traditional Chinese weapons; mainly staffs, spears, and swords, as well as a few of the Chinese halberds known as guandaos. Rohini grabbed a staff, Guangming chose a guandao, and the Guanzi picked up a sword. Jane had gone to her chamber to grab her gun, but she quickly rejoined them, grabbing a sword as well.

"Have you kept up your practice, Sinéad?" Zhongkui said, as he saw her grab a sword.

"Not as much as I'd like, Mentor. I'm still much better with this," she said patting the gun in her shoulder holster.

"Wait, you two know each other?" Rohini said. "You didn't tell me you knew Zhongkui,"

"I didn't realize I did. This is my Elder mentor, Rohini. He never called himself Zhongkui. I only knew him as my mentor. I'd never even heard the name Zhongkui until Guangming told us about the society.

"And Sinéad, is that your real name?" Rohini said.

"Sinéad MacGowan, in the flesh. It's the Irish version of Jane Smith," Jane replied.

Hearing the commotion, the two old monks had come out of their chambers.

"What's happening?" one said. "Why are you arming yourselves? Are we under attack?"

"Not here. The temple in the valley," Guangming said. "We're going to try to evacuate them through the old tunnel. Zhongkui knows the way."

The two shared a confused look, and then were even more startled when they saw Zhongkui step out of the armory. Their first instinct was to begin prostrating themselves before him, but he would
have none of it. "Please, that's not necessary and we have much grav-
er matters to attend to," he said, helping the old monks up from the
floor.

"Please Guanzi," Guangming said. "Stay here. We can't risk losing you."

"He's right," the old monk said. "Let the young ones go. Stay
here and let us protect you."

"You're probably right," the Guanzi said. "I guess I'm not as
spry as I used to be, this sword feels much heavier than I remember,"
she said, laughing.

Zhongkui led the others out of the chamber and back towards the
stairs, descending again. Rohini, Jane and Guangming hadn't been
below the main chamber before. Rohini wondered what they would
find. As they descended the stone steps in the lantern light, it became
clear that the lower level was much deeper. It took longer to reach the
chamber below. It was similar to the main chamber above in that it
appeared to be a naturally occurring cave which had been enlarged in
places. It seemed to be a store room as there were large bags of grain
and ceramic jars on shelves, as well as crates and boxes piled around
the perimeter of the chamber.

"Here, we must move these," Zhongkui said. Setting down the
lantern he had been carrying, he began to move a stack of boxes out of
the way. Grabbing the lantern again, he held it up towards the ceiling.

"It must be here somewhere," he said. "Ah, there it is."

It was faint in the dim lantern light, but from where she stood
Rohini could just make it out; the Big Dipper was carved into the
ceiling of the cave. She watched as Zhongkui reached up and pressed
on either side of the handle. Nothing happened.

Rohini remembered the chamber at the monastery below with
the figure pointing to the Dipper on the ceiling and what the abbot had
said about the two invisible stars along the handle, "The attendants,"
she said.

"Yes, Rohini. The secret stars of the Dipper. This must not have been used in many years if no one here knows of it. Let's hope it still works," Zhongkui said, pushing again, this time straining harder. Again, nothing happened.

"I hope we've got a Plan B," Jane said.

Zhongkui moved back to the wall where he had cleared a space. Closing his eyes, he reached out with his free hand. There was a muffled grinding sound as a section of wall slid aside, revealing a dark void beyond. Rohini stood still, mouth agape. "Careful, you'll catch flies like that," Jane said, snapping her fingers in front of her face.

"Let's go," Zhongkui said, diving into the passageway; the others followed, hot on his heels.

# 49

Gruber's team waited for sundown for their insertion. They had been breathing pure oxygen for the last half hour in the belly of the Transall C-160, in preparation for their jump. High Altitude Low Opening jumps were a specialty of Gruber's team. When not on assignments they practiced the protocol over and over until their jumps had become like clockwork.

After meeting at their rally point in the far end of the valley and stowing their parachutes, they quickly made their way toward the temple compound in the twilight. Staying off the main trail, they fanned out through the orchards, closing in on three sides; the cliffs at the rear of the temple would prevent anyone escaping that way.

Their orders, as usual, called for minimum necessary force—not that they expected much resistance from a bunch of old monks at a mountain temple. They were to secure their targets, then get out quickly. Innocents they encountered would be left unharmed—if cooperative—but silenced if necessary.

Securing the main gate as well as one small side entrance they'd found, the raid began. They blew the lock on the gate with minimal noise using a small shaped charge. Once inside, the plan was simple: roust anyone they encountered and herd them all into a central location until they located their targets.

Once they'd located their targets, they'd leave, disappearing into the night. The monks would have nothing to go on and a simple snatch and grab in the remote wilds of the Qilian Mountains wouldn't be a high priority for the local police, especially if their targets were trying to keep a low profile. Gruber assumed their disappearance might go completely unreported, but a massacre would undoubtedly result in unwanted attention.

If all went according to plan they'd leave nothing but boot prints and take only their targets. It had become a bit of an informal motto for their team after one of the American members told Gruber about the hiking saying: Leave only footprints, take only photographs.

As they began searching the outer ring of buildings, they hadn't encountered anyone yet. *They may all be in a central hall somewhere. Perhaps we are just in time for dinner.* Ops always made Gruber hungry.

# 50

Jimmie was summoned to the dining hall for dinner and had just begun eating when he noticed a monk rushing towards the Abbot. The monk leaned down and whispered something in the abbot's ear. *Something must be up*, Jimmie thought. *I hope Rohini is safe*. Jimmie saw the abbot's eyes widen slightly and the hair stood up on the back of Jimmie's neck. The abbot whispered something back to the monk who rushed out of the building as quickly as he'd come. Then the abbot stood.

"Your attention, please, the temple is under attack by unknown intruders. They are heavily armed. As you know, we are not. I assume they are after our guests. We must protect them, as well as the Guanzi, at all costs. They must not know where they have gone. We'll retreat towards the cave of Tianyinzi where we'll hide our remaining guest. The Guanzi has sent word that they have found the way into the old tunnel which leads there. Let us hope that if all these intruders find are a bunch of old monks, they will leave us in peace. My brothers and sisters, please be vigilant. Try not to provoke these intruders, but we must defend the Guanzi. As long as she lives, so does the society. Go now."

Everyone stood and made their way out of the dining hall. Jimmie was impressed at the calm, orderly manner of the monks and nuns as they left. The abbot and another of the senior monks approached Jimmie. "Come this way."

\* \* \*

Rohini and the others followed Zhongkui through the tunnel. They'd been traveling at a steady jog for about fifteen minutes. As the tunnel sloped downhill, they were making quick time. *It shouldn't be long now*, Rohini thought. *I hope we're in time.* As it happened, they were close. Zhongkui slowed suddenly as did the rest of the group.

"What is it?" Jane said.

"There are small openings along this part of the tunnel which look out over the temple; we should be able to see if the soldiers have entered the temple yet from here," Zhongkui said. "Here's one," he said, leaning into a small window-like opening in the side of the tunnel. "They're already inside. Sinéad, take a look. Tell me what you see."

"It looks like they're closing the noose, working their way in from the periphery," Jane said. "They'll gather everyone in a central location to make sure they haven't missed anyone."

"Yes, I agree. Fortunately, that will work in our favor. It will take them a little time and unknown to them they'll be flushing everyone our way. But we must hurry," Zhongkui said, beginning down the tunnel again.

As they passed another of the window-like openings, they heard a sound which sent a chill down Rohini's spine: gunfire. "Jimmie!" she said. "We've got to get down there." They picked up the pace.

After what felt like an eternity to Rohini, but was only moments, they skidded to a halt at what looked like a dead end. Zhongkui held up his lantern near the wall, illuminating it. In the circle of light was a lever which Zhongkui grasped. *Fingers crossed*, Rohini thought.

This time the mechanism worked. As Zhongkui pulled down on the lever, a doorway opened in the cave wall. "Quietly now," Zhongkui said as he led them into the passage. They'd gone only a few steps when they ran into a startled Abbot and a few of the older monks and nuns huddled in Tianyinzi's cave.

"Come, into the tunnel," Zhongkui said. The monks stared at Zhongkui as they passed, but followed his direction. "We heard gun fire, Long Daozhang. What's happened?" Guangming said.

"I'm afraid some of our fiercer brothers sought to challenge the intruders. We had almost been cut off from reaching the cave, but the brothers from Wudang came to our aid. They killed two of the intruders and ran back to help the others. Your friend Jimmie went with them," the abbot said. As he spoke, more gunfire could be heard outside.

"How many people were at the temple, Abbot?" Jane said.

"There should only be about a dozen left after us. Please get them all to safety, if you can," the abbot said.

"OK. Go on into the tunnel, Abbot. It still leads to the Abode of the Guanz. We'll get everyone to safety," Guangming said.

"Be safe, all of you," Long Daozhang said, before ducking into the passageway.

"We've got to find the others and get them into the cave," Jane said. Even with Zhongkui's skill we'll be no match for so many guns. How many do you think there are?"

"I thought I saw at least a dozen in my meditation," Rohini said.

"That still probably leaves at least ten then. I'd be OK with those odds if we weren't bringing knives to a gunfight," Jane said. "But as it is..."

"I will create a diversion, drawing their attention away from the cave. If you see them approach the cave before I return, close the passage and retreat," Zhongkui said. "I will return by other means if necessary." Then he was gone, running deeper into the compound.

"Meet back here in five minutes," Jane said. "Rohini, someone needs to stay here."

"No way, Jane, I'm going with you. I've got to find Jimmie," Rohini said, unable to hide the worry in her voice.

"I'm sorry, Rohini, but no," Jane said, grabbing her by the shoulders. "Look at me. If he's out there, we'll find him, but someone has got to stay here. If we get cut off, we've got to get that cave closed to cover our escape and protect the others."

"Alright, Jane. I don't like it, but you're right," Rohini said. "Now, go find Jimmie."

Jane and Guangming jogged off into the night looking for the remaining Daoists, moving from building to building, shadow to shadow. As they encountered stragglers they directed them to the cave.

After a minute they heard a commotion off in the night. *It must be Zhongkui*. Rohini heard shouting and gunfire which were quickly silenced. There was a sudden flash followed quickly by a boom which split the night. *Please let them all come back.*

Moments later she saw several people running towards the cave. It was more of the Daoists, but there were still several missing, and still no Jimmie. "Have you seen Jimmie?" She asked, as she ushered them into the passageway at the rear of the cave, but no one had seen him. Then she heard others coming—she recognized Guangming, but he wasn't alone, he was followed by a larger figure. *Who is that?* she thought, before realizing what she was seeing—it was Jane carrying someone. As they got closer the image became clearer; Jane had Jimmie in a fireman's carry, her left arm looped around one of his legs, holding onto his arm, leaving her right arm free to use her gun. She was running as fast as she could under his weight, the strain showing on her face as she passed through streaks of moonlight.

Rohini ran out to meet them, but Jane shooed her back. "Rohini, I've got him. Get back in the cave. They're coming."

They hurried back through the hermit's cave and into the tunnel, "Watch his head," Rohini said, as Jane shuffled sideways through the doorway at the back of the cave.

"We're clear, close it, Rohini," Jane said.

"But what about Zhongkui?"

"Believe me, he'll be fine." Jane said.

"Don't move!" Two men in black tactical gear had slipped quietly into the cave behind them. In the faint lantern light of the tunnel, they were like ghosts, except for the very real guns they held levelled at the trio. Rohini heard a wet gurgling sound as a sword tip suddenly sprouted from one of the men's throats, followed by a spray of blood as the sword was quickly withdrawn. That was all the distraction Jane needed. She raised her gun and fired, taking out the other masked man with a single shot to the head.

The two men fell almost in unison. Zhongkui stood behind them, blood dripping from his sword. "Let's go," he said, stepping over the fallen bodies of their pursuers.

# 51

Rohini pulled the lever closing the hidden passageway as soon as Zhongkui cleared the door. As it slid closed Rohini rushed to Jane, who with Guangming's help was laying Jimmie down on the ground.

"Oh, Jimmie, what did you do?" Rohini said, as she knelt next to him. "What happened, Jane?"

"He's been shot. I don't know how many times. I didn't have a chance to look him over out there," Jane said. "Guangming, get that light over here."

As Guangming held the lantern closer, Rohini could see the blood soaking the front of Jimmie's shirt. Jane began pulling it up to determine the severity of his wounds. "Shit," she hissed. "That doesn't look good at all." Rohini's heart leapt into her throat when she saw the extent of his wounds. His chest and stomach were awash in blood. It looked like he'd been shot at least three times, maybe more.

"He's still got a pulse," Jane said, feeling for his carotid artery. "But it's fading fast. What I wouldn't give for a med kit. Give me your shirts, now, both of you; we've got to get this bleeding stopped."

Rohini and Guangming dropped their jackets and stripped off their shirts. Rohini had a tank top on under the flannel shirt she'd been wearing; Guangming was bare to the waist. They handed their shirts over before putting their jackets back on. They'd be no use to Jimmie or anyone else if they got hypothermia.

Jane got to work. She tore the bottom half of Rohini's shirt into three strips, taking one and folding it over several times before placing it on Jimmie's chest wound and binding it with Guangming's shirt. She repeated the same process with a second piece, binding it with the top half of Rohini's shirt, tying the sleeves together over a wound on Jimmie's abdomen. Seeing she still needed one more dressing, she dropped her coat and took off her own shirt, tearing it as she had Rohini's, and repeated the process once more.

As they shifted Jimmie to one side to slip the third wrapping under his back, she noticed a large exit wound on his lower back; it didn't look good. It was too close to the spine for comfort. *If he makes it out of here at all, he's definitely done with action movies,* Jane thought. She turned and looked up at Zhongkui.

"I understand," Zhongkui said. He closed his eyes for a moment. "The Guanzi is sending the fastest runner they've got with a medical kit. If Jimmie can be moved, we should keep heading up the tunnel, he'll reach us sooner that way."

"I'd like to, but he's got a nasty exit wound on his lower back. I don't want to move him again until we can get him stabilized. Is there anything else you can do?" Jane said.

"My skills lay elsewhere, I'm afraid," Zhongkui said. "I've always had more of a knack for destruction than healing. If he were possessed it would be another matter, but I'm afraid bullets aren't the kind of extraction I'm skilled at. We each have our own gifts."

"Wait, if you can't heal his body, can you move the bullets out? Can't you move them the way you moved the door?" said Rohini.

"It's possible," Zhongkui said after considering it for a moment. "My only reservation is that we could cause more damage pulling them back out. Let me see if I can sense them well enough to see if it is safe." He knelt down and looked at Jimmie's body for a moment, then held out his hand. "There is a bullet lodged in his chest still and one in his abdomen. The third has gone completely through, resulting in the wound on his back. The bullet in his chest appears safe, it's lodged in the muscle and doesn't seem to be affecting his breathing, but I'm afraid attempting to remove the bullet from his abdomen would risk more damage, it's right next to an artery."

Rohini had been listening to Zhongkui, but her attention returned to Jimmie as he began to stir. His eyes flickered open, and a small gasp left his throat. "Jimmie, can you hear me?" Rohini said, as she rested her hand gently on the side of his head.

His eyes found her face. "Rohini," he croaked. "You're safe."

"What were you doing out there? You should have hidden with the abbot," Rohini said.

"I was, but when two of the monks from Wudang went out to fight, I had to go help them. I figured we could buy the others some time."

"Always trying to play the hero, huh? But this isn't the movies, Jimmie. Those are real guns out there." Rohini said.

"Yeah, might not have been one of my best ideas," Jimmie said, his voice growing quieter.

The sound of footsteps in the tunnel drew everyone's attention, along with a light flickering in the distance. *The runner! Thank God, he's almost here*, Rohini thought.

But her attention returned to Jimmie, as she heard a gagging sound. Rohini saw blood sputtering out of his lips. "Oh God, he's choking! Help me." They rolled him onto his side to allow the blood to clear his airway before he asphyxiated, but it was no use, he was bleeding out. After a deep gasp, Jimmie's body fell still. Jane put her fingers back on his pulse as Rohini looked to her expectantly. She met Rohini's eyes, and shook her head. "I'm sorry, Rohini."

"No!" Rohini cried, cradling Jimmie's head in her lap, her pants and hands covered in his blood.

# 52

Bartholomew Simms was ensconced in the back of his Bentley limo. He'd just left his estate on his way into the city, when he received the call.

"Gruber, what news have you got for me?"

"I'm afraid we were too late, sir. If they were there, they must have moved on. There was no one there but a bunch of monks," Gruber said.

"That's unfortunate. Keep looking. They couldn't have gotten far. They should be easy to spot in the mountains if they're still on horseback," Simms said.

"We've covered the whole mountain with drones. There are no heat signatures anywhere. We'll keep looking, sir, but there's something else. I don't think these were ordinary monks. Not only did a few of them resist, they actually killed several of our men," Gruber said.

"What? Were they armed?" Simms said.

"They were only armed with swords, but they definitely knew how to use them. I've never seen their like," Gruber said. "I thought they only knew how to fight like that in the movies. There was also an explosion during the raid so with that and the bodies; we thought it best to destroy the temple to cover our tracks. Fortunately, with their energy infrastructure, we were able to make it look accidental. Unless they get some real demolitions experts in there, the authorities shouldn't suspect anything."

"Good. I've always appreciated your ability to deal with unforeseen challenges, Gruber," Simms said. "Keep looking. We'll move ahead with our plans in the meantime. Is everything still on track?"

"Yes, sir."

"Excellent."

# 53

The runner arrived less than a minute after Jimmie's last breath, but there was nothing to be done. They remained in the tunnel for some time as Rohini grieved, until a large explosion shook the tunnel, showering them with dust and small rocks.

"We'd better move," Jane said. "If there are any more of those, this tunnel might not hold. Come on, Rohini," she said, grabbing her by the arms and helping her up.

"What about Jimmie?" Rohini said.

"Don't worry," Zhongkui said. "I will bring him." He began to pick up Jimmie's body, Guangming helping him.

"I was worried there for a moment you might make him a *jiangshi*," Guangming said, after they'd walked a short distance up the tunnel. "But they must just be a myth, right?"

"*Jiangshi* are quite real, at least they were in my day," Zhongkui said. "But I am more than capable of carrying him back to the grottos, and I assume it would be quite upsetting to Rohini if I animated his corpse."

"I don't think any of us could handle it right now," Guangming said.

Arriving back at the storeroom, Rohini's gaze drifted up to the faint impression of the Dipper Stars as they passed under them. *I hope you're on your way, sweet Jimmie.*

"Jane, take Rohini, we'll take care of things," Guangming said as Zhongkui closed the passage behind them.

"Alright, let me know if you need me. Do we have any way to know if they're heading this way? Do you have lookouts or something?" Jane said.

"I'll send out my awareness from time to time," Zhongkui said. "But I believe they are preparing to leave. We are safe for now."

Rohini was in a daze. She let Jane lead her upstairs to her room. She helped Rohini clean up and found her some clean clothing. Several hours later she left Rohini's room and ran into Guangming.

"How is she doing?" Guangming said.

"She finally went to sleep. She's been alternating between crying and shock," Jane said. "What's happening?"

"Zhongkui was right. The soldiers have left," Guangming said. "They were picked up by a helicopter in the valley a short time ago."

"Hopefully it's for good. We should lay low for a few days at least. If they're still looking for us I'd hate to be caught out in the open," Jane said. "I'm going to update the president, see if they have any new intelligence."

"OK. You should be able to get a line of sight in the valley outside the entrance," Guangming said.

Jane retrieved her satellite phone from her pack and headed outside. Holding up the phone she turned around trying to find a signal. *No such luck.* The line of sight was fairly limited in this narrow valley. She'd either have to try again later or see if there were any higher vantage points she could use which wouldn't leave her too exposed. While their pursuers were gone for the time being, there was a good chance they might still be surveilling the area. *How did they find us, anyway?* After their tails had been intercepted by Tenzin she thought they'd be in the clear. They must have had eyes on the area somehow to have located the monastery. *Either satellite access or drones.* She couldn't think of any other likely explanation. *Which again leaves us with the question of a mole or else just a group with very deep pockets.*

She headed back inside. It had been a long night. *I might as well get some shut eye myself,* she thought, but she wanted to find her mentor first. It had been such a pleasant surprise when he'd appeared in the Guanzi's chamber the night before, yet the events ever since had been a whirlwind. She'd hardly had time to process the fact that he was actually here.

Guangming was still in the main chamber when she returned. "Any luck?" he said when he saw her.

"No, I couldn't get through," Jane said. "I'll try again in the morning. I figure I'd better try to grab at least a few hours' sleep. Have you seen Zhongkui?"

"He's downstairs with Jimmie still. He and some of the monks have been cleaning the body and preparing it for the funeral rites. Since we don't know yet if we'll be able to perform them down at the temple—or even what's left of the temple—they thought they'd better prepare to hold them here. They wanted to retrieve the others from the valley below, but Zhongkui convinced them they'd have to wait."

"Good. Our pursuers could still be watching the area, better to play it safe for now," Jane said, before heading downstairs to see her mentor.

As she entered the storeroom, she saw that much had changed in her absence. Jimmie's body had been laid out on a table and most of the room had been cleared out. The blood had been washed off and he'd been dressed in fresh white clothes. Zhongkui was standing near the body, quietly reciting prayers. Jane waited silently until he spoke.

"Sinéad, my pupil," Zhongkui said. "It is so good to see you again. I only wish it were under happier circumstances."

"So do I, Mentor, so do I. He was a good man," Jane said, looking at Jimmie's body.

"And how is your pupil holding up? I understand she had strong feelings for this man," Zhongkui said.

"Yes, they hadn't known each other long, but they'd grown quite close. She's sleeping for now. She'll recover in time. She's very resilient," Jane said. "Will you be staying with us, Mentor? Or will you be leaving soon? During our training I never knew when to expect you or how long you'd stay."

"I will stay until I am sure you are out of danger. If that is until the Elders return for the ambassadors, so be it," Zhongkui said.

"Where have you been for so long, Mentor?" Jane said.

"I must apologize for my absence, Sinéad," Zhongkui said. "It was not my intention to leave you for so long without an explanation."

Then Zhongkui told her the story of Guanyin, how she had stepped down as Guide and had returned to the One, and his decision to go into retreat which had followed.

"I understand, Mentor. I'm sorry to hear of your loss," Jane said.

"Much time has passed, Sinéad," Zhongkui said. "Though I must admit, ten years sometimes seems like only a day, when you have lived as long as I have. Seeing loved ones pass is something we all must face, Immortal or not. The price only goes up with immortality—the longer you live, the more death you'll see."

"Yes, I guess that's true," Jane said.

"You seem distracted, Sinéad. If you have other matters to attend to, please do so. I assure you I will still be here in the morning," Zhongkui said.

"You're right. I have another duty to fulfill. I also have those I answer to here on earth. I need to let them know what's going on, but I haven't been able to communicate with them yet. I can't get through with my satellite phone right now."

"You know I can help with that," Zhongkui said.

"Let me try one more time. I'll ask Jingyi, the Guanzi's assistant, if there is a higher vantage point. I'd like to talk to the president myself. There are things I think she should hear directly from me. Besides, I know you've never liked sharing your thoughts," Jane said.

"I still don't, but sometimes it's necessary," Zhongkui said. "Many things have changed since we were last together ten years ago, Sinéad. I'm afraid we no longer have the luxury of our preferences—our petty likes and dislikes. Time is of the essence now. There is a threat looming which has changed the Elders' opinions of many things. The council is considering a drastic course of action not seen since the Great War. There is much we must discuss, Sinéad, but that will be for another time. I must consult with the council again first, to see how they wish to proceed."

Jane found Jingyi upstairs. Everyone was still awake, the evening's events keeping everyone on edge. Jane asked her about the satellite phone and Jingyi knew just the place. There were other openings to the outside in the cave complex like the one in the Guanzi's chamber. Jingyi led her up several flights of stairs and down several passageways until they came to a door which let out onto a ledge just below the peak. From there a short flight of stone steps had been carved which led right up to the very pinnacle. There was a flat area from which she had a completely unobstructed view of the night sky. *This should do the trick.* She made the call.

The president called her back a few minutes later. Jane told President Powers about the attack on the monastery and their escape through the tunnel back to the Guanzi's cave complex. She had been hesitant to involve Zhongkui at first, and considered giving the president a sanitized version of the events, without telling her of Zhongkui's involvement—or her own relationship to the Elders—but the stakes were too high. She bit the bullet and told the president everything, from the Elders' bloodline and her mission to protect Rohini, to the return of her mentor, Zhongkui.

President Powers was a bit shocked, to say the least. There was a long silence when Jane finished her story. Eventually she spoke.

"Is that everything, Agent Smith? You're not hold anything else back?" the president said.

"Yes, ma'am. That's everything," Jane replied, sheepishly.

"Good. I'll expect you back in Washington ASAP. I've spoken to the other world leaders and we've been unanimous in our determination to carry through with the Ambassadors Program. Under the circumstances, I think it only fitting that you be a part of it."

"I understand, ma'am," Jane said.

"We've all agreed that continuing with the program is the best way to honor the memories of the fallen ambassadors. They are already being thought of as martyrs to the cause of a united humanity and the restoration of Earth."

"Plans for a complete renovation of the Lincoln Memorial are already underway, fortunately the most extensive damage was limited to the steps and the façade," the president said. "I've put out the call for submissions for a new memorial design honoring President

Johnson and the ten Earth Ambassadors lost on that fateful day to be incorporated into the restoration."

While much of the world's attention had turned to the tragedy and its aftermath, efforts at ramping up renewable energy production continued. As new generating capabilities were brought online, old coal and nuclear plants went offline, signaling the end of an era, one most of the world agreed they never wanted to revisit. The collective mood of the global community was one that said, "For once, let us learn from our past and not repeat our mistakes, as we have time and time again."

But there were still those who opposed the new order of things. There was still the question of who was pulling the strings behind the SOC. After the attack on the monastery they at least had another piece of the puzzle. The number of groups or governments who could have pulled off that kind of operation under the noses of the Chinese military was limited. They might still be looking for a needle in a haystack, but that haystack had just gotten much smaller.

# 54

The next morning, Rohini awoke to find Jane on the small cot next to her. It was comforting, at least for a moment, until the events of the previous night came flooding back. The tears threatened to start falling again, until she pulled herself together. *Time for a stiff upper lip, Rohini,* she told herself. *You won't be any use to anyone, if you fall apart now.*

Jane woke at the sound of her stirring. She sat up on the edge of the bed and put a hand on Rohini's shoulder. "How are you doing?"

"I'll be OK," Rohini replied. "I just need to push on through. How long have I been out?"

"For a while, it's almost 10am," Jane said, looking at her watch. "The immediate threat has passed. The strike team is gone, but we're laying low in case they've got any surveillance on the mountain."

"I want to see Jimmie," Rohini said, sitting up and wrapping her arms around herself.

"Are you sure you're up to it?"

"Yes," Rohini nodded. "I need to see him one last time."

"Alright. I'll take you. He's still downstairs. They're setting up an altar and making preparations for funeral rites still, you should be able to have a few minutes with him."

"Jane, there's something else," Rohini said, taking in a deep breath. "Yesterday, while I was meditating in the grotto—before Zhongkui came and all hell broke loose—something happened. I remembered what happened."

"What do you mean?" Jane said, cocking her head. "Remembered what?"

"In college," Rohini said. "I remember what happened to me, and what you did. You were there for me even then. All this time I had no idea."

"I'm sorry you had to go through that, Rohini. I wish I had found you sooner," Jane said, hanging her head slightly.

"It's OK, Jane," Rohini said, squeezing Jane's hand. "I'm just glad you were there at all. How did you even know?" Rohini said. "Weren't you a spy back then or was that just a story?"

"I was based in DC during much of your time at George Washington. I'd leave on assignments, of course, but when I was in town and had the opportunity, I kept an eye on you. I had a bad feeling that night and knew something was wrong, call it intuition, or maybe some of my Elder heritage starting to manifest itself, I don't know. I'm just glad it did."

"Me too," Rohini said, giving her a smile.

"Are you sure you're OK, Rohini? This is a lot to take in at once."

"I'm OK. I'm glad I got to process it here, like this. I think being in the grotto helped. It felt like I released all of the bottled-up emotions connected to it. I'm pretty sure it would have wrecked me if I'd remembered in my old life, before all of this," Rohini said, holding up her palms. "Now, let's go see Jimmie."

When they went downstairs, the chamber had been transformed once again. An altar had been set up for the funeral rites. Rohini gave it a cursory glance as they passed. There was a lamp in the center flanked by two candles, along with cups of tea, water, and rice, and five bowls of fruit. But what caught her attention were seven lanterns which had been hung from the ceiling in the pattern of the Big Dipper. As her eyes fell back down in the chamber, they came to rest on Jimmie.

They walked over to the table on which Jimmie's body had been laid out. "He looks so peaceful," Rohini said. Despite his clean face and the fresh, white clothes he was wearing, she flashed back to how he'd looked the night before, covered in blood as he lay dying. Her knees buckled slightly at the thought.

Jane grabbed her arm, but Rohini had already caught herself. "I'm OK," she said, steeling herself. She reached out and gently stroked his hair. "Oh, Jimmie," she whispered. Bending down, she gently kissed his forehead. "Goodbye, my sweet man," she said, placing a hand on his chest. It felt hard and cold to the touch, even through his clothing. She knew Jimmie was truly gone. Just his body remained. After a minute, she turned to Jane. "OK, let's go."

Back upstairs they ran into Jingyi, who asked them if they had eaten anything.

"I'm fine. Thanks, Jingyi. I'll wait and eat with the others," Jane said. "Rohini?"

"No, I don't have much of an appetite, but thank you," Rohini said.

"At least let me bring you some tea," Jingyi said. "The Guanzi has been speaking with Zhongkui and Guangming in her chamber, she requested you join them. I'll bring you some tea."

"OK. Thank you, Jingyi."

Rohini and Jane followed Jingyi upstairs to the Guanzi's chamber.

"Ah, Rohini. Jane. Please, join us," the Guanzi said. "Zhongkui has been telling us a little about the Elders' world. It's quite fascinating."

After Jane and Rohini sat, the Guanzi turned to Rohini with a concerned look. "And how are you doing, my child? I know this has been especially hard for you."

"I'll be OK, Guanzi. Thank you," Rohini said, quietly, fighting back her tears.

"We've been discussing our next steps, as well," Zhongkui said. "Jane, were you able to speak with your president?"

"Yes. She's expecting us back as soon as possible. They're moving ahead with the Ambassadors Program and she wants Rohini and I to be part of it," Jane said.

Rohini shot Jane a surprised look. "Really? You'll be going too? I have to say, that's a bit of a relief."

"I told her the truth," Jane said.

"About the bloodline?" Rohini said.

"The bloodline. My mission from the Elders. Zhongkui returning. Everything," Jane said.

"Wow. How'd she take it?" Rohini said.

"She was a bit shocked, but you know the president, she's tough. She took it all in stride," Jane said.

"It's probably for the best," Zhongkui said. "The level of cooperation that will be required between our worlds going forward can only be built on honesty. That being said, there are things which the council have not decided to share with the leaders of earth at this time. I hope that by the time the delegation returns, they will be ready to."

"Can you at least tell us, Mentor?" Jane said.

"I would like to. Let me speak to the council first," Zhongkui said. "The Guanzi and I have been considering something else which will also require the council's approval. I will need to go into meditation to communicate with the leader we call the Guide. It will take me some time. By tomorrow morning I will have an answer for you. Now I must prepare myself, if you'll excuse me."

Rohini's curiosity was piqued by Zhongkui's enigmatic answer. Once he left, she asked the Guanzi what they were contemplating.

"Zhongkui has told me about a group of Elders on their world called the Watchers. We were both struck by the similarity with the title and office I hold as head of the society," the Guanzi said. "These Watchers are those most talented at viewing other worlds in spirit. They keep an eye on things and let the council know of anything which warrants their attention. Zhongkui feels that I would be particularly suited to this due to my current abilities, and of course as a carrier of the bloodline. He suggested that once you are safely back in the protection of your government, he take me back to their world to train with the Watchers. I would of course return—I wouldn't be leaving for good—but this would also be another way of forming a relationship with the Elders. I must say I'm quite excited about the prospect of such a trip!" she said, breaking into her signature infectious laugh.

Rohini couldn't help but smile. *She's still such a child at heart.*

Later that evening they held the funeral rites for Jimmie with the Guanzi presiding over the ceremony. After the services, Guangming explained some of the meaning to Jane and Rohini.

"First the Guanzi and the monks chanted scriptures, this is often done as a form of building merit, and to release the dead from the suffering of darkness. This goes along with the lanterns which are meant to serve as guides to Jimmie's spirit," Guangming said.

"Is that why the lanterns were in the pattern of the Big Dipper?" Rohini said.

"Yes, just like in the Hall of Ascension. The ceremonies are designed to lead him to the heavens, and away from the earth or the underworld," Guangming said. "The other parts of the ceremony all essentially had the same goal; they were all meant to relieve Jimmie's suffering and smooth his transition in various ways. Believe it or not, this was a very concise service. Sometimes these can go on for a week."

By the next morning, Zhongkui had returned from his seclusion. They all met in the Guanzi's chamber again. "It seems the Guide approves of our idea, Guanzi," Zhongkui said. "The only question remaining is when we will leave."

"You shouldn't have to wait long," Guangming said. "The society has arranged to get us back to the plane in Lanzhou with a security escort. We can be back in the United States soon. When we came here, we were trying to be inconspicuous, but now I think playing it safe means having protection and being visible."

"I think you are right. Nevertheless, I will escort you as well. I can return here to retrieve the Guanzi, or else she could come along, and we could travel to the Elders' world as soon as we've seen you safely back to your president," Zhongkui said. "I was also able to convince the Guide that all of you can be trusted with the Elders' secret, the real reason we have come to earth at this time." And so Zhongkui told them of the Others.

"Are they really that bad?" Rohini said. "Can't you fight them somehow? Will the Elders actually have to leave their world?"

"They are worse than you can imagine. Words cannot do them justice. Let me show you," Zhongkui said. "I am not as gifted as the

Speaker, Dayan, the one who shared his thoughts with the leaders of earth. I cannot send my thoughts across the globe to many people at once—at least not ordinarily—but come, if we go into the grottos I think I will be able to show you all."

There was just enough room in the Lower Guanyin Grotto for Zhongkui, Rohini, Jane and Guangming. The Guanzi had stayed in her chambers. She would be seeing what the Watchers saw soon enough when Zhongkui took her to the Elders' world. Rohini couldn't help but feel a bit of déjà vu as they sat down on the stone seats in the grotto. Yet this time it wasn't the Guanzi, but an Elder seated across the cave from her.

"Just clear your minds," Zhongkui said. "It will only take a moment."

When the moment came, Rohini almost cried out. The horror and suffering they'd been shown was heart-wrenching. In her raw emotional state, she couldn't help but weep. World after world of beings had been conquered by the Others. The death and destruction they left in their wake was hard to fathom. Those whom they didn't kill were enslaved, forced to serve their new masters, supplying the Others with resources until their worlds were completely bled dry.

Rohini felt like she'd just been shown Dante's Inferno. They all exchanged looks of shock. "Now you understand what the Elders are facing," Zhongkui said. "Now you see why simply fighting them doesn't seem to be a viable option."

They slowly filed out of the grotto and returned to the Guanzi's chamber, sitting down once again. "I can see from the looks on your faces that the situation is dire, indeed," the Guanzi said. "We must not give up hope. One way or another we will face this challenge."

"So, Mentor," Jane began. "Are we to keep this knowledge a secret for now or can I share this with the president? I think it would be better for everyone if we all knew what we were dealing with."

"If you think it best. The Guide trusts your judgment," Zhongkui said.

"Zhongkui, I propose we both accompany them and speak with the president ourselves," the Guanzi said. "Something tells me she will appreciate the candor, and from everything I have heard about her, I'd like to meet this woman who is now in the most powerful office in the world."

They set out the next day when the security team from the society arrived. They'd arranged for a helicopter to get them back to the jet in Lanzhou. They took the old tunnel, coming out into the cave of Tianyinzi on their way to meet the chopper. Rohini half expected the bodies of the soldiers to still be there, but they were gone. Much of the monastery was a smoldering ruin. While no fires still burned, smoke hung in the air. The monks and nuns had begun to scavenge through the wreckage, salvaging what they could. More people and resources would be sent in by the society to rebuild, but it would take time.

The security team met them there and escorted them out to the chopper. Their security detail would follow in a second chopper, while some stayed behind to secure the monastery. While they didn't expect the soldiers to return, they weren't taking any chances. As they passed through the monastery a figure caught Rohini's eye as they passed. It was the statue from the Hall of Ascension. The building appeared to have collapsed around it, yet the statue itself appeared unharmed, its hand still pointing to the stars. Rohini's thoughts turned to Jimmie. She took it as a sign that he had moved on to a better place.

"Look," Rohini said to her companions, pointing to the statue as they passed.

"How auspicious," said the Guanzi. "The Immortal points the way."

# 55

*State Highway 51*
*20 miles South of Bruneau, Idaho*

Trooper Erickson had a feeling. *Something's off.* Not that this was the first rental truck he'd ever seen broken down on the side of the road. They put on a lot of miles and most rental companies didn't exactly have a stellar reputation for maintenance. *I don't know where they're moving.* Other than the Bruneau Sand Dunes and the old ghost town at Wickahoney, there wasn't much out here but sagebrush. *Unless they're headed to the Duck Valley Reservation.* The only other thing nearby was the new solar array that had gone online last year. Then he remembered the recent attack in Nebraska. *Oh shit.* He called it in.

The bomber hadn't seen the trooper pull up. He was busy under the hood of the rental truck. He'd seen the temperature gauge creeping up, but had hoped he'd be able to make it the last few miles before the engine overheated. When steam started pouring from under the hood, he'd pulled over. *Maybe if I let it cool off for a little while I can still make it,* he thought.

He didn't have any extra coolant and he only had a small water bottle in the cab of the truck of which he'd already drunk half. *That won't be any help. I'll just have to pop the hood and wait, I guess.* He popped the hood and went around front to open it, but the radiator was still steaming. He'd have to wait. A moment later he heard a thump. *Was that a car door?* He hadn't heard anyone pull up over the hissing of the radiator. He drew his gun from his shoulder holster and peaked around the side of the truck. *Oh shit.*

Trooper Erickson exited his patrol car and made his way towards the truck, checking the side mirror to see if anyone was in the driver's seat. Not seeing anyone, he began to make his way forward on the shoulder of the highway, his hand on his sidearm. He'd already clicked the safety off. *Let's hope it's nothing.* He had every intention of making it home to his family tonight. As he got closer to the front of the truck, he could hear the hissing of the radiator. *Typical,* he thought, but then a figure jumped out from around the front. His sidearm was up before he'd even consciously registered the gun in the figure's hand.

The hissing of the radiator was drowned out by a flurry of gunshots. Trooper Erickson felt a searing burn across his left shoulder as he saw his assailant fall. *I hit him at least twice, center mass.* He moved forward quickly, kicking the gun away from the assailant, who was already coughing up blood. *He's not long for this world.* Trooper Erickson rolled him over, holstering his sidearm, and cuffed him. He called it in, eyeing his own shoulder. *I'll need some stitches, but at least I'll make it home tonight.* The bullet had just grazed him. He'd been lucky.

His backup was already on the way, and so was EMS, but it took them close to a half hour to get there. The perp died long before they arrived. Trooper Erickson had returned to his patrol car and found the med kit and roughly dressed his wound. Holding a pressure dressing to his shoulder, he sat on the rear bumper of his patrol car.

Eventually his backup, Trooper Strong, arrived, screeching to a halt before throwing his cruiser in park and jumping out. He ran to Erickson. "Bob! Are you alright?"

"I'm OK, he just grazed me," Erickson said, though he was starting to feel a little woozy now that the adrenaline was wearing off, and his arm stung like hell. It was starting to stiffen up.

"Where's the perp?" Trooper Strong asked.

"He's dead. He's in front of the truck," Erickson replied. "I haven't checked it yet."

They walked over together, and Trooper Strong opened the back of the truck. One look and they immediately backed off. "Holy shit, Bob! That thing's rigged like Oklahoma City," Strong said. He had been an Explosive Ordinance Disposal Specialist in Iraq. What they found in the truck told him they didn't want to be anywhere near it.

They returned to wait in Trooper Strong's patrol car. He made a quick sling for Erickson to immobilize his arm and helped him into the passenger side, then he backed the patrol car up several hundred feet to wait for the EMTs and the bomb squad.

\* \* \*

*The White House*
*Washington, DC*

It had been an auspicious sign. Their trip back to the US had gone off without a hitch. Rohini and her companions had met immediately with President Powers in the Oval Office upon arriving in DC. After learning about the Others from Zhongkui and Jane, the president's expression turned grave.

"I agree with you both, "President Powers said. "I think it's best for the time being we keep that information under wraps. It's just the kind of thing that would feed into the public's worst fears about the danger aliens might pose. The public's psyche is fragile enough right now, we can't take any chances."

As she recalled the meeting, Rohini was struck by the sheer absurdity of it, having regained a bit of her old sense of humor in the intervening weeks. *There I sat,* she thought, *with a Daoist Abbess, and immortal alien, a spy, and the President of the United States.* She smiled as she recalled something else from the meeting. The president had been quite taken with Zhongkui. It had seemed so incongruous at the time that Rohini had second-guessed her impression, but Jane had noticed it too. *I don't suppose you can blame her,* Rohini thought. *He is quite dashing in his own intense, brooding sort of way, and she is a widow after all.*

The truth about the Others hadn't been the only revelation to come out of the meeting. President Powers also had news—both good and bad. The bad news was that there had been another attack. The good news was that it had failed. She went on to tell them about the failed attack in Idaho.

When the solar installation was searched they found it rigged with charges which required remote detonation. A photo of the bomber was quickly circulated and they got their first lead. The clerk at Tiny's Beer and Bait, in nearby Bruneau, had seen him with another man earlier in the day. The bomber had an accomplice.

After a dragnet was put in place—which was surprisingly effective for such a rural location—another suspect was apprehended.

A brief standoff with ATF, FBI, and DHS agents at a roadside motel left him wounded. The suspect had tried to shoot himself after it was clear his escape was cut off, but his gun jammed, allowing him to be captured alive. When his prints were run, they came back as another deceased service member, just like in the attack on Rohini, but this time they had a living, breathing body to go with those prints. He'd rolled over quickly, once he'd failed to commit suicide.

The mercenary worked for a private security outfit operating out of Switzerland, their headquarters just outside Zurich. He and many of his fellow recruits, though by no means all, were former US service members with a penchant for bending the rules, who now got paid handsomely to break them altogether. They'd been recruited and their deaths faked, in Iraq and Afghanistan, years before with the promise of big money working in the private sector. While he wasn't able to identify his ultimate employer—whoever had hired the firm—he was able to lead them to the remnants of the SOC.

They'd been hiding out in a dusty backwater town along the Iraqi-Syrian border all these years and from what the operative told the FBI, they were basically as defunct as everyone had believed, until whoever hired the contractors had put them in touch with the terrorist group. There had been some debate about whether to try to send a Special Ops team in to potentially apprehend them, but when that didn't appear feasible, a quick drone strike had wiped the map clean, ending the SOC for good.

The attacks had been carried out by the SOC largely in name only, most of the logistics being taken care of by the private contractors. The company itself had destroyed all records in their headquarters—a failsafe system virtually incinerating everything inside their offices. The company's personnel had gone off the grid as soon as their operative was apprehended, so the trail to whoever hired them and was ultimately pulling the strings had been severed—at least for the time being—but before they left, President Powers vowed that those responsible would be brought to justice, no matter how long it took.

After the meeting at the White House, Zhongkui and the Guanzi had left immediately, disappearing in a flash of light directly from the Oval Office. Although it wasn't the first time she had seen it, it still amazed Rohini, and it had certainly left an impression on President Powers. Afterwards, Jane had taken Rohini home to see her father, and Guangming had gone to the Chinese Consulate to speak with the Chinese Ambassador to the US. He would be rejoining Rohini and Jane, as well as the rest of the new Earth Ambassadors soon.

\* \* \*

Bartholomew Simms' resolve remained firm. *I might have lost this round*, he thought, but he was determined not to lose the fight. His co-conspirators may have abandoned him, but he didn't need them anyway. *Cowards.* Once the going got tough they had all backed out. That hadn't really come as a surprise, but now that he had lost the cover of the SOC to take the blame for his mercenaries' dirty work, he would have to come up with a new strategy.

*That's alright, I can wait.* He'd acted rashly before, which was uncharacteristic. He usually took more of a long view, crafting his plans carefully, knowing that was what paid off in the end. *You can't worry about the daily ups and downs of the market, you have to look at the long-term trends.* When others ran scared, pulling their funds, that's when he looked for opportunities, and there were always opportunities. *It's the long game that sets the real players apart from the dilettantes,* Simms thought, and he knew he would be able to find others who felt the same. While his cabal had fallen apart, one of the members, James VanHouten, felt guilty about abandoning him and had mentioned that he had some business contacts in Russia who felt as strongly about the aliens as he did. He'd promised to make an introduction. *Perhaps something will come of that.*

# 56

Several weeks later Rohini, Jane, Guangming, and the other new ambassadors sat chatting along with the rest of the crowd in the General Assembly Hall at the United Nations. President Powers was there, along with the leaders of the other nations participating in the Earth Ambassadors Program. The selection process had been much quicker the second time around, narrowing it to those with the Elders' bloodline had made the list much shorter.

Although the terrorist threat had been removed as far as anyone knew, it was thought prudent that the Earth Ambassadors train together in a secure facility. Since it had worked well for Rohini and Jane the first time, and the group of ambassadors was relatively small, they had returned to Quantico.

As they sat in the assembly hall at the UN, the feeling in the room was upbeat, the excitement palpable. They had been there for a few hours already, not knowing exactly when the Elders would arrive, yet no one's enthusiasm was flagging. The awaited return of the Elders was being broadcast live all over the globe. Though it was a weekday, many businesses were understaffed, people calling in sick to watch the days' events—the "E-flu" apparently making the rounds. Sports bars and other establishments with televisions, on the other hand, were packed, even though it was only 10:30am on the East Coast.

All talk was suddenly cut short as a bright flash filled the room. Everyone's attention turned to the dais, the same spot where the Elders had appeared out of the blue six months before. The silence in the hall surprised Rohini, considering how many people were packed into the chamber. There were now a group of figures standing on the dais, where none had been only a moment before.

Many people stood to get a better look, including Rohini and Jane. It was then that she noticed there weren't just four Elders standing on the dais—this time there were six. There, among the Elders, Rohini recognized two familiar faces smiling back at them. Zhongkui and the Guanzi had returned. But the Guanzi looked different. She still had the same mischievous grin and twinkle in her eye, but she appeared to be a good twenty years younger than she had been the last time they'd seen her.

Rohini felt a strong sense of déjà vu, recalling the UN Conference on Climate Change which had brought her to this very spot six months before. So much had happened since then. *It's been an incredible journey. But the real adventure is about to begin.*

The End

# ACKNOWLEDGEMENTS

Just as none of us are self-made—despite the hubris which leads some of us to believe so—no book would be possible without the work of many people. We are all part of a network of connections: connections with the natural world, connections with our social networks—whether real or virtual—and connections to those who have come before, leaving a web of thoughts, ideas, and stories in their wake.

I discovered a love of storytelling later in life. Maybe it was inevitable, as I'd tried just about everything else along the way. As I think back, I realize it was an inherited trait. When my brothers and I were growing up, my father used to tell us stories about the history of different things; the provenance of words or expressions, or how something came to be the way it is. These stories were usually true, but on occasion he enjoyed telling us ones that bore little resemblance to fact. They were always plausible and there were no search engines at the time to verify or disprove them. As a result, we all developed healthy BS detectors. My parents were also responsible for raising a family of voracious readers. Instilling in us, through example, a love of books.

Thank you to my early readers, especially Julie Marcus and Julianne Zhou, whose feedback proved invaluable in shaping the final manuscript, as well as my publisher and editor who gave the book a chance and helped polish it. Thank you to all the Daoist teachers, scholars, and translators without whom I'd know nothing of the Dao, especially Miriam Levering, my first professor of Chinese religions, Livia Kohn for her entire body of work, and Lao Zhichang for his continuing teachings.